Praise for Peter Orner's
LOVE AND SHAME AND LOVE

California Book Award in Fiction Silver Medal
Finalist for *Hadassah Magazine*'s Ribalow Prize
A *New York Times Book Review* Editors' Choice
A *San Francisco Chronicle* "Lit Pick"
A *Chicago Tribune* Editor's Choice

"Teeming yet not hyperactive, full of emotion without being mushy, elegant yet intimate, this is a book that gets into your head and makes itself at home there....Like the James Salter of *Light Years* and *A Sport and a Pastime,* with their acutely observed domestic and sexual tension. There's something noble and moving about Popper's resolute sorrow, about all the Poppers' largely unsuccessful struggles to connect to their times, to their city, to others. *Love and Shame and Love* doesn't end so much as fade into a Lake-Michigan-in-winter mood of quiet devastation. It doesn't grab for glory, but it wins a big share anyway."

—Maria Russo, *New York Times Book Review*

"Beautiful....Think Saul Bellow (Chicago setting, rollicking Jewish-style comedy) mated with Chekhov (unassuming, devastating detail), set to the twangy thump of early Tom Petty. Now that promises quite a love child....Orner is the rare sort of writer who not only exactingly paints life's bewilderments and suffering, but induces the experience itself in the reading....Again, apt that Chekhov is invoked here, because Orner's prose showcases a twenty-first-century version of the Russian's unvarnished mastery....What drives this slideshow is inventiveness and craft—or art—condensed into seemingly simple images and stories. It's the kind of nostalgia-fest that finds you settling deeper into your cushion, leaving you slightly bereft when the last image gives way to a bright white screen."

—Ted Weesner Jr., *Boston Sunday Globe*

"Peter Orner's inventive coming-of-age story finds the drama pulsing through the most seemingly conventional lives.... 'I start things and I stop,' Alexander Popper admits. 'It doesn't connect. Nothing ever connects.' Not so with this fine novel, which resonates thanks to Orner's understanding that the more disparate the elements, the more complete the portrait of family life."
                              —David L. Ulin, *O, The Oprah Magazine*

"Both challenging and worthwhile. Instead of a sustained narrative, hundreds of snapshots from Alexander's past are pieced together—though 'snapshots' suggests something static, and each of these eye-blink vignettes is animated by yearning.... They soon coalesce into an emotionally inflected mosaic of Alexander's past. 'Isn't history as much about tearing things down as it is about building things up?' Alexander asks. Mr. Orner has found a way of making loss and reclamation exist side by side."
                              —Sam Sacks, *Wall Street Journal*

"Though Peter Orner is quite purposeful and precise in his nonlinear approach to storytelling, reading his latest novel, *Love and Shame and Love,* can evoke the sensation of unpacking a box full of memories in brief, frequently lovely chapters, vignettes, and letters, which ultimately coalesce to create a powerful and heartfelt family history.... But this is less a semiautobiographical bildungsroman or a sad chronicle of one family's ascent and decline than it is an ambitious, kaleidoscopic novel of the Jewish experience in Chicago.... *Love and Shame and Love* serves as an ode not only to the history of Chicago, but to Chicago literature itself. In Orner's erudite, quotation-filled prose...there is, of course, more than a hint of Saul Bellow. The novel is...remarkable for the specificity of its characters and the settings they frequent...But the more universal story of the Poppers' thwarted dreams and loves will likely resonate with those who have never set foot in Chicago or its northern suburbs."   —Adam Langer, *Chicago Tribune*

"This book evades quick reading, and rewards the kind of close attention paid to poetry.... The pleasure is in the language and the characterization, both of which are sharp and particular. It is clear that Orner knows these people deeply."

—Malena Watrous, *San Francisco Chronicle*

"Like Jeffrey Eugenides's Detroit, Orner's Chicago is the microcosm of the twentieth-century European immigrant experience. The 'white-but-not-white-enough' immigrants: exiled, persecuted, over-worked, caricatured, yet still suffered just enough power by the domi-nant culture to occasionally rise above the huddled masses.... Peter Orner has written a magnificent book—magnificent in its unassum-ing details that nevertheless burst with meaning."

—Lauren Eggert-Crowe, *Los Angeles Review of Books*

"From his first story collection, *Esther Stories,* on to his most recent novel, *Love and Shame and Love,* Peter Orner has established himself as one of the most distinctive American voices of his generation."

—Ted Hodgkinson, *Granta*

"Part epic, part bildungsroman, Peter Orner's *Love and Shame and Love* is a refreshing departure from the shtetl nostalgia shtick that has come to typify contemporary American Jewish fiction. Orner's characters are complex, but their quirks, like their Jewishness, are the stuff of real life. And like life, this novel is at times terrifically funny; at others, hopelessly sad. Always, the writing is meticu-lously crafted and evocative.... Often, *Love and Shame and Love* brings to mind Saul Bellow and his depictions of Chicago, that land of opportunity and loneliness, and characters—like Moses Herzog—who are helpless in the face of destiny. In the world of this novel, as in much of Bellow's oeuvre, Jewishness is not something external to the characters; it's embedded in their psyches like childhood traumas, like Chicago, but more so, inextricably a part of who they are."

—Shoshana Olidort, *Jewish Daily Forward*

"*Love and Shame and Love* is an epic book—epic like *Gilgamesh* and epic like a guitar solo. When I finished it, my head was buzzing, my heart was pounding, and I was pumping my fist high in the air for Peter! Goddamn! Orner!"   —Daniel Handler, author of *Adverbs*

"Reading Peter Orner's work is like breathing different air, or moving through a different kind of time—I feel like I'm stepping off some mental treadmill and looking around at a world which isn't trying to sell me anything. It's exhilarating and finally necessary."   —Paul La Farge, *Bomb*

"The Chicago men and women who inhabit these pages exist in a world we recognize, where government is as common a topic of thought and conversation as relationships, work, and kids. Drawing on his own history, Orner sifts freely through three generations of the Popper family, which moves from Chicago to Highland Park in the great suburban expansion after World War II. They're 'a modern ironical family' who say proudly, 'We're Democrats before we're Jews.' Alexander Popper, the youngest son of the last generation, serves as the modest but haunting central character....Melancholy anecdotes are held aloft by wry humor....Orner has a fine ear...but the most striking aspect of the novel...is its airy structure....What emerges is the history of a man trying to feel loved, watching his parents and grandparents falling apart, and seeing politics as some larger expression of belonging that never quite satisfies....Orner is unusually gifted at creating freighted moments of despair that generate far more impact than their size would suggest. There's a short piece in *Love and Shame and Love* about a fishing vacation—'Chain O'Lakes'—that's line-by-line perfect, from its hilarious opening image of Alexander's mother sitting in the boat in her mink coat to its mournful climax. An anecdote about gym class—'The Hill'—plays with the clichés of middle school, but then sneaks up and devastates you....As Alexander says, 'I'm trying to write a sad story, a good, sad story.' Orner has done that."
     —Ron Charles, *Washington Post*

"Orner, who comes from Chicago in the way that James Joyce came from Dublin, uses the Second City to explore what amounts to serial romantic and political monogamy. The book is about politics and passion...like a sonata, it does a hundred things at once. It makes you laugh against your will....This is the laughter of Kafka and Welty, a laughter that asks you to take seriously the vagaries and violences of human life, but also to distance yourself from them....A tour-de-force novel."

—Katie Kane, *The Missoulian* (Montana)

"In his magnificent second novel, *Love and Shame and Love,* Peter Orner proves he is one of the finest American poets of family weather....The novel unfolds like an epic in miniature. Since his 2000 debut, *Esther Stories,* Orner has refined working in short chapters to a prose poet's art....Entire worlds are created within them....Where does a family mythology go when there is just one person to tell it? *Love and Shame and Love* forms the only answer possible. You remember, and even when there is hardly a happy arc, you tell its story anyway. With a ferocity that can only be called love."   —John Freeman, *Toronto Star*

"Vibrant and captivating, this novel about three generations of the Popper family of Chicago resonates with the truths about human nature. Sure-footed control of his narrative gradually discloses information that conveys emotion and physical atmosphere. A richly layered, intimate picture of a distinctive but also typical family enduring life's vicissitudes and stoically carrying on."

—*Publishers Weekly* (starred review)

"*Love and Shame and Love* will break your heart, but in the best possible way."   —Anna Pulley, *San Francisco Weekly*

"It's easy to luxuriate in Orner's language, which blends poetic rhythms and a foreboding tone....The novel is remarkably earthbound and emotionally complex."

—Mark Athitakis, *Minneapolis Star Tribune*

"*Love and Shame and Love* is a finely crafted family album, told in comic and heartbreaking snapshots, of America in the twentieth century. Orner has captured his characters in motion, bringing the past exquisitely and precisely to life even as he illuminates the present, timeless struggle to make family, and life, meaningful. This is a big, smart, generous, important novel."

—Antonya Nelson, author of *Bound*

"In this emotionally saturated yet briskly episodic novel about a brash city on a Great Lake, and a family navigating the rough waters of ambition and disappointment, pain and sorrow, Orner achieves a remarkable mix of psychological nuance, imaginative storytelling, and historical verisimilitude."

—*Booklist* (starred review)

"A masterful, multifaceted novel. Readers will find both love and shame in abundance in Orner's teeming fictional world."

—*Kirkus Reviews* (starred review)

"A keen-eyed observer of American life and history, Peter Orner strips every layer of pretense from his characters, not to diminish but rather to reveal them. This is a real and memorable America."

—Yiyun Li, author of *Gold Boy, Emerald Girl*

"Peter Orner's new novel is a deft character study of a family hiding the usual secrets and lies of contemporary life, but it's also a well-observed portrait of a city as rich in history, dirty tricks, and deception as any of the people he puts in it. Orner excels at stripping away artifice and revealing the complicated, often contradictory workings of the human heart.…Love, anger, shame, sorrow, regret, betrayal, and, finally, acceptance: these, then, are the factors that propel the Poppers." —Connie Ogle, *Miami Herald*

"*Love and Shame and Love* is a marvel. It left me with that feeling we all crave when we read — the sense of wonder you wake with after a dream, realizing just how mysterious is this world."
— Marisa Silver, author of *The God of War*

"I consider Peter Orner an essential American writer, one whose stories unfold with a flawless blend of ease and unpredictability. Every sentence he writes is wide awake to his characters' hearts, and it is for the clarity with which he makes me feel time working its changes in their lives, and by extension in my own, that I keep returning to his books. *Esther Stories* was among the best story collections of the last decade. *Love and Shame and Love* is among the best novels of this fresh new one."
— Kevin Brockmeier, author of *The Illumination*

"A beautifully written book about the ghosts of family hovering over us all, and the often tenuous perch the tribe has in a gentile world." — Neil Steinberg, *Chicago Sun-Times*

"Each chapter is a solitary memory, dusted off and glowing with latent emotional residue.... It stands as a feat of laudable literary skill that Orner manages to use one-off vignettes to get at the really big happenings in life."
— Jessica Gelt, *Los Angeles Times*

"A captivating family epic that stretches across four generations and fifty years, Orner's second novel is a vibrant masterpiece about what it is to live in America — and what it is to live. Orner's characters, the children, parents, and grandparents of a Jewish middle-class family, are exquisitely rendered, and though he is not always kind to them, they are easy to fall in love with, no matter their faults." — Emily Temple, Flavorpill.com

LOVE
AND
SHAME
AND
LOVE

A NOVEL

Peter Orner

BACK BAY BOOKS
LITTLE, BROWN AND COMPANY
NEW YORK   BOSTON   LONDON

Copyright © 2011 by Peter Orner
Illustration copyright © 2011 by Eric Orner
Reading group guide copyright © 2012 by Peter Orner and
Little, Brown and Company

Back Bay Books / Little, Brown and Company
Hachette Book Group
237 Park Avenue, New York, NY 10017
littlebrown.com

Originally published in hardcover by Little, Brown and Company, November 2011
First Back Bay paperback edition, November 2012

Back Bay Books is an imprint of Little, Brown and Company, a division of Hachette Book Group, Inc. The Back Bay Books name and logo are trademarks of Hachette Book Group, Inc.

The publisher is not responsible for websites (or their content) that are not owned by the publisher.

The Hachette Speakers Bureau provides a wide range of authors for speaking events. To find out more, go to hachettespeakersbureau.com or call (866) 376-6591.

Library of Congress Cataloging-in-Publication Data
Orner, Peter.
Love and shame and love : a novel / Peter Orner. — 1st ed.
   p. cm.
ISBN 978-0-316-12939-8 (hc) / 978-0-316-12938-1 (pb)
   1. Families—Fiction.   2. Domestic fiction.   I. Title.
PS3615.R58L68 2011
813'.6—dc22   2011022547

10 9 8 7 6 5 4 3 2 1

RRD-C

Book design by Fearn Cutler de Vicq

Printed in the United States of America

CONTENTS

Part One

Part Two

Drawings by Eric Orner

For K and P

In Chicago I had unfinished emotional business.

—Saul Bellow, *The Actual*

Visit to the Judge

Chicago, 1984

This is how it was for certain boys in Chicago, the sons of lawyers. In some families, Alexander Popper's included, forget the bar mitzvah. To leave boyhood behind, you went to see Judge Abraham Lincoln Marovitz for a chat.

He was a great man, a learned man, bosom buddy of the mayor himself, the machine's favorite judge. In the words of one West Side precinct captain, "The yid really classed up the joint."

A federal judge! Think, son, of the heights to which you yourself might one day rise!

A bachelor, father to no one and so father to everybody. Popper's brother, Leo, once presented the judge with a drawing of him and his namesake. In the picture, Marovitz and Lincoln are sitting on a bench talking politics. The caption beneath their feet reads: *Just a Couple of Abes.* Marovitz got a big kick out of that. "Just!" he roared. "Just!"

In the index of Mike Royko's *Boss*, the judge is listed like this: *Marovitz, Abraham Lincoln, 41–46; and Mafia, 42; amateur boxing career, 41; association with underworld figures, 42–43; influenced by "friendships," 43–44; friendship with Richard Daley, 44–45; preoccupation with Abe Lincoln, 41–42.*

———

Now to this day, Popper has no truck with Royko's insinuations. He remains a loyal, if wayward, stalwart. And hey, if Judge Marovitz was crooked, he wasn't that crooked, which in Chicago, as everywhere, if everywhere was as honest about being dishonest, means something.

It wasn't a chat. Popper remembers how he sat there, swallowed up in that tremendous leather chair, afraid to even move because of how loud the crinkle would sound in his ears, and how he listened. But take a step back—before he listened, Popper waited, and in that waiting was a silence so absolute it was like drowning in the lake, out past that point where the sandbar gives way to blue emptiness. Him in there alone, his father in the judge's anteroom, pacing. And the judge staring at him. His face and ears and bald pate were ruddy, as befitted a man who kept his chambers heartily cold. His single thick eyebrow was like a centipede crawling across the top of his face. And his eyes beneath that thicket of brow were full of motion, and to meet them straight on (as Popper had been told by his father to do) caused a churn in Popper's stomach. Above him, as if to enforce the power of the judge's gaze a hundredfold, an armada of images of Lincoln. Paintings, photographs, etchings, silhouettes, drawings by other boys like Leo who'd been encouraged by their father to give the judge a present. (Popper himself presented him with a piece of cardboard, the judge's great name spelled out in pennies.) And on the tables, busts of Lincoln, statuettes of Lincoln. And they were all watching him, too—this was a test—and the silence was broken only by the judge's sporadic wheezing. The fourteenth floor of the Federal Building. Afterhours, February.

The judge slowly raised one hand and waved it around a little, as if to summon the force of all the Presidents who were all the same President. Then, with the index finger of his other hand, he pointed to a framed picture on his desk, a man and a woman dressed in black. Lined faces, hollow-eyed peasants from Lithuania. His parents. The judge played traffic cop, exhorting him to look around the room and at the same time at the little picture. But he got it. Popper had been prepared by his father to get it. Moreover, he was given to understand the miracle that was this country itself, this city. From a Kentucky log cabin to the White House. From the shtetl to the U.S. Courthouse. *Look at him. Look at them. Now look at me. My father was a peddler. My mother sewed buttons for the landowner's wife. My mother first got wind of the Great Emancipator at a meeting of socialists in Podberzeya. She heard that after he freed the slaves, Lincoln got shot in the temple. In the head, Mother, it means in the head! Nothing could convince my mother that Lincoln wasn't a Jew!*

And the two of them, Popper and the judge, laughed, but the judge stopped laughing earlier, so Popper's laugh hung there alone, between them, like an insult. And the judge's ruddy face drooped then, became sad. Sad because there were some boys, there were always some boys, who failed to embrace the opportunity that was being handed to them on the silverest of all platters. Maybe you yourself are one of those boys who will squander God's gift of Chicago. One of those boys who will take this vast gift for granted.

The judge talking less to him now than to an audience of ghosts who seemed to have gathered at the darkening windows, just behind the half-closed blinds.

Not that any gift worth salt comes without a price. You think a gift is free? Remember this for all time. But, by God, here we are free to live. No Ivan the Terribles, no Cossacks, no Stalins. In this city they wouldn't know a pogrom from the St. Patrick's Day parade. And here we answer only to the

United States Constitution and Robert's Rules of Order. With, note, one unwritten stipulation. Some call it patronage, I call it friendship. Everybody needs somebody else. Just as in the old country, everybody serves Caesar. The difference is, here you get a shot at playing Caesar in the movie. And so does your neighbor. And your neighbor's cousin Bobchinsky. We scratch each other's back in this city. I scratch you. You scratch me. Nice to have your back scratched. Especially those places you can't reach. This is how we build our buildings tallest of the tall. Our highways, fourteen lanes across. Sears, Roebuck, Marshall Field's, Wiebolt's, Goldblatt's, Montgomery Ward, Carson Pirie Scott, Hart Schaffner Marx, Polk Brothers. Back scratchers all. Do you think we could have reversed the flow of the Chicago River, this kind of engineering marvel, if not for the scratch, scratch, scratching of one another's back?

The judge sneezed then, an internal, handless sneeze, the sneeze of a man for whom sneezes were not an obstacle to straight dope. His little body jolted.

And it wasn't absurd. If it sounds absurd, it is memory's fault and not the judge's. The truth is that it was a show — a show Popper studied for, a show he rehearsed for, but there was something fundamental about it that wasn't a show at all. Himself in the big leather chair with his cold feet; it was less the judge's words or all those sorrowful Lincolns than the incoming dusk of the city, the gray doomful light settling over that room through those half-closed blinds. He was being told in no uncertain terms: Don't be cute. Your flesh will wither, too. Don't be cowed into the old hoodwink that you are actually young, that you've got your whole life ahead of you. Even cows aren't so stupid. And then the old judge gulped a breath and laughed, really laughed this time. A terrible, high-pitched whinny of a laugh. His eyes disappeared beneath his brow. The skin around his skull seemed to tighten, and all at once his ruddy face went pale — dead.

That day Popper, too, felt dead in that winter office light.

Relieved, though, as well. Because he'd been prepared for this also. *Make it past the laugh,* his father had said. *All you have to do is make it past the laugh and you're home free.* The judge reached to his shelf and pulled down the Pentateuch. He began leafing, seemingly at random, until he came to his favorite book, Numbers. Then he intoned: "And all the congregation lifted up their voice and cried; and the people wept that night. And all the children of Israel murmured against Moses and against Aaron; and the whole congregation said unto them: 'Would that we had died in the land of Egypt.'"

The judge slapped the book shut, leaned toward him over the great desk, and began the test: "How did Moses respond to this cowardice and ingratitude?"

"First he put his head in the sand, Your Honor."

"And then?"

"He pleaded with the people, Your Honor."

"And then?"

"The people still wouldn't listen."

"Yes! And then what happened?"

"Well, the Jews prepared to stone Moses and Aaron, Your Honor."

"Conclusion?"

"Accept to be stoned."

"Accept to be stoned for what?"

"The greater glory, Your Honor."

"Right. True. Well done. And then?"

"God had enough of the Jews. They were too rebellious, too defiant. He wanted to smite them out of existence but Moses convinced him to give them another chance. God agreed, reluctantly. After a couple of minor plagues for punishment — fire and snakes and also a few men over twenty sucked into a crack in the earth—they moved on again. Moses wanted to get to the Promised Land already. Forty years of wandering in the wilderness gets tiring."

"Sustained. And did Moses reach the Promised Land, Mr. Popper?"

Popper hesitated, purposefully. Weighed his answer with the heavy burden of study, of knowledge, of the sad irony of it.

"No, Your Honor, he never did. In the end, Moses too failed God and—"

"Yes? *And?*"

"God brought him to Mount Nebo and let him have a look at the land of milk and honey but Moses never set foot in it."

"In summation?"

"Moses died alone. No family, no friends. Nobody even knows where he's buried. An angry God isn't much of a friend, Your Honor."

The skull nodded and the judge began to clap. The doll-like hands in slow syncopation, clap, clap, clap. The room all shadows now. Forget Moses. Goodbye, Abe. Your days are done. You were good stories, good men. But this, my son, is Chicago. We don't go it alone. For a while longer they sat together in the new darkness, until it was time for the judge to ring the little bell. *Tinkle, tinkle.* Then, at last, his secretary came in—the light draining into the room as if from another world—and she took Popper by the wrist (he still thinks of her moist grip) and towed him out to where his proud father waited with his hat in his hands.

PART
ONE

1096 Olivia

1

PORTRAIT OF THE ARTIST
AS A CREATIVE WRITING MAJOR
IN THE AUTUMN OF MIKE DUKAKIS,

OR

FIRST LOVE

Often he thought:
My life did not begin until I knew her.
—Evan S. Connell, *Mr. Bridge*

BUNNIES

In the early seventies there was an epidemic of Playboy Bunnies hurling themselves out windows of the John Hancock Building. Leo informed him that these bunnies weren't rabbits. They were women, women with long pointy ears and puffballs over their breasts. Popper was five. He would imagine them falling, all that air speeding past those ears. But these bunnies never landed. Theirs was a free fall that went on and on — and on. And even then he thought he understood why they did it. That if you spent so long so high, so so high, it was only inevitable that you'd need to feel that drop, Hugh Hefner and Chicago itself be damned. If it's time to fall, let's fall.

LETHE

T he scene: the basement of the Undergraduate Library at the University of Michigan, the most hideous concrete mistake of a building ever architected by man, i.e., the UGLi.

It's 2 a.m., Tuesday.

The UGLi is a raucous place, loud conversation, coffee, beer, music, a little dope in the bathrooms, some isolated studying here and there. Popper's not studying. He's in his cubby, half-sleeping, half-reading William Blake. Not for class. Popper likes to carry certain books around and announce before anybody even asks: *This book? No, actually this isn't for class. And it's not pleasure reading either. There's no such thing as pleasure reading. It's all pain, pain—and more pain.*

> *If you trap the moment before it's ripe,*
> *The tears of repentance you'll certainly wipe;*
> *But if you let the ripe moment go*
> *You can never wipe off the tears of woe.*

She's a mere four cubbies away. At first he spies only the back of her head, her blond-brown ponytail rising above the plywood like a beacon. He ducks beneath his desk and eyeballs down the row of legs. Her running shoes are off her feet, one socked foot scratches a naked shin.

Blake admonishes, nay, threatens—

Sooner murder an infant in its cradle than nurse unacted desires.

Popper stands up and laps the cluster of cubbies six, seven times, as if pursuing great thoughts. All the while, *surreptitiously*, observing her in this basement light, in this noisy purgatorial fluorescence. Each time he passes, he peers a little closer over the rim of her cubby. Never has a square of plywood held so much promise. Details? At present she is eating a Butterfinger. Very unique candy bar. Famous yellow wrapper. Concentrate. Don't babble. Tell your head to stop babbling. She places her index finger and her middle finger over her mouth when she chews. She is reading intensely. He can almost see her eyes move across the words. God, if I could only read like that. I read two sentences and my brain wanders to Tegucigalpa. Her face, describe her face. Why is it so hard to describe a face? May as well describe a soul!

(Question for Creative Writing Professor (adjunct), Tish O'Dowd Ezekiel, author of a good, sad novel called *Floaters*, which refers to those small black wings that rain down our eyes:

POPPER: *Professor O'Dowd Ezekiel, why is it so hard? Why are things like trees or cars easier, when we spend much of each day staring into faces?*

PROFESSOR O'DOWD EZEKIEL: *Ah, but do we, Mr. Popper? Do we really ever truly look at each other, see each other? It would seem to me that we spend our days not looking into each other's faces.*)

Body easier. Legs easier. Breasts easier. Always. Because men are inherently infantile? Something to do with our relationship to the memory of our mothers? Hers? Only rising hints of sweat-shirt. Small undiscovered planets? You know they're there, but they're so distant they may as well be conjectures.

Retreats to his own chair. Spies low again. She crosses her legs, one way, then another, then uncrosses them. For no recordable reason, Popper thinks of the word *lethe*. He gets up again and approaches the dictionary, the great dictionary that stands alone in the middle of the room, beneath all that buzzing light, like a weird pulpit nobody ever sermons from. Popper flaps the pages of truth and/or metaphor. *The stream of oblivion in the lower world, hence, forgetfulness.*

Maybe I'm spelling it wrong?

Ah, *Lithe*. Supple, bendable, that's better. Supple, an exciting sort of word. Back again to his cubby headquarters. Use it in a sentence. *I hope you don't mind my saying hello. I find you beautiful but also lithe, not to be confused with lethe, which means something else entirely, having to do with memory, or rather loss of it, yet as it is, I can't forget you. Are you by any chance a dancer?*

She gets up to talk to a friend sitting in another cubby. The friend's face hidden, nothing but a mass of curly hair.

"How's it going?"

"I'm so bored of psychology I could go on a shooting spree," Mass of Curly Hair says.

Gripping Blake for courage, Popper makes his move and drops the note on her desk. He notes the title and the author of the facedown book. *The Need for Roots.* Simone Weil. Never heard, must look him up.

And flees to the bathroom. Popper, hiding in a stall, waits. In the bowl, a forlorn unflushed turd the color of knockwurst. But even in there, he hears her laugh. A blasting, honkish, gooselike sound. The UGLi goes quiet. He'll learn this. How this girl could laugh entire rooms — banquet halls — into silence.

Lindy, seriously, look at this, some doof's writing notes.

At Yu Lin's

W ait, you're a what?"

"It's a new undergraduate major."

"Weird."

"You?"

"Philosophy."

"Philosophy. Interesting. Really. And difficult. Wow, philosophy, wow. I've read Kierkegaard. God ordered Abraham to murder his kid and Abraham said, Okay okay, whatever you say, not a problem. He didn't even try to get out of it. He didn't run away to Nineveh, which sounds to me like a pretty fun place. That's faith? I mean, at least Jonah gave defying a totally unreasonable God a shot. And Kierkegaard says Abraham's a great man? To me, he just sounds like a bad dad. Did I miss something?"

She just let his gibberish float there between them without answering. Lunch at a Chinese restaurant on South University. The place was dark, the blinds drawn against the afternoon sun. Above each table a small round bulb; Popper thought, Each table its own sad moon. This isn't going very well at all. She is from Wisconsin and her name is Katherine but her father had called her Kat since she was six minutes old. Kat Rubin. *I'll never see her again.*

"Who do you read, then?"

"Oh, you know, lately a lotta Ray Carver."

"Who?"

"People call him a minimalist, but that's really a misnomer. Carver just doesn't use a barrel of words to say something he could say in half a phrase. He's the poet of modern despair. Drunken, laconic husbands. Lonely, cheating wives. You know, the gritty truths—"

"Fuck that. Are you related to Karl Popper?"

"Never heard of him."

"How many Poppers could there be?"

"I'm not sure there needs to be any more."

"He's this supposedly important philosopher." She waved a tuffle of rice squeezed between two chopsticks before his eyes. "It was Karl Popper who brought scientific rigor to the so-called soft sciences. You have something on your chin. Some sauce. Karl Popper said, for example, that astrology was bunk and sociology was even bunkier." She licked her finger and reached across the table to his chin. She touched his chin with her licked finger. She touched his chin with her—

"How did he feel about Scientology?" Popper asked.

"Quick," Kat said. "Name the lovechild of Karl Popper and L. Ron Hubbard."

He shrugged.

"Cher?"

She honked a brief laugh. "Nice. Not that I've ever read Karl Popper. Nobody reads him anymore. I guess he served his purpose. To bring scientific rigor to whatever whatever whatever. Seems kind of obvious to me. Systems need proof. Okay, next."

She pressed her chopsticks to her lower lip and watched him watch her. Popper took this in about his relation. A kinsman rendered irrelevant, these days unknown even to his own family.

"And Kierkegaard?"

"Oh, Kierkegaard's just romantic. That's a different deal altogether. Abraham was prepared to kill Isaac because he loved him *and* he loved God. And God didn't make him do the deed because He loved Abraham. In Kierkegaard, everybody loves everybody. I'll take Kant. If we're estranged from ourselves, how can we not be estranged from other people, much less love them? Kant says that what we don't know—or wait, maybe that's the existentialists—"

Popper gripped the side of the table. The entire lunch he hadn't once used his chopsticks. Sitting there half listening, watching her eat, her fingers brilliantly, acrobatically, tonging those thin little wooden sticks while he shoveled food into his mouth with a common fork like a hayseed. Possible to switch to chopsticks now, this late in the game?

He opted to stop eating altogether.

"Something wrong?"

"No!"

She stood up and stretched, fluttering her arms toward the ceiling. "You're done? I think I'm done." He watched her go up to the front and pay the bill for both of them. On the sidewalk outside, the sun white and bulbous, she said, "Did you notice nobody working there was Chinese? A Chinese restaurant should have at least one Chinese person—What are you up to now?"

What am I up to now?

It was the autumn of Mike Dukakis. What could possibly go right? In a month, Popper would cast his first vote in a presidential election. And on the other side of campus, the bells in the tall clock tower ring, the bells ring…

On the Rug

K at refused to live in the dorms. What am I, a lab rat? She smelled of lip gloss and sweat. Amazing, and also deeply disturbing, how fast two near-strangers can go from Chinese food to a wrestlingish tussle on a worn-out rug in an attic room amid the trees. Her walls were practically all window. No furniture, only the bed they weren't using. Skin that seemed as far away an hour ago as, say, the Yukon Territories is now right here beneath his shocked fingers, his entire body (led by his still blue-jeaned pelvis) in a state of ecstatic flux, now spastically, aimlessly, freakishly thrusting, a twitch, and aw no no, shit, shit, shit—

To distract, to buy time, to cover up, to ward off the unwardoffable, he clutches her and he tells this stuff about the Yukon Territories, trying to remain calm, casual. "Isn't it amazing how a clothed person is another country? For instance, earlier today, to me, you were—your body, I mean—was the Yukon, Canada's northernmost—"

"Are you a little repressed or something?"

She reached inside his boxers. His heart banged deep in the well of his ear.

"Oh, I get it." One goose-honk, two goose-honks.

"Just give me a little time."

"You know what you need to do?"

"Just a little time—"

"Grip yourself. You know, when you're still stiff. You want to cut off the blood flow, like a tourniquet. Plus, you'll probably enjoy—"

"Please stop talking."

"It's called shunting."

"I'm begging."

"I'm only trying to impart some friendly advice."

"Do you do this with everybody?"

"Give this sort of advice?"

"This. After a lunch date. Come back to your place and—"

"Are you a monumental prick? Metaphorically speaking since as far as I can tell—"

Kat rolled over and pushed the hair out of her eyes and began sliding downrug. Describe the attic room with windows on three sides, her on that frayed rug, his ecstasy, his shock, his humiliation, his what? The dappled afternoon light. The tall oaks lurking outside like voyeurs. Her chin edging down his chest. Describe it. Her chin—Why not just say happy? For once? Why not say joy, as derived from the thirteenth-century word originally connoting rejoice?

"Cool apartment," Popper connoted.

She tongued his knee. "Don't talk."

"Where have you been my entire life?"

She paused, looked up. "You believe in that?"

On, Wisconsin . . .

Fourteen degrees with the wind chill, October, Michigan versus Wisconsin. Eighty thousand drunk fanatics bellowing for blood, nothing whatsoever at stake, Wisconsin's 1–7; the only team they've beat is Northwestern.

How to even begin to describe this ocean of complete idiots?

Popper and Kat scrunched, huddled, blanketed. Popper making a point of holding Stendhal up in front of his face.

"Watch the game," Kat says.

"*The Charterhouse of Parma* has more excitement in its pinkie than anything in this entire stadium. Fabrizio sleeping is more interesting. The public's tax dollars go to support this sort of quotidian stupidity. Do you have an idea how much Bo Schembechler gets paid?"

"Have more Jim Beam."

"It's like a Nazi rally. Hitler entering *liberated* Vienna and the crowd goes wild for the Führer—Anyway, you're for Wisconsin—"

"Fuck yeah, Badgers!"

And their voices lost in the loud, more white breath than words.

"Don't you need a hat?" Popper says. "Your ears are going to splinter off."

Kat raises the bottle to her lips and swigs, hands it to him.

"Drink the hooch, Popper."

There's a certain kind of cold that merges people in the same way that two metal objects freeze together. You can't pry them apart until you inject heat. He thinks about how long it will take them to warm up in that tree-house room. How his feet, even in the morning, will still be cold. He thinks of her hungover breathing, her mouth open, her eyes half-open. He takes another view of his brethren. Humanity encapsulated in this great oval of inanity, and yet he could love these people, every million one of them, he could—

"And please don't use the word quotidian in ordinary conversation."

Kat hiccups whiskey and he thinks this, thinks—

On, Wisconsin! On, Wisconsin! Plunge right through that line . . .

GNATS

A May evening and the sun squats motionless above these stately roofs. Two women sit in front of their little house, one on the humble stoop; the other on a chair on the lawn. They are reading. Both books are thick. (Textbooks? After all, we are blocks from the university.) And yet the two women read gently, almost lazily. There is no doom in the Midwest tonight. Only rows and rows of words. Small hands turn pages without haste. One of the women on the lawn has red hair; the other has on some sort of bonnet. The City of Trees is at peace. The gnats roam down the sidewalk in waves.

There's more, right?"

"What do you mean?"

"I mean, is there more?"

"You hate it."

"I like it."

"What do you mean by more?"

"Isn't something supposed to happen? Is it a poem?"

"You think something has to happen?"

"Is that so terrible?"

"Requiring something to happen is tantamount to literary tyranny. Think of all the people who nothing ever happens to. How could we ever do them justice on the page if we're always giving their lives some kind of arbitrary action? Some people just read in the yard while sitting in a chair."

"Their entire life?"

"Yes."

Kat took another look, holding the paper above her head and mouthing the words as she read. They were in her attic, in her house of windows. Popper watched them both in the multiple reflections, two people on a bed, in the light, one lying on her back reading a single typed piece of paper, the other sitting up and watching the one read. If she could read his mind at this moment, which she could have done if she wasn't reading his story, she would have said, Popper, you watching yourself watching me isn't watching me, it's watching you. I'm only incidental to the process, the reader as ornament. The real star is you—

"I got an idea," Kat said. "What about if before these two started reading, they ate some shrooms? That way nothing would have to happen, but they'd think something did. Let them hallucinate a little. This is how all the people you were talking about get through their lives. They do a little drugs, they dream, or they watch TV or go snowmobiling—which is awesome, by the way, snowmobiling is the greatest thing ever invented and don't let any pansy tell you—or they—"

"What do you think of the gnats?"

"The gnats I like."

"Kat?"

"Yeah?"

"I love you."

"You what?"

The Kitchen Chair

Her room had three kitchen chairs and no kitchen table. They were arranged around the idea of a table. She said, Who needs a table when you've got three chairs? She sat on one of them with her feet on a second, being his model.

For this portrait, he don't need no easel. Give this man a pen and paper and he'll create fission with words —

Christ, if he had even a modicum of talent, he should at least be able to describe her face.

"Hurry up, Popper, I've got class. We're doing Hegel today. I am who I am not because I am 'I' at the moment, but because of who 'I' will become, which is unknown. Thus, I am my future self—who knows who this is?—and yet at the same time, that self exists. It's only time that's in the way. And since time itself is nothing, meaning from the point of view of our perception of it, not in the Newtonian sense, then we're our future selves right now. We just don't know who the hell we are. Isn't that awesome?"

"Turn your head a little?"

"I'm unknowable. Why even bother? Don't write about my double chin."

"You don't have one."

"Good. Or my weird tooth."

"What weird tooth?"

"Excellent. You make a fine painter in prose."

"Where were you last night?"

"What?"

"I came by around eleven."

"You want to know where I was?"

"What's wrong with that?"

"You're talking like I have to tell you."

"Stop moving your eyes, your face keeps changing."

"I'm late to class."

"You're right, I have no right, no right at all to monitor——"

"I slept in the antiapartheid shanty."

"In the middle of the Diag? With who?"

"With other people who think apartheid is a scourge on the face of the earth——Hugh, Paul, and some girl named Polly."

"You think I don't think apartheid's a scourge on the face of the earth?"

"I really don't know what you think about apartheid."

"I think apartheid is very bad. Does this mean you have to sleep with Hugh and Polly?"

"Listen, Popper, I got to get to class."

For a long time after she left, he stared at her empty chair. Torn vinyl. Light blue. Little rubber feet on all four legs. A sad little chair empty of her body. Maybe it's only in absence that we can get at it? Someone is gone, either to class——or clear out of your life——then fragments of a face emerge in a cold, still kitchen like a haunt. Joyce says absence is the highest form of presence. A small-boned face, high cheekbones, hidden ears only the tops of which poked out from her brown yellow hair, a chipped front tooth (a day camp accident involving a picnic table), slight upcurving nose, red from allergies. Roaming coffee eyes —

She won't come together. Her face with her hair falling all over it.

In the Diag

Age-old problem: if she chose him, there has got to be something wrong with her. So he followed her. Every Tuesday afternoon for a month, he'd wait for her after her class in Angell Hall and trail behind as she wandered around campus. It made sense at the time. How could he penetrate her secret realms if he himself was always hanging around?

The way people walk when they are with someone could not be more different from the way we walk alone. Alone, she was more timid than he'd expected, less charging around. With him she walked fast, sometimes stomped, laughed often, commented on everything and everybody. *Now, those red boots I'm liking.* And yet alone she seemed to blend in on the sidewalk. Suddenly shy, she looked at her feet when she walked.

To Popper, these revelations were thrilling: *I'm dead, it's like I'm watching my own nonexistence. With me, Kat strong, vivacious, brave. Without me, timorous.* Popper would duck behind bushes and construction equipment and watch her sit against the same tree in the Diag (a tree he had no idea she had any relationship with, a tree they'd walked by together dozens of times and she'd never said, Here, this tree means something to me, let's sit here) and pull out a book. He thought it must be Emerson. She'd been carrying him around for weeks now. She'd read a sentence, then put the book down and think about it. It may have been: *Man is timid and apologetic; he is no longer upright; he dares not say 'I think,' 'I am,' but quotes some saint or sage.* She'd gnaw on her lower lip, throw a stone at a drunken squirrel. (People said they'd done atomic experiments on Ann Arbor squirrels in the fifties, which explained the fact that they walked on their hind legs and gibbered at people all day long in fourteen different languages.) From her tree, she'd watch life go by on the crisscrossing diagonal sidewalks.

After a while she'd begin picking out a single person to follow with her eyes. A girl on crutches, a white-haired woman with clunky shoes, an angry tomato-faced professor, a fraternity pledge in a coat and tie, carrying an old tire slung over his shoulder. She'd follow each of them out of her line of sight as if they were heading out to sea never to be heard of again. Her eyes pinched into a sorrow he'd never seen on her face before. She even mourned the dork with the car tire.

It took spying on her a few times to understand that she wasn't watching for herself—meaning the lack of herself in other people. He came to see she had nothing to do with this at all. It was only about the people she watched until they were gone, how they could just disappear like that. Because people just vanish. Around a corner, into a crowd, down the street, across town. Isn't this a kind of death? To watch someone out of sight? Sure, some of them she might run across again, but most—even in a dinky city like this—she would never lay eyes on again.

Arboretum Postcoital

Bedraggled blanket Wednesday in wettened spring, missing class, Kat and Popper spent, drained, languid, pants pulled back up; Kat on her back, bridged across Popper's thighs, stares at the trees; he's reading, the sunlight polka-dot through a stand of ash — a place deep in the Arboretum known as School Girl's Glen. Earlier, Kat said, I'll show you a schoolgirl, Glen—

POPPER: Listen to this.

KAT: You never look at trees.

POPPER: It's Faulkner. From *The Wild Palms*. It's about a couple. Faulkner's one Chicago book. Part of it's even set in Wisconsin. Then this couple, they flee to Utah, where they almost freeze to death. It's a strange book, very passionate.

KAT: These are white ash trees, you can tell by the waxless leaves. Or maybe they're box elders. Read the Wisconsin part.

POPPER (*clears his throat*): *They say love dies between two people. That's wrong. It doesn't die. It just leaves you, goes away, if you are not good enough, worthy enough. It doesn't die; you're the one that dies. It's like the ocean; if you're not good, if you begin to make a bad smell in it, it just spews you up somewhere to die. You die anyway, but I had rather drown in the ocean than be urped up onto a strip of dead beach* — Damn. Urped not burped, now that's fucking writing.

KAT: What the hell's he yattering about? This isn't very Wisconsinesque.

POPPER: Her, it's a her talking. It's Charlotte. She's talking to Harry, the guy she's run off with. She left her husband, Rat, because he was too respectable. There's nothing Charlotte detests on the planet more than respectability. She's an artist. Not a very good one, but this only makes her more passionate about art. In the book, she makes figurines and she sells them to Marshall Field's. Harry's a doctor, or almost a doctor. He's poor and he's never been in love before, which is part of the reason she's run off with him. To, among other places, Wisconsin. To prove to him that love actually exists. I'm not reading this for class. Also, Charlotte left her two daughters with Rat. They don't really figure in the story. Forget family, kids. Charlotte's basically saying that in love it's all or nothing. You half-ass it and you're doomed — that's when the bad smell —

KAT: The husband's name is Rat?

POPPER: Apparently it means student, like a freshman, according to the helpful note at the back of the book.

KAT: Read the urped part again.

POPPER: *You die anyway, but I had rather drown in the ocean than be urped up onto a strip of dead beach and be drifted away by the sun into a little foul* —

KAT: Charlotte's nuts.

POPPER: Why?

KAT: Because it makes no sense. Anybody who drowns is eventually burped up onto the beach.

POPPER: Urped. Not everybody. What if you're tied down by something? She's talking about staying on the bottom for good. She's talking about going down with the ship of love and never coming back to the surface—

KAT: And I'm saying eventually you wash up—She wants to drown in love and not be urped. She can't have both.

POPPER: It's a metaphor.

KAT: Meaning what?

POPPER: I just said it. If you're not up to love, if you falter, if you lack the courage, it dies and you end up—well—urped. No better word for—

KAT: Urped! We're all urped, Popper. Either way, urped no matter what we do. And her leaving her husband had nothing to do with running from respectability or family. Charlotte's afraid of something like everybody's afraid of something.

POPPER: What?

KAT: Other choices. Everybody's afraid of other choices.

Silence. He turns the page. The wind in the leaves. Kat watches the regal white ashes hardly sway. Or maybe they are box elders . . .

POPPER: What about this? *I mean us. Love if you will. Because it can't last, not even in Utah.*

KAT: I like that better.

MANCHILD IN THE PROMISED LAND

She wasn't just from northern Wisconsin, she was from the top of the top of northern Wisconsin. Ashland, on the south shore of Lake Superior. Her father taught at Northland College. Where hippies go to freeze, Kat said. Her neighbor, the alcoholic astronomer lying on his back in the yard with a bottle of Jim Beam, raging at the clouds about the aurora borealis, how there's no aurora borealis like our aurora borealis and everybody else's borealises can go fuck themselves. Her high school boyfriend. He had a van with orange shag in the back where she lost her virginity, an idiot phrase if there ever was one, Kat said, because she also lost actual things back there, too — her keys, a comb, a roach clip, ten bucks, a Guatemalan necklace. Her parents' wedding in Duluth. How her mother's mother and her father's mother refused to sanctify the union of a lace-curtain Irish girl and a radical anarchist Jew by attending the ceremony, so they sent their respective husbands, who came and played their parts. Her mother's father, his long ruddy face stoic. *Your mother's heart, dear, will mend with the advent of children,* and her father's father, a wobbly kibitzer pointing to Kat's mom and muttering, *A beautiful strawberry girl, why all the fuss, why all the disunion over a strawberry girl?* Their house on Broadway Street, Superior at the end of the block, the ore docks reaching out into the lake like skyscrapers flat on their backs.

Her room, that attic tree-house room. 1096 Olivia, Ann Arbor. Three sides of windows and a bed. All the days and nights of 1096 Olivia, the branches scratching against the panes. What about the day her roommates were gone and the landlord came over while they were fucking and jammed his finger in the buzzer like he knew what they were up to up there? From the window Popper could see the top of his head and Kat said, *Hey, faster, I think it's the landlord.* And when they finally went downstairs and she opened the door to him, Kat said, "Terribly sorry we took so long, Mr. Delano, we were just finishing screwing." The man looked at her with bafflement and then with real fear, and, smiling with his teeth, backing away, said, "I'll come back Sunday to plaster."

Her books. They line the low shelves. V. S. Naipaul, Doris Lessing, Chomsky, *The Autobiography of Malcolm X, Walden Two, Raise High the Roof Beam, Carpenters* and *Seymour: An Introduction, The Brothers Karamazov, The Book of Laughter and Forgetting, Ward Six and Other Stories, Manchild in the Promised Land, Call It Sleep.*

Popper fingered *The Brothers Karamazov.* "My dad's like the father in this one."

"Are you going to murder him?"

"I haven't decided."

College? What else is there to remember? In college, I wrote small stories where nothing much happened; read books nobody asked me to — It's where I met Kat —

Try to not remember.

———

Always more. The mole inside her left armpit. The way she always ate with her hand over her mouth. The time she wanted to legally change her name to Bernadette Peters. *Because isn't she the perfect concoction of brains and beauty and airhead? Why shouldn't the state recognize my right to honor her?* Or the time they listened to *Astral Weeks* for two hours a day for six weeks and could air-violin all the violin parts on "Madame George." And what about the storm on that canoe trip? The storm on that island beach in the Quetico, the hours and the hours of that storm, the two of them in the leaking tent, drenched sleeping bags, drenched clothes, the thunder above their heads, ceaseless like some gagging god, Popper trying to plug holes with sogged underwear, and Kat saying, "Aw fuck, Popper, we're going to die Canadians."

1308 Lunt

2

A BACKGROUND GIRL

After all, an entire nation consists only of certain
isolated incidents, does it not?

—Fyodor Dostoyevsky, *Winter Notes on*
Summer Impressions

Century of Progress

Chicago, 1933

What is the temperature?

This question asked every day, not only by the millions who are attending the Century of Progress, but also by people all over the globe who are not fortunate enough to see these wonders, is being answered for you and yours by this two hundred foot high thermometer that the Indian Refining Company erected as a monument to Chicago's climate.

—Sponsored by Havoline Motor Oil

Bernice Slansky scoffs, unimpressed. Even she knows they can make a thermometer small enough to fit in your pocket. And to jam up other places just fine! This is how they are going to pull the world out of its messes, by building Jack and the Giant Beanstalk thermometers? *Fee-fi-fo-fum!* Not that she cares. No, the world can do whatever it likes. Bankrupt is fine with me. I'm going to be a dancer. Don't tell Mother. Then I'm going to move to Moscow like Isadora Duncan, marry a Bolshevik, and dance, dance. Because the world will always need and not need dancers in the same ratio, progress, no progress, she thinks as she twirls across the mass of hats and women in clackety shoes, looking for her lost in the crowd father.

September 4, 1944

Mrs. Seymour Popper
1308 Lunt Avenue
Chicago 26, Illinois

Angel, I got through today pretty well considering how much I miss you and the children—At least the schoolwork is easing up, thank God—the toughest course is navigation, which is right up my alley—All those hours up and down the Calumet River—You know, New York is a funny place—The Jews here for instance are in such numbers that they don't make any bones about their existence—They broadcast it—going to the ball game in Brooklyn I passed a building with a sign on it: SCHNORRERS CLUB—I almost fell off my seat laughing—Oh, Beanie, I don't know what to do—At times I have such a great feeling of exhilaration and I'm all for going through with this with all the resolution I can muster—Praise the Lord and pass the ammunition—Other times I'm down in the dumps again and my heart cries out just to be with you and the babies and the hell with everything—Counsel me, darling, I'm here all alone—

Seymour
Fort Schuyler
Bronx Station, New York City

BERNICE

Chicago, 1951

She stands before the mirrors in the ballet studio on East Jackson Boulevard. Sweat leaks down her face, her neck, her chest, soaking the front of her leotard. This body, this sweat. It all might be over, but nobody can take away this body, this sweat. Even at this small-time level. And, yes, once there was more. Yes, once the great Lincoln Kirstein himself had seen her dancing for Ruth Page in *Frankie and Johnny* at the Chicago Opera. Bernice was only a background girl, nobody special, but after the performance—how often does she remember this?—while the principals, Fay and Irene, and the rest of the pratty titterers were talking a mile a minute, he approached her, bland Bernice, his huge forehead gleaming, and said, as if nothing could be more simple, *Why not come dance in New York?*

So she didn't have the talent to stay. Who says anybody has to have the talent to stay? She went, didn't she?

Bernice extends her arms, slides, runs a step, a *grand fouetté* right, then half-turns. Pauses. Muffs a *tour jeté*. Lands, turns, slides right, slides left, and is about to leap again—

Telly, the office girl, pokes her head into the studio. Long-boned, storklike, dreamy, can dance.

"Bernice?"

"Yes."

"Your son's here. Handsome."

Bernice grips the bar and raises her left leg. In the mirror she examines the small pouches below her eyes. No matter how much sleep she gets — the unstoppable droop.

She was nineteen. She came home from New York four months later.

"Tell him I'm busy. My handbag is on the bench. Tell him he can take what he needs."

Her body slackens. Her men, their need. Seymour came back from the war terrified of his own children. Esther's crying in the night used to send him over the edge of the bed. *Man overboard!* The man will never get over the war. He felt so alive, he says. They should have sent women to fight the Japs. We wouldn't have come back sentimental about it after. Drop the bomb and be done with it. We got kids to raise. And now Philip's growing up like his father. All the talk, the charm, the confidence — but, like Seymour, isn't something missing? She leaps. Again. Lands wobbly and thinks she knows. Hell, you don't even need talent. Only a little grace. It's free, Seymour, Phil, it's free, my precious dolts. You don't have to scheme or lie or cheat or bluster for it. Nijinsky knew and he was crazy. He said, I merely leap — and pause.

When did I start forgetting this myself?

Now again:

Grand battement to fifth position — effacé. Right foot in back. Arm in arabesque. Toes never leave the floor. No fancy stuff. Pinch fanny. Front back front. Plié turn and hold it.

The room begins to fill with students. Bernice stops and mops her neck with a towel.

September 18, 1944

Mrs. Seymour Popper
1308 Lunt Avenue
Chicago 26, Illinois

Angel,

Now I certainly know how you feel—Look, all I can say is that there still happens to be a war on—a tough one—I wish I wasn't in it, but if I had to do it all over again I suppose I would do it the same way—We both know so many people who broke their necks to stay out—I still can't say I admire them for their actions—Men like Sid and Milt, yes, they stayed home with their families—But imagine the world, Beanie, if every man shrugged his duty, what would it look like? You think these Japs are kidding around? Your package came today—You certainly sent enough cheese! Thanks a million—

Seymour
Fort Schuyler
Bronx Station, New York City

Seymour

Chicago, 1953

Schnitzel and *pfifferling* and a hard-cooked egg. You eat on the run like a man of this city—standing up. We are men at feed. One thing these Krauts know how to do is stuff a sausage. Two-dollar lunch at Berghoff's. Like a mead hall of old. Don't I remember my *Beowulf!* Eat. Drink. Go out and kill Grendel. Waiters sail by, hoisting silver trays. Fellow upstarts munch their sandwiches. *And when you're done with him, go and kill his mama.* He'll tell it back at the office. See if any of the literary types know what's what. Seymour reaches for the crown of his hat and nudges the brim closer to his eyes. Little piece of fat between his front teeth. He niggles it with his tongue. Can't dislodge. Need toothpick. But not an unpleasant thing, a little fat. Damn, the things I squeeze a little enjoyment out of now. In the war I used to prop my mouth open with toothpicks to stay awake. Prick your gums and you can go for hours. *They're calling this shootout in Korea a war now also. Soon every little pissant fistfight they're going to call a war.*

Seymour eats alone—in the company of fellow hats, true, but it's not the same. There's no camaraderie. And the money game? More brutal in spades than shooting. And there's no such thing as loyalty in the business of business. He looks out the big window at the scurriers winging by on West Adams, a slither of soap-white light peeks from between the buildings.

He might have gotten lucky. Yanked offstage early. Lost at sea! Wouldn't that have been something? Typical dream of the sailor returned. When did I become so average? Long live Seymour; he died in the Pacific, his whole life ahead of him. *You hear about Sy Popper? Christ, what a shame. Two kids. Drop-dead wife. Bernice was a ballerina, wasn't she a ballerina before she married Sy? My God, the man had the whole shebang. Poor Bernice. Not even a rock to go visit.*

1308 LUNT AVENUE

Chicago, 1959

Twenty-three years at 1308 Lunt in Rogers Park and Bernice knows every creak in the floorboards. The one at the top of the stairs by Esther's room that always moans long under her left foot. And what about the little window in the attic, just under the peak of the roof? Once—only one time in all these years did she stoop and look out of it. Impossible to see much through the grime. She'd spat, tried to clean the window with her fingers. The view disappointed her. Only Lunt Avenue through a blur of spit and dirt. The brown lawns, the leafless trees, the new sidewalk, the cars lined up and down the street like ants, bumper to bumper. What had she been expecting to see?

And tomorrow? Tomorrow we will box ourselves up and move northward to become a new address. But we lug our old ones around with us, don't we? Isn't a new house number a sham? At least in the beginning, before it begins to weigh anything? Like those first few hours in a wedding dress when you're lulled into thinking the ring on your finger will change things.

Tomorrow, piece by piece, the furniture will be carried out of here, only to be plumped down again on the North Shore: 38 Sylvester Place, Highland Park.

It's not that she doesn't want to leave. It's that she always wants to leave. After the North Shore, where?

At the Century of Progress, Bernice remembers wandering into a fortune-teller's tent and having her future read by a bug-eyed white lady done up to look like a Gypsy. The white Gypsy had gripped her arm and held tight when Bernice laughed in her face.

"Your eyes, missus, why do they always run?"

October 2, 1944

Mrs. Seymour Popper
1308 Lunt Avenue
Chicago 26, Illinois

Look, let's be clear, I know the score somewhat better than you appear to be willing to give me credit for—I intend to come home to make you and our children a lovely happy life—I'm not quite playing cops and robbers here—This is just one of those things a man has to do—except occasionally a guy likes to feel that at home someone has some understanding—or even God forbid a little pride—we leave for Virginia on Friday—

> *Seymour*
> *Fort Schuyler*
> *Bronx Station, New York City*

ONE OF US

Northbrook, Illinois, 1961

It's called the Villa Venice, a nightclub and casino in the suburbs, done up in red tassels with waiters dressed as gondoliers. They row you to your table in a real boat down a real canal with water and everything. Sam Giancana owns the place, and his friend Sinatra and his boys, Dean Martin and Sammy Davis, are appearing at the grand opening as a favor. Bernice and Seymour Popper are in the crowd, at a table with Sid and Babette Kaufman. Sid got them tickets. Sid Kaufman always gets them tickets.

A woman at the next table says, "No, he's a real Jew. I hear he's got a rabbi and everything."

A man says, "Irene, Sammy can buy a rabbi and stick him on the lawn. Hey, you know what they call him in Harlem?"

"What?"

"The kosher coon!"

"Oh, Bill, shush."

Dino comes out first and stumbles around a melody, murmuring: *Drink to me only, that's all I ax, ask, and I will drink to you...I left my heart in France and Cisco.* The crowd laps it up. Dino's so saucy. How can you not love Dino?

Sinatra follows and does a solo number, but he's languid. Nobody in Chicago wants to hear "Chicago." It's embarrassing.

What, you think we're a bunch of yokels out here, Frank? He slows the tempo a little. *Toddlin' town*, he says, not singing, talking it, *swingin' town*. Still, the crowd doesn't go for it and the song's a bomb.

Finally, Sammy comes on and everybody starts waking up. He introduces himself as Harry Belafonte and starts with a hammed-up "What Kind of Fool Am I?" At first it gets a laugh. Sammy smiles wide, but then keeps going with it, goes deeper into the song. The crowd stops laughing and starts listening. Sammy, my God, that voice. Even mocking Belafonte, even without trying. The man sings a joke and still he sounds like an angel.

Why can't I cast away the mask of play and live my life?

The mobsters in the crowd start scratching themselves. The boy can sing, can't he now?

Then the highlight of the night, Frank and Dean join Sammy onstage. This is what everybody came for, the clan clowning. You want to listen to their music, put on a record at home.

Sammy sings, "She's Funny That Way." *I've got a woman…crazy for me…She's funny that way…I ain't got a dollar. Can't save a cent…She wouldn't holler…*

"Wouldn't holler?" Dean says. "That's too bad."

(Crowd giggles.)

She'd live in a tent.

"Jewish people don't live in tents," Frank says.

That Frank. He's not funny till he's funny, but by God when's he's funny—biggest laugh of the night goes to Sinatra.

"Don't live in tents!" Sid Kaufman howls. Even Babette laughs a little, and it always takes a lot to get Babette Kaufman to smile. Bernice doesn't laugh. She only keeps looking at the stage. All night, she's only been looking toward the stage.

Dean's still doubled over. Sammy, too. He can hardly breathe,

Sinatra's so goddamn funny. But watch Sammy closely when he comes back to the mike. He's still laughing, but his eyes are through with it. Sammy gazes out at the crowd, as if he's looking for somebody.

Seymour too is roaring along with everybody else. He smacks his knees. He gulps his drink. *Oh, that Frank.* But he thinks, I'm with you, Sam. You're one of us now. No matter how high you build yourself, they'll always find a way to tear you down. Damn right we don't live in tents, not anymore. Now we live out here in the suburbs with the rest of the musketeers.

With his free hand he reaches to rub the back of Bernice's neck. She shifts in her seat, only inches, but enough for his fingers to dangle, for a moment, before he retreats them to his drink. *Why can't I touch you, Beanie? Why do you always pull away?*

October 18, 1944

Mrs. Seymour Popper
1308 Lunt Avenue
Chicago 26, Illinois

What do you think about when the lights go out at home and you crawl in? You don't tell me what I want to hear—I'm sending you all my remaining war bonds—So if you wish to get that silver fox jacket, and Jules will extend us some credit on the strength of those—then go ahead—I don't want you running around to luncheons and be the only woman present without some fur—I'm being sarcastic, my lovely—Chatter says we ship out next month—
                                    Seymour
                                    Camp Bradford
                                    Norfolk, Virginia

PS. If you only knew how I look for your mail, you would never stop writing.

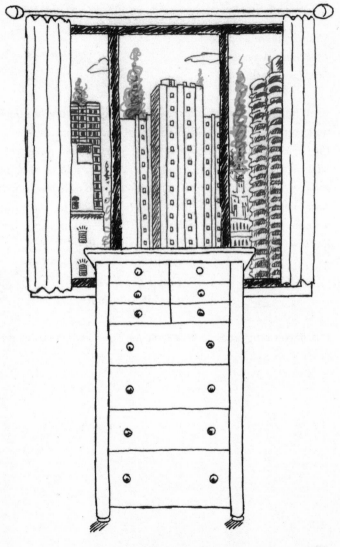

1444 North State Parkway

3

CHICAGO'S NOT A PLACE YOU LIVE

"A woman ought to be careful who she marries,"
said Mr. Dooley.

—Finley Peter Dunne, "Home Life of Geniuses"

MIRIAM

Fall River, Massachusetts, 1956

Miriam's father collected paperweights and phone books. The paperweights Miriam understood. She remembers one was of Robert Burns. The farmer poet, the great lover of freedom, her father always said. It was Burns who said, "Liberty's in every blow!/Let us do or die." *How's that for a man?*

Miriam used to ogle the poet's face. A beautiful man, high forehead, small tuft of hair, about to speak, sing, forever trapped in the thick glass of the paperweight.

But the phone books baffled her. Once she asked her father why. She was standing in his study and roaming her fingers across the rows and rows of Fall River directories.

"Why do you collect books that are all the same?"

He was sitting in his swivel chair with cigarettes in both his ears, entertaining her. She didn't want to be entertained. She simply wanted to know why. Why all the books that are the same book?

"All the same? Every year the dead and gone, and every year the born and added. God's math in its most fundamental form in these books. Same? Whose kid are you? Was there a mix-up at the hospital? Names, Squeezeface, don't you know, all those names, name after name after name, constitute the hope of all us fools.

We give our children names, Miss Foxglove, as if it makes any difference if they're called Jehovah or Omar. And still we do it, every day we do it. We stake our lives on names! Let's call him David, that one over there with the button head, how about Saul? Let's call him Jimbo, her Mary, her Sunshine. And you, you, my darlingest darling, let's call you, let's see. Hortense! No, what about Eleanor? Too Roosevelty. Hmmmm…Wait! I've got it. Miriam. How's that sound?"

"Why of all the names on the planet did you have to—"

"Have you not yet read Hawthorne's *The Marble Faun,* unworthy child?"

"I tried. Six times. Dull. And Mother says Miriam's life's tragic."

"Dull! Hawthorne! And Miriam's not tragic, she's mysterious. Wouldn't you like to be mysterious? Not to mention that Miriam was Moses's only sister and a prophetess in her own right until God gave her leprosy. Wonder why he did that?"

"I'd rather be Judy."

"Hawthorne, funny, a good marriage, but haunted, so haunted. I wonder what by—"

"Or Nancy."

"—the past, of course, what else? His and everyone else's. But even so, you'd think the gloom would lift once at the sight of his Sophia—"

"Sophia's nice."

"*Call me Nancy.* No, no ring to it. There's always got to be a ring in a name. Otherwise—"

"Even Susan, I'd take Susan over—Otherwise what?"

Her father didn't answer. You wouldn't be you and who would I be if you weren't you? I can't even imagine. But he didn't say it. Because wouldn't it have shot a hole in everything he just said?

Instead, he began to take the phone books one by one off the shelf. He piled them up in his arms until they towered past his head and swayed for a long moment as he intoned, The heaviness of names, the weight of names, names, each name in each of these books contains multitudes, a life, an inexplicable, never-knowable life...

> Kantowitz, David (Anna) Prime Poultry and Meat Mket
> Osb 7-9311
> Kanuse, Geo W (Rita) custdn City Hall Osb 5-7055
> Kaplan, Walt (Sarah) treas Kaplan Furniture Osb 6-8571
> Karagianes, Thos M. Pres Central Ice Cream Co Osb 9-5642
> Karitan, John (Shirley) taxi driver Osb 9-6411

In Spain

It wasn't that she betrayed him by leaving. Even he knew she was always going to leave. It was that she took the first boat out of Fall River without hardly looking over her shoulder.

Chicago? My Miriam left me for Chicago. You don't live in Chicago, Chicago's not a place you live, Chicago's a place you've heard of, read about in Upton Sinclair, that stink, maybe you visit for a convention, but live?

And where did you meet this Chicago?

I told you, I'm calling from Spain! I met Philip in Spain.

Never send your kid back to the Old World. How many generations did we spend getting the hell out of there? Spain! Don't you know Franco lives in Spain?

Tell Mother, don't worry, he's Jewish, and he's studying to be an attorney, and he'd like to run for office. He's got a terrific sense of humor and—This call is costing too much—We're getting married.

Is he kind, darling? It's my humble contention that kindness is still rarer than even Jews. And lawyers? Politicians? Comedians?—Sarah! Sarah! Your daughter's engaged to Bernard Baruch—

What?

On the phone, Sarah, she's on the phone—Spain—She says she's calling from Spain. Hurry, the charges—

55

It didn't mean she didn't love him. It wasn't even rebellion. At first she thought it was only relocation. She'll betray him again. When the time comes — not far off — she will sell his phone books, and if no one is foolish enough to buy them, she'll leave them on the sidewalk for the rain.

November 3, 1944

   So we had services here at the base in Puerto Rico this morning—There were about fifty other Jews, men and officers, and a rabbi who has only been in the Navy for a month—He did a fine job, though—He's a sad sack, too, leaving a wife and a 15 mo. old baby—You get religion when you're in an outfit like this—I want you to be sure that the children go to Sunday school and learn what it's all about—Get a little prayer book and let them learn a few prayers—Will you please go and have your pictures taken? When the ship goes down, I'll need something to hold—You and the children and you alone—Make them 5 x 7s. Go to Mandel's—Ask for Larry—

ROSEHILL

Chicago, 1961

An unmarked grave in Rosehill Cemetery on North Ravenswood in Rogers Park. Philip wanted him to be buried up north, near the old house on Lunt Avenue. Miriam didn't care what ground, what neighborhood. What could that possibly matter?

At a crossroads on the northwest side of the cemetery, near where Western Avenue meets Peterson, there is a tree with a white arrow that directs cars to go one way. From this tree walk south (away from the road) until you reach the Mortimer Kahn family plot. Then walk fifteen paces to the right. Should the tree ever be gone, the Mortimer Kahns never will be. They have perpetual care. From the Kahns walk fifteen paces to the right. Between the Felsenthals and the Braudys there is a small patch of slightly sunken grass.

She's forgotten other things, but not where his little bones are. He was so small he was hardly there at all. In more than forty years she hasn't gone back.

So long as she remembers.

They went out there in the rain with an assistant rabbi. He was kind. He was too young. He kept pushing hair out of his eyes.

Miriam tried not to look at his face. She was twenty-three years old. Philip stood back, blinking into the wet wind. She had insisted on no other mourners. She hardly listened to the words, but she remembers this, that the young rabbi recited something that he called a half Kaddish. And then lines from Deuteronomy, which ended with the words "And there was no strange god with him."

Later, she would sometimes think of him, not in the ground but somewhere out on the streets of the city, how if he headed west out of the apartment her dead boy could walk for days and never run out of sidewalk.

No strange god? The iron sky, thick and close. Miriam in the rain, March 1961.

1444 North State Parkway

Chicago, 1964

PHILIP (*in front of the TV, wagging a drink*): Johnson leads
   Goldwater by 65,000 votes in Kansas. In bleeding Kansas!
MIRIAM (*in the kitchen, making herself a martini, her one-year-old
   son, Leo, draped across her shoulder, balancing himself, his little
   legs and arms stretched, reaching*): And if Kansas goes for Big
   Daddy, who else can resist?

I t will pass. They aren't naïve. Good news always does. A lot
quicker than other news. They know that tomorrow will be
only another tomorrow and they'll again wake up alone, not lonely,
alone, and wonder why. Why so alone if we're here together?

Right now, though —

They turn out the lights and go to bed, but keep the TV going
in the living room all night, half-listening.

Leo sleeps in his crib to the lullaby of a landslide.

Their bookcase in the glow of the city undarkness: *Immortal
Poems of the English Language*, O'Hara's *Sermons and Soda-Water*, *The
Rubaiyat of Omar Khayyám*, Sandburg's *Lincoln: The Prairie Years, The
War Years* (Philip's, an unread gift from his father), Ferlinghetti's
Coney Island of the Mind (Miriam's), Sexton's *To Bedlam and Part Way
Back* (Miriam's), O'Neill's *Long Day's Journey into Night* (inscribed,

7-15-60, Dear Miriam, I hope you enjoy this trip as much as I have), Gold-stein's *Trial Technique*...

The television speaks in the dark:

> CHET HUNTLEY: We have received word from Providence that Lyndon Johnson has taken 89.9 percent of the vote in Rhode Island...
>
> PHILIP (*mumbles*): Khrushchev doesn't get 89.9 percent in Moscow. Come here.
>
> MIRIAM: I am here.
>
> PHILIP: I mean here here. All the way with LBJ.
>
> MIRIAM (*laughs, laughs*).

Because he used to make her laugh, Leo years later would tell his brother about the years before he existed. Explosive, croakish laughs. Leo said he used to lie in bed and worry she was choking.

THE FIRES

Chicago, 1968

Miriam watches the city burn. She stands motionless in front of the west-facing windows in the apartment on North State Parkway. A holy address, an address Philip, Miriam, and even Leo will later sometimes repeat like a prayer. *Oh, 1444 North State, it really was the perfect little starter apartment. The doorways had these chapel-like arches. There was a breakfast nook perfect for three, beautiful built-in walnut bookcases, and those huge west windows. Those were good years—*

But tonight. Dr. King is dead and tonight Chicago is destroying itself in his honor. All the lights in the apartment are off, and Miriam, motionless, stands at the window and watches the soft glow of the fires pulsing like a creeping second sunset. She's not afraid. She's never been a worrier. A little more than a mile away, but West Madison may as well be a different country. It is a different country. Up here there's no sound, only the thrum of the air conditioner. Miriam turned off the radio hours ago. *The rioters are moving west and burning as they go.* And the mayor said, *Stand up tonight and protect the city, I ask this very sincerely, very personally. Let's show to the United States and the world what the citizenry of Chicago is made of...*

Philip is away on business downstate. The phone rings often. She doesn't answer.

Leo's in his room, in his bed, his blond curls spread across the pillow. He's awake. In the darkness he listens to his turtle, Adlai, as he meanders around his tank, slow churnings in the sand.

Is this, Miriam wonders, what they call the march of history? And even if she doesn't fully understand, it doesn't mean she can't appreciate the need, the periodic need for some people to resort to gasoline, rags, and matches. Doesn't it always come to this? Isn't history as much about tearing things down as it is about building things up?

Out the window the rising band of fires glows wider.

Leo emerges from his room holding Adlai by the shell. Stubby green feet crawl the air. The turtle is used to this, being carried around the apartment by his five-year-old keeper.

"The fires are still?" Leo says.

"Yes, but they won't reach us."

"Why not?"

Miriam looks at him. His face is pale and serious. Leo and his questions. Leo's not five. He's never been five. Even holding a turtle he's not five.

"Because the police will protect us and the fire department will put out the fires."

"But why?"

"Why what?"

"Why do they want to get us?"

"Not us."

"Who, then?"

"They don't know who. That's the trouble. They're searching. But even if they did know, it wouldn't be us."

Leo shakes his head. He won't be had. "The bosses," he says. "They want to burn up the bosses."

Leo doesn't move. His wide eyes are mesmerized by the light.

"Honey, take Adlai back to bed."

Burn it. Burn it all and maybe they will listen.

Who?

I know who. My kid just told me who. Mayor Daley and the rest of the kings who rule the planet.

"They want to burn us, too, Mom."

"Leo, we're not the bosses. You and I will never be the bosses."

"We're not?"

Miriam watches her son. She smooths her rising stomach. Leo holds the turtle up to the window. Adlai claws across the emptiness.

November 19, 1944

Here we go—Tomorrow morning at 0800, destination unknown, length of time unknown—But my guess, my darling, is not too long, because when these Japs find out I'm on the way, they'll probably give up from laughing—And cripes, I forgot to tell you—You have to turn the water off to the hose connection in the yard so the pipes won't freeze—There is a little drain at the shutoff that should be opened, too—

A House with Trees

My God, what's wrong with us?
> —Arthur Schlesinger, Jr. (August 1968)

My thanks to you all and now it's on to Chicago and let's win there —
And Philip weeping, the story goes, Philip weeping, he can't stop weeping, kneels down to explain to Miriam's stomach that—contrary to what he or she inside there might be thinking now—the world, in addition to housing murderous rampagers, has, among other things, zoos, peacocks, and begonias. And Miriam laughed. She laughed through her own tears, even though all along she'd been for Gene McCarthy. Like a lot of people, Miriam loved Bobby more, so much more in newborn death than she ever did when he was alive.

"Now we're stuck with Humphrey," Philip said to her stomach. "And we know what Tricky Dick will do to him."

Still laughing, crying—Miriam—and then she wasn't laughing.

"Phil?"

"Yeah?" (His lips still on her stomach.)

"I want a house with trees. I want a house with trees and grass for the children. A lawn like a tablecloth."

"All right."

"Grass, lots of grass."

"Okay."

"A backyard *and* a front yard."

"Got it."

105 RIPARIAN LANE

We hear some very fine people are a bit disturbed over the settlement among us of some excellent families of the Hebrew faith. Tastes do differ, but why object to the sons and daughters of Abraham? We don't object to them, rather we commend them, for they pay their bills one hundred cents on the dollar every time and pay promptly and cheerfully any obligations they make... We will welcome the Hebrews here.

—*Sheridan Road Newsletter*, March 15, 1901

...and so northward to the new Jerusalem. It was what certain Chicago Jews did. When your time came, you migrated from the city to the North Shore.

Those who had the money went to Highland Park. Jews who didn't have means (the migrators liked to tell themselves) either stayed put in Rogers Park or they went north and inland away from the lake, to Skokie.

The young Popper family had the money and they didn't deviate. Plus, Seymour and Bernice had already paved the way to Highland Park, years before.

The moving van—a stuffed green Mayflower—creeps up the Kennedy Expressway, northward. Philip, Miriam, Leo, and the baby—Alexander. Having been delivered prematurely at Michael Reese Hospital in October of 1968, five and a half pounds, four ounces, the new kid was promptly robbed of his birthright. *So long, Chicago, I never even knew ye.*

The Poppers follow their furniture, giddy, apprehensive, beloved city shrinking behind them. The problem with any Promised Land is what you do after you get there.

Highland Park! (Leo shouting in the backseat.) No yippies! Better schools! Grandparents! No black people! Safer! I hate it already...

Shhhhhhhhh, precocious one, shhhhhhhhh.

A high place where the prairie convulses into ravines and the scalloped bluffs rise above the lake. It is part of what is known collectively as Chicagoland, a mythical place, a kind of parasitic hinterland that exists solely in the mind of those who dream of the city from a distance. Just half an hour away, depending on traffic. How do you begin to remember a place you've never left? It's not yet full winter, and memory is always November. The trees are stripped bare. Now you can see all the setback houses you hadn't been able to see in summer.

Welcome home, Alexander. We're making this sacrifice for you. A white colonial three doors down from the lake. 105 Riparian Lane. Two lawns—front and back—a flagpole, and matching wrought-iron benches on both sides of the front door.

SIR EDMUND

A half-open door, a triangle of light stretching across the kitchen floor. Miriam looks out the window at the new dog loose in the backyard. A Lhasa apso. Philip named him Sir Edmund Hillary. Nobody really got the joke, the dog especially. He's digging holes again. He doesn't bury anything. Sir Edmund has nothing to hide. He just digs holes. Upstairs, in the guest room, the new baby wails. *Maybe all this quiet wasn't such a hot idea.* On the counter curdled bacon soaks through a yellowing paper towel.

Lake Michigan, Winter

4

THE EAST WINDOW

Childhood recollected is often hallucination.

—Mavis Gallant, "Rose"

THE LAKE

His father taught him to swim by tossing him off the fishing pier at Cary Avenue Beach. Cold drizzle. Sink or swim, kid. Popper was four. Lake Michigan in his mouth, his ears, up his nose. The lake calm that day and rain was falling slowly. So calm he could concentrate completely on the cold. It was like being dropped into an icy bowl of cloudy soup, and it felt oddly right, the rush, the flailing around for breath itself.

And his father on the pier shouting: "Pull, Alexander, pull the water. Fingers together, thumbs locked — and now pull!"

Lake Michigan is 307 miles long, 118 miles at its widest. A total area of 22,300 square miles. "What's so great about the lake?" Philip would say, and Leo and Popper would shout, "No salt!" Ever since, Popper has imagined God with a huge salt shaker — his grandfather Seymour's, the one in the shape of Uncle Sam — so enormous God needs to hold it with both hands as he scatters salt and ruins the world's oceans. Yet God left the Great Lakes pure, because we in the Midwest are made of superior moral timber. The lake is always east. East is always the lake *and so is Jerusalem.* At ten, he will swim to the sandbar off Cary Avenue Beach and stand on top of blue itself, his blue, Lake Michigan! Sixth-largest lake in the world and young, very young. At 10,000 years, in geological terms, Lake Michigan is a punk. But that first time, bobbing upward, the sky upside down, his father vanished, Popper wasn't thinking about salt or size or even of water, though water was all there was and ever would be—water and his own skin, the uproar in his ears, and the way the cold made him nothing.

AT THE AMBASSADOR EAST

Remember a John-John haircut in the basement of the Ambassador East Hotel downtown. The place was very red, and the walls were padded. Old black men with graying hair and steady hands would cut Popper's hair gently, soothing him, *All right now, all right now.* Rubbing his neck sometimes with warm fingers. Didn't matter. Still, he screamed bloody murder. Why? Because he was moppy-headed and he wanted to stay moppy-headed.

Also, his hat. In order to get a haircut he had to take off his hat, *the* hat, given to him by his favorite Uncle Mose.

The sight of Uncle Mose's big blue honker coming through the door of Seymour and Bernice's house at 38 Sylvester Place. *Hail the family loser.* There was just something about the man. He rarely said very much, but he liked to come out to the suburbs every once in a while and see the family, the only family he had. Also, he needed money.

Mose walked with a limp and had a droopy face that swung from side to side like a basset hound's. His very blue nose was colossal, and his nostrils were like the hairy mouths of caves. He was Seymour's much older bachelor brother. Bernice once said at least he should have married somebody. People ought to get married, Bernice said, if only for the sake of appearances.

It was said Mose was a sad man—but his sadness seemed to manifest itself in a bunching of his forehead that always made him seem perpetually surprised, as if everything about the world—opening a door, sneezing, being broke and asking for handouts from Seymour—was all cause for wonder.

For a living, he sold suits on the Southside, not very far from where he and Seymour grew up. This, according to the family, was an almost unspeakable tragedy, given the relative success of his brother. Because he'd never thrived, the family was forever trying to diagnose him. What's wrong with Mose? *Oh, the man simply isn't a striver.* Once, he gave Popper an old hat of his, a sunken brown fedora with a missing band, and Popper lived under that protection for years.

Leo?
Yeah?
Were you asleep?
It's four in the morning.
What happened to Uncle Mose?
What?
Uncle Mose. He gave me my hat, remember? What happened to him?
He must have died at some point, no?
Wouldn't we have heard?
Call Dad and ask him.

Mose? No, he died in . . . hmmm. When did he . . . I always liked him. Didn't amount to much, but I for one always—

But wouldn't we know it if a man, a member of the family—

Alex, the man sold raincoats on South State Street. I have enough trouble with family that's living. I never see you, you never call. When you do, you talk about nonsense. Ask my mother.

My God, Mose is long dead! But you know something, dear, it's very strange. Seymour's brother. I honestly don't remember if he died or not.

And Leo upstairs in the lobby in Queen Elizabeth's chair (the one she graced when she visited Chicago), chatting up the concierge. We used to live right near here at 1444 North State Parkway, but my brother had to be born, I guess, and so we moved. Not that my parents don't regret it. Every day they regret—

The basement of the Ambassador East Hotel. How red the barbershop was, those puffy walls he always wanted to bang his face into. Plunked hatless in the chair, shoulders waggling, feet scissoring.

All right now, all right now, hold steady—

His father: Stop that fidgeting.

His mother: Come on, Phil, at least let him hold his hat.

Upstairs, Downstairs

The leather chair upstairs in the TV room. Her father's old chair. After Walt Kaplan died, Miriam had it shipped to Chicago from Fall River. Philip decreed it too ugly for the living room, so it was lugged upstairs to the TV room. After dinner the boys would race to it, that ancient veiny leather chair. The loser had to sit on the green couch. Leo would change the channel to *Upstairs, Downstairs* and turn up the volume. Not because he liked the show, or maybe he did, but mostly to drive his brother bananas. Or maybe, no. Maybe Leo had a strategy. Why not drown out the kitchen voices with some uproarious British comedy? Popper didn't know, at the time didn't care. All he knew was that he hated that show and he'd throw Paddington Bear at the screen, Babar, that toucan, what was the name of the toucan? A butler chases a skirty maid around and around a table with a candlestick, her tithering as if she doesn't like it, but she likes it. Popper knows she likes it. And the butler growls under his breath like a mad terrier.

The East Window

Or the grandfather clock downstairs, how Philip would never forget to wind it. He'd pull the chains and set the hands with his finger, and it would start again, the relentlessness of that tocking (no ticking, only tocking), and for years it lulled him until, at no time he can pinpoint, it stopped being a comfort. This is all he knows. That one night it soothed him and the next night and forever after—it didn't. His room. With the built-in white cabinets and the blue horseshoe wallpaper. Popper would lie there and listen to that tocking all night long, trying to hold the moment of the silent pause between beats.

Now he's certain he never slept an inch in all those years in that house, although of course he must have. He must have. It stands to reason. In order to wake up you have to sleep, but he doesn't remember ever opening his eyes in that room, because they were always already open, staring out at the dark east window, waiting for the first light to come slantwise from out beyond the lake.

THE SLAUGHTERHOUSE

Seymour claimed the stockyards as his birthright, his bloody inheritance. He'd tell the boys how he clawed his way from the slaughterhouse to the suburbs. The stench, he'd say. Once that death gets in your nostrils, it's up your nose for good. I take a snort of a flower and I still smell guts. My first job out of high school was to yank out the cow intestines with my bare hands and toss them out the window into Bubbly Creek. They called it Bubbly Creek because guts are hot. The next guy down the line would rip off the legs, the next guy the head, and so on. *I tell you, boys, the killing is nothing compared to the tearing apart.*

Seymour, behind his slab of desk like a tomb. Beside him the globe that seemed to be the exact circumference of his head. Remembering or inventing, what's the difference? He wanted his grandsons to understand the patent ugliness of this world. He worried they might become as soft as their father. His heroes were Don Rickles and Barry Goldwater, in that order. He said a man had to be bold. He said that the meek might well inherit the earth. They can have it. For the time being, grab your Cadillac.

———

"Jews didn't work in the slaughterhouses," Philip says. "I'm not saying we always had it so easy but we never packed meat: the Irish did that. Maybe some Italians."

They are walking back to Riparian Lane from Bernice and Seymour's house, about a mile away. The snow wanders down the sky and lands on his brother's hat, melts. His father's hat and melts.

"After high school, my father went straight to college in Champaign. And after college, he went to work for his old man selling insurance on Garfield Boulevard. When my grandfather Leopold died, he took over the business, expanded it, relocated downtown, pretty much wrecked it—but the man never once killed a single—"

"Seymour was in the Pacific theater," Leo says.

Popper slapping slush but listening. Who knew the little mute was listening?

"Theater is right," Philip says. "By the time he got in it, the war was practically over. He missed it. Why do you think it's so important to him? The man was thirty-nine years old when he signed up. He begged to go. Anything to get out of the house."

"What about Okinawa?" Leo says.

They walk over the bridge over the ravine. Popper sticks his head between the slats in the guardrail. The tall trees rise from his country of dead leaves.

"He watched Okinawa from his boat like he was at the movies. Grab your brother before he falls in the ravine."

"Bubbly Creek," Popper says.

Leo yanks Popper back from the guardrail, bonks him on the head for good measure.

Philip stops to shake the snow off his hat.

"I remember the day he came home. He walked into our house

in his full-dress blues. Esther and I ran up and started pulling on his legs. Daddy! We were faking it. We didn't know who the hell he was. Don't hit your brother."

Seymour told them many other things. He often sang of the beauties of insurance. *It's the dream protection business. Isn't life insurance a glorious thing? Can you imagine a more brilliant business plan? Deodorant follows the same concept. Creating need where none existed before is the great illusion of capitalism. And insurance is the crown jewel, a thousand times better than even deodorant, because it's all in your head, and what won't the people pay for a little calmness in their heads? They think if they pay up each month they won't die.*

He also had faith in the GOP and Quaker Oats. Every time he saw the Goodyear blimp on television Seymour's heart surged. You know what's also a very good product? Lubriderm. Hell of a stalwart product, a man's got to moisturize, too. Don't forget that, boys.

Jake Arvey in the Lobby of the Standard Club

"Who was I? A nobody! Nobody knew Jacob M. Arvey.
Yet I was elected alderman...I came to the attention of the
people."

—Jake Arvey in Milton Rakove's
We Don't Want Nobody Nobody Sent

Chicago, 1972

Jake! Philip says. But something in Arvey's face says, Not so
loud, kid. Not so loud. And so Philip leans toward the old
man and says, low, gruff, comradely, "Haven't seen you around
much, Jake."

Jake Arvey, the ancient political warhorse, stands, one foot
forward, one back, a boxing stance, on that lobby carpet that has,
since the thirties, been the same dark maroon of coagulated
blood. Teddy, the hat check man, watches, his mouth sealed shut.

Arvey says, "Talk a sec, Phil? In Teddy's office?"

"Sure, Jake." Philip follows Arvey through the little half-door
of the hat check. Arvey nods to Teddy, who doesn't nod back with
his head exactly, more with his eyes, so it only seems he's nod-
ding. And that's Teddy, graceful, beloved by the men who daily

entrust him with their coats, their hats, their secrets. Wives in the front door, girlfriends in the back door.

"My castle's your castle, Colonel Arvey," Teddy says.

Arvey laughs, and parts the coats. A sliver of a room, and yet isn't a coatroom like a tiny forest you can disappear into? Philip breathes up the animal smell of wet wool. Outside, it's sleeting. Arvey, an old friend of Seymour's from the war. It was Arvey who got Philip started with the city in the early sixties.

Phil, your father tells me you've hung out your own shingle.

It was simple, Colonel. I made myself a senior partner in half an hour.

Type of law?

Anything I can get my hands on, sir.

Listen, call the mayor's Mary Mullen at the Central Committee. Tell her you're Sy Popper's kid, that your old man sold insurance on Garfield Boulevard. Maybe get yourself a little city business. What was the address?

Which address?

On Garfield! Seymour's office. The mayor will want to know where you come from. How can he do anything for you if he doesn't know where you come from?

322 East Garfield.

Tell Mary that. Tell her 322 East Garfield. The Third Ward. And that I sent you. She'll get you an audience with his honor. Mary Mullen has opened more doors than Paul and Silas. And don't forget to send a contribution to the Party.

Of course, Colonel, of course...

In the coat check, Arvey squeezes his shoulder.

"The jig is up, kid."

"Which jig?"

"All of it. Every last nickel of it."

"You need money, Jake? Just say the—"

"Mortality, Philly. You'd think I would have thought about it by now, but I tell you, I woke up the other day and it occurred to me for the first time. Isn't that incredible? I'm going to Miami Beach to croak. I booked a room at the Doral. They asked me if I wanted a view. I said, What do I need a view for?"

He stares at the old man. Arvey's bony jowls the cartoonists used to make such hay out of. Philip digs his hands into his pockets and tinkles a little change. And then he thinks he gets it. Ah, all of it, all of it. Politics isn't what it used to be. The havoc of the '68 convention, riots, Vietnam, a lot of nonsense. The machine's decaying, petrifying. The mayor is still standing. The mayor will never be a man who needs to be propped. But for how long? And when he dies, they may as well bury his chair along with him. May as well dig a hole big enough for the whole fifth floor of City Hall while they're at it. And nationally? George McGovern? God save us. No, the jig is up up up.

Philip sees it, the state of their world. He grins. "You'll outlive us all, Jake," he says. "You're a horse."

Arvey sighs. He takes off his hat, and there's that shiny head in all its glory. Was it not Jake Arvey who whispered to Truman, *Come on, Harry, give the Jews a little country, haven't they been through enough?* But influence in the world is one thing, influence in this city something else entirely. For decades Arvey was ward boss of the mighty Twenty-fourth, the Democratest Democratic ward in the country. It's true he could even have been mayor, but when his time came—back in the forties—Henry Horner was in Springfield, and a Jew governor and a Jew mayor would have been too much for the Irish. Not that anybody in this city has ever given a damn who's governor. It was the principle of the thing. Two Jews would have been bad for the machine, bad for the party.

Arvey puts his hat back on, then spies another he likes better.

He trades his for it, a newer fedora of a slightly darker shade of brown.

"Fits, huh, Phil?"

"Not bad, Jake."

Philip stares at the rows of hats. Hats, Philip thinks, hats. In this city we men still wear hats.

"The sun will do you good," Philip says.

"Think so? I'll miss the weather here. It strengthens the character."

"Listen, Jake, I'm thinking about running for something. Chuckie Dalver's seat in the legislature—"

"There'll be time for that, Phil. You're not ready. Meantime, keep getting rich. How are your boys?"

"The older one's quite the artist."

"And pretty Miriam?"

"A bit bored in exile."

"Didn't I tell you?" Arvey says. "You want to talk about dying. Who does that girl have to talk to out there, the grasshoppers, the dandelions? And Seymour? How's the old lion?"

"My old man and I don't see eye to eye, Jake, never really have—he's voting for Nixon again."

"So is Vito Marzullo. What are you going to do? A good man, Seymour. How's his business?"

"Shaky."

Arvey sighs again, longer this time. A bloated sigh, and Philip waits in anticipation of more wisdom he'll remember. He feels for his own hat. It's gone. He already checked it with Teddy. He wants to ask him again about Chuckie Dalver. He looks at his shoes and listens to the old man breathe—then realizes it's his own breathing. Arvey's gone. Marched right out of the hat check and straight through the revolving door without a word. Philip joins Teddy at the half-door. They watch Arvey out the window hailing his own cab. It's still sleeting.

"He took somebody's hat," Philip says.

"Judge Epstein's," Teddy says.

"What are you going to do?"

"About what?"

"When Judge Epstein comes for his hat."

What kind of question? Colonel Arvey wants a hat, he takes a hat. Teddy stands silent in his yellow vest. The sleet drains down the windows. On the sidewalk, the old man bellows: "Yellow! Checker! Chariot of any color! I have no preference!" South Loop call of the wild.

Sleet makes a different sound than rain, even hard rain. Philip wishes he could put this washing-away noise into words, but he can't.

THE STAIRS

Leo stuck him in a sleeping bag and launched him down the stairs. He flounced slowly down and thumped into the front hall like a sack of laundry. Then he mudged up the stairs, the sleeping bag following him like the train of a gown. Again, Leo, do it again. Leo sent him with more force, and when he hit the floor, he careened and banged into the wall. In the kitchen, they stopped. His father stuck his head out the swinging kitchen door, the one that opened into the front hall.

"What was that?"

His mother's head appeared from the other kitchen door around the dining room corner. Her face raspberry, her hair tucked behind her ears. "Did you just throw your brother down the stairs?"

Leo, a hatless Mad Hatter cackling at the top of the stairs, shouts, "This house shall be a democracy!"

"What?" Phil says. "What the hell are you talking about?"

"Again, Leo! Do it again!"

HOLLIS OSGOOD

Miriam and Philip hired a houseman. Everybody else in Highland Park seemed to have a maid; only the Poppers had a man. He put up the storm windows. He ran errands in Miriam's VW Bug. Hollis babysat. He cooked. He slept in a small room in the basement from Tuesday to Friday. Mondays and weekends, the Poppers were on their own. At cocktail parties Hollis would wear a light blue shirt with ruffles and a black bow tie, and serve drinks with jokes and aplomb that always left the guests shrilling: We simply *love* Hollis. Where on earth did you find him?

A huge man, nights he'd fall asleep in his basement chair, by the Ping-Pong table, reading by the white light of the television. He liked his novels thick and endless. *Shogun* and *Clan of the Cave Bear. The Thorn Birds.* Popper would crawl over the mountain of him and sneak the clicker (one of those prehistoric ones that sounded like a staple gun) out of his hand and lie on the carpet beside his chair and change the channels until the racket would wake Hollis up and he'd say, Rodent, turn it back to Johnny Carson before I count to one and a half.

He smoked mentholated Kools. He said he had a daughter who lived in Cleveland. But the way he said the word, separating it out, *Cleave Land*, it sounded, to Popper, as if he meant to say she was dead—or so far away from him that she might as well be. A Korean War vet—Korean Emergency, Hollis called it. Precisely whose emergency, I'm still trying to decipher. He lost two fingers during the battle of Chosin. One was shot off, he said. The other froze off.

"Zander, which do you think I'd rather go through again?"

"Shot off. You already told me."

When he gripped Popper's neck, there was always something missing. There was strength, yes, he was strong, but there was also emptiness, and not only because of his missing fingers.

His stomach, solid as a refrigerator. Popper would make running starts from the back door, sprint into him, and bounce off. Hollis would shout, "Do it again and I'll call my lawyer on you." Philip was his lawyer. Philip was everybody's lawyer.

Hollis Osgood was born in Alabama. After Korea, he moved to Chicago to look for work. Miriam found him in the *Sun-Times* classifieds. You get born into a family. You get found in the classifieds.

Philip stands in the kitchen, squeaky galoshes. "Hollis, you think this floor is mopped? Do I have to do these things myself? Do I have to come home from an endless day and mop this myself?" In memory, Hollis is always taller than he actually was. He wasn't more than 5'7", about the same height as Philip. His stomach made him not only bigger but also more substantial, more rooted to the floor. He remembers being worried for his father. Couldn't Hollis at any time have decided to knock his lawyer down with one lazy swing of his hand?

STREETLIGHT

Their neighbor to the west, Mr. McLendon, used to throw rocks at the streetlight on the corner at three in the morning. His aim wasn't great, and some nights it would take him more than an hour to shatter the bulb. The thing was, he did it buck naked. The only thing he wore was shoes. It must have been that he only did this in summer or on warm spring nights, but Popper can't keep himself from remembering that he was also out there in the snow.

Mr. McLendon worked for the phone company, in the yellow Illinois Bell building on Second Street across the street from where Stasha's (Vienna Beef) used to be. It was said that he married Mrs. McLendon for her love, not her money. Whether she spent any love on him is still open to speculation, but the word was that Mrs. McLendon had tons of money, serious money. She was part of what people called "Old" Highland Park (meaning: before the Jews came). Her house looked like some Southern plantation airlifted to northern Illinois by genies. It had huge white pillars you couldn't even wrap your arms around. Parked in the garage, a black '67 Lincoln Continental and a surrey. They never saw much of Mrs. McLendon, but they often saw her dog. Mrs. McLendon had a black miniature schnauzer named Cassandra, actually a succession of miniature black schnauzers named Cassandra. When one Cassandra died, which they did with alarming frequency throughout Popper's childhood, she got another, the new one meaner than the last.

And some nights, Mr. McLendon out in the street, throwing rocks at the light. A thin, pale man with hairless legs the color of bone. In the morning, he'd leave the house, an ordinary man in an ordinary suit, a *Tribune* under his arm.

"Alex, wake up. He's out there again."

He followed Leo back to his room and they watched him out the window.

"His wife won't love him," Leo said. "He'd rather be dead. But since he lacks courage, he takes it out on Commonwealth Edison, which isn't a bad choice, really."

"Why doesn't he put some clothes on?"

"This sort of thing needs to be done as purely as possible."

"And in the morning?"

"In the morning what?"

"In the morning does he want to be dead?"

"In the morning he works for Illinois Bell."

"Oh."

Here is a useless revelation. Popper and his brother witnessed some petty vandalism and (possibly unintentional) exhibitionism in 1973.

One day he died. There was no announcement, no obituary in the *Highland Park News*. No one dropped by to pay their respects. Miriam, though, sent over a card. Mrs. McLendon went on calling her dog. Popper would like to call the phone company and ask about Mr. McLendon, but there is no Illinois Bell you can call anymore. The streetlight must have shined into his bedroom window, the one he shared or didn't share with Mrs. McLendon. But Mr. McLendon's hatred for it went beyond the light in his eyes, the light that exposed what he didn't want exposed, Leo told his brother, to the idea of the light itself. Couldn't it leave Riparian Lane's little miseries alone? His wife won't love him. Isn't this bad enough? Let a man sleep. Not white but yellow, an unnatural, radioactive egg, that light on the corner of Riparian and Sycamore.

Men's Room

I n the private men's room, the second floor of the Standard Club. The attendant, Mr. Hopkins — white pants, white shirt — sits straight-backed, listening to the radio murmur, a towel draped over his forearm.

Philip and Arvey, side by side, the tall marble urinals, ice and fruit at the bottom. Hot piss cracks the ice.

"You're not dead, Jake."

"How do you know?"

"Tell me something I can use."

Arvey's finished but remains standing before the urinal as if it's a lectern. Mr. Hopkins coughs into his hand.

"Something regarding what?"

"Politics, Jake, what else is there under the sun?"

"Enough of politics. Napoleon said politics is destiny. And you know what?"

"What?"

"What did that French midget know about Chicago? Politics is vaudeville."

"The colonel returneth!"

"And power?"

"Yeah?"

"Power is my old friend Harry Truman."

"The bomb?"

"Forget the bomb. I'm talking about Doug MacArthur. Compared to MacArthur, Nagasaki was a tennis ball. Truman canned MacArthur not because he was the better man but because he wasn't and could fire him, anyway."

The light in the men's room. The gleek of the ice cracking. A near-forgotten old man sermonizing to a not-so-successful disciple. The two men move to the sinks to scrub their hands.

Mr. Hopkins stands silent, washcloths at the ready.

"Jake?"

"Yeah, Phil?"

"I'm going to do it. I'm going to run for Chuckie Dalver's seat. I think the man's ripe."

Arvey takes a towel from Mr. Hopkins and dries his hands slowly, thoroughly, each finger. "He's not," Arvey says. "Not yet, anyway. Dalver's a zero, but he's got another two terms in him at least. But go ahead, what's the worst that can happen?"

January 25, 1945

Incidentally, I didn't like that crack about us never being rich, but we'll be happy anyway—I have every intention of being rich, and I for one have the utmost confidence in my becoming so, and if I had you right here at this moment, I'd make you rich—It's got to be rich as hell with all this saving up—and this ship has such a lovely motion— How are things at home?

At the Kitchen Table

Come into the house through the garage, the mudroom with its retired platoons of rubber boots and galoshes and crinkled sneakers, toes pointing upward, like crushed little boats. Into the kitchen with the small round table about the size of a wagon wheel, the four of them would crowd around, the black iron light fixture, the fat bulbs hanging so low they sometimes grazed their heads. The blue china wedding dishes with the rusty cracks. The kitchen never smells of anything because Hollis spends so much time scrubbing and disinfecting. Dinner, the four of them. Hollis always eats in the basement, though Miriam was always saying we really ought to get a bigger table. Finally Hollis said, "I appreciate the sentiment, Mrs. Popper, the truth is, I prefer to dine alone."

Miriam reaches into the freezer for Philip's Schlitz, and for a moment there's a loft of snowy air before she shuts the door. Her fingers snap off the top of the silver can and toss the sharp tab in the garbage. She pours the beer down the glass.

He's not one of them. They try not to show it. Philip returns from gladiating downtown to a conspiracy of silence.

To say something, anything, Leo says, "Did you hear the news? Alexander Butterworth says there's a taping system in the Oval Office."

"Butterwho?" Philip says.

"Alexander Butterworth. An aide to Nixon. He says there's tapes. That Nixon tapes everything. The truth is going to be on the tapes."

"Is it?" Philip says. "The one and only truth? And this Butternut has it? You believe that? Even I'm beginning to sympathize with Nixon. The thing's become a witchhunt. They're looking for bodies in every closet."

"It's all recorded," Leo says. "Everything. Recorded."

Beyond Miriam's head, the window above the sink that looks out into the backyard, where Popper would often see her standing, years of her standing, the sheeny curtains the cat, Louise, tore up. On the counter the little television the President will resign on. The iron pots hanging from long hooks. Above the stove, those mustard-colored tiles in the shape of bells.

PHIL POPPER PHENOMENAL

Philip's campaign for the Illinois State Senate, Thirty-second District. Popper remembers the blazing orange bumper stickers, loud as a crossing-guard sash, emblazoned with the three P's: *Phil Popper Phenomenal.* They were more common around the house than on anybody's cars. It was Miriam who came up with the slogan. It barely fit on the stickers. She was campaign manager and loved it. It got her out of the house.

"Phenomenal what?" Philip had asked.

"Oh, just phenomenal phenomenal," Miriam said.

Those bumper stickers. And those *Phil Popper Phenomenal* pens that Popper used to like to take apart and then put back together minus the little spring, so that when somebody went to write with one it wouldn't work. His father gave anti-Nixon speeches to small yawning audiences across Lake County, Miriam applauding wildly. At home, they strategized at the kitchen table late into the night.

"You're not connecting to your audience, Phil."

"Maybe I should talk more about Vietnam."

"Vietnam is over, Phil."

"Is it? I read the other day it was still going on. That Kissinger and Ford —"

"Don't save the country. Nobody wants the country saved. What if you talked about crime?"

"Crime, in Lake County?"

"People can't get enough of crime. When it isn't there, they still want to hear it is coming to get them. You need an issue, Phil, an issue people care about, or at least think they care about."

"My issue is, I'm not Chuckie Dalver. What kind of name is Chuckie anyway?"

"American."

The two of them, Miriam and Philip, at the kitchen table, their knees touching beneath the table, between them precinct maps, call lists, cold coffee. Sir Edmund asleep on his mat, the little TV on without volume, the late-night movie on CBS.

"How do you feel about ERA?"

"I like women, you know I've always liked women."

"I know, Phil. What about equal pay?"

"Sure."

"The Zion nuclear power plant. What's your position?"

"Of course they'd build a nuclear plant in Zion."

"I like that. You even might be able to use it. But it's not a position."

"I'm for the plant."

"No, you're not."

"I'm against it."

"No."

"Damn it, Miriam. I can't be both."

"You can. You love the energy source and the jobs. *And* you're scared to death of nuclear power. You can't sleep you're so afraid of nuclear power. Depends on who asks and how they ask it."

"This is serious, I'm trying to—You've got everything all twisted. What am I trying to—I want to stand for something."

"But you don't, and since you don't, my thought is—"

"All right."

"People don't elect people, they elect visions of themselves, and you've got to do something to connect—"

"I said all right."

Leo interrupts, strolling into the kitchen with his little brother hostaged in a headlock. "What about the Crosstown Expressway?"

"What's that got to do with Lake County?" Philip says.

"State money's going to build it. You think the people out here want to give money so Mayor Daley can build another highway? There's an issue, Dad. Think local."

"Go back upstairs, both of you," Philip says. "And by the way, if Mayor Daley wants to build a highway, I'm going to send you out there to help tar it, Leo."

Still holding his brother's head in a headlock, Leo says, "Alexander wants juice." On the little TV, Shelley Winters screams soundlessly, flailing, drowning. "Hey," Leo says. "Isn't that *Poseidon Adventure?*"

As a family, they went door to door to door. They handed out literature in front of supermarkets, the post office, banks, the A&W in Crystal Lake. In some place called Lincolnshire, Leo and Popper stood on a corner holding *Phil Popper Phenomenal* signs for three hours until Miriam came to pick them up. Leo lied and said one person honked, and Miriam cheered, "See? We're getting our message across!"

"Wait, what's our message again?"

"Shush, Leo."

During the last week of the election, they rented a double-decker London bus and wandered Lake County looking for votes in grand style. From a loudspeaker, Philip extolled ERA. "You know, I've always loved women…" Hollis drove and spoke in an English accent that Popper sometimes repeats to himself in his daydreams like a chant… *Cheerio! Cheerio! Won't you be so good as to vote for my dear friend and yours, Phil Popper, for the State Senate? Quite frankly, and there really is no other way to put it, he's simply phenom—*

On a side street in Lake Forest lined with oaks, a PPP volunteer, a friend of Bernice's named Gert Zetland, got hit by a low branch and knocked unconscious.

A 22 percent drubbing. Chuckie Dalver? The man died in office in the early nineties after eight and a half terms, and even then nobody much remembered he'd been in the legislature all that time. But there's this. In 1974, Philip Popper ran against him. In October of that year, toward the end of the campaign, Gert Zetland got upended by a tree and needed eighteen stitches in her forehead, a fact that remains remembered in stone.

5

IN THE COUNTRY OF DEAD LEAVES

February 3, 1945

*I bought you the perfume and stockings in Panama—
Well, I have to say, Colón is some spot—girls—everywhere—
White, black, brown, cream, every other color you can
imagine—Panamanians, Nicaraguans, Costa Ricans, Bra-
zilians, Indians, Africans, Cubans—One waiter even pointed
out a Russian—They all speak about ten words in English—
We were all drinking something they call a Blue Moon—
They call it that because it makes you think the moon is
blue—It was strong enough to eat cement—Most of these
girls are very young—Of course, they're all good and all
have their crosses around their necks—Finally the pretty
one sitting next to me said, "Me pussy—Doctor says O.K."—
She had been acting so dignified and then this "Me pussy"
business—Then the tag line—She wanted $15—I must have
made an impression on her because the other fellows couldn't
do any better than $25—There's life in the Navy for you—Of
course, darling, I didn't indulge—What kind of s.o.b. do
you take me for?*

38 Sylvester Place

Summer and chaos in the trees. Carcasses rain from branches. Lawns wear coats of brittle, crunchable bodies. Pebbles of eyes stare up at the sky. Over breakfast, Miriam explains their sudden appearance. "These harmless insects emerge out of the ground every seventeen years in order to have intercourse. That's enough sugar in your cereal, honey. Then they die. In Mexico, people consider them a delicacy."

"Intercourse means screwing," Leo says.

"Leo, stop educating your brother. You don't want him to resent you when he's older. And remember, the only certain thing is you'll be brothers forever."

Far freakier, though, is the noise that is beyond noise, an hysteria, a never-ceasing throb that rises and falls all day, all night, a perpetual seethe. They sleep to it, wake to it. And yet after a few weeks it is as though this has always been the sound of all the days and nights, and the truth is, they have always been here, lurking beneath, waiting, biding the years patiently before it is time to crawl out of the ground, whoop it up, and screw and screw and screw—and then die happy.

Nobody ever went into the living room of Bernice and Seymour's house on Sylvester Place. It was a room for entertaining in an era that was over, a no-man's-land of too thick carpeting, crowded with unused furniture. There was a plush rose-colored sofa. If you sat on it, your assprint was impossible to rub away. Rub the cushion all you wanted, it still looked sat on and would be proof that you had crossed the border from the den into that forbidden zone. There was a fireplace with old, unswept ashes. On the wall was an abstract painting made up of red and brown slashes. It was said to be by someone well known. There were heavy drapes that allowed no light.

One night, Dean Martin and Sammy Davis, Jr., had sat in that very room. Sinatra was supposed to come, but sent his regrets. Milton Berle, Dinah Shore, Ruth Roman, Raymond Burr, Nipsey Russell, Danny Kaye, Barney Ross, the boxer. Former Vice President of the United States, Alben Barkley—all, at one time or another, had graced the living room. Cloris Leachman also. Bernice said she had a snorty laugh and that she fell asleep on the plush sofa. Cloris Leachman slept through the party. All this fame and fortune in the house because back in the day Bernice and Seymour were grand pals of a famous Chicago gossip columnist Sid Kaufman and his wife, Babette. Sid Kaufman knew anybody and everybody, since anybody and everybody has to, at least once in a while, grace Chicago with their presence. And when they do come, someone has to write about them. So: who didn't love Sid Kaufman?

Chicago does not go to the world, the world comes to Chicago! Who needs New York? Who has taller buildings than our tall buildings? Who's got a busier airport than our airport? You want

Picasso? We got Picasso, big Picasso. Nobody can make heads or tails of it. It's a lion? No, a seahorse. Looks to me like a radiator with wings. Who gives a damn, people, a Picasso's a Picasso.

During the period of this long friendship, the Poppers themselves often appeared in Sid Kaufman's column... *We hear that old man of the sea Capt. (and insurance magnet) Sy Popper caught a 150 pound blue marlin off the coast of Bimini, but we'll have to see the pictures and the official measurement data to believe it, as the good Capt. is prone to exaggerate... In the bibs and diapers department, it's a boy! Leo Morris, to Philip and Miriam Popper (née Kaplan) of North State Parkway... Heartbroken young men of Chicago, unite, the beautiful Esther Popper's engaged to a doctor, hear that, boys, Aphrodite's off the market... Philip Popper has been recognized by the Cook County Bar Association as one of the Chicago legal profession's Next Generation Leaders, our hats off to this young Brandeis...*

And back in those days Sid would sometimes want to show his famous friends and clients the view from the North Shore. He'd call Bernice in the afternoon. *Beanie, listen, Tony Bennett's in town, says he wants to meet some real people for a change, some flesh-and-blood people. Eleven-thirty all right? We'll come after the show at the Airie Crown tonight. Oh for God's sake, Beanie, forget the beauty parlor, your hair's terrific stuff.*

All that years ago. The friendship ended. Sometime in the mid-sixties Sid and Babette dropped the Poppers from their set. It was said to involve money, but who ever knows? Friendships, like friends, they die. All those gone nights of witty conversation, all those nights of lots of laughs.

In the summer of '76, his grandparents went up to New Buffalo for a few days. Before they left, Bernice asked Miriam to check on the house. To Popper, the long-since-sold house on Sylvester Place remains a rambling, endless place with yet-to-be-discovered walk-in closets. The laundry chute where he and Leo practiced Morse code. The upstairs with all those small boarding-house bedrooms. That house, even when it was filled with people, had always felt like a lonely hotel. Drawers still filled with Philip and Esther's old clothes. The master bedroom. Bernice's beauty table with those little lights he loved to unscrew and those two rock-hard twin beds separated by a nightstand. The alley between those beds. Seymour's paperbacks stacked on the nightstand. *The Case of the Borrowed Brunette; The Case of the Screaming Woman; It's Loaded, Mr. Bauer; The Girl in the Turquoise Bikini; Death Commits Bigamy.*

A quick check of the house and all is well. No gang of thieves has broken in. The Zenith is still lording in the den. There has been no explosion, no gas-main leak. No flood in the basement. A tree has not fallen on the roof. Popper leaves his mother in the bedroom, where she's picked up one of Seymour's books and begun to read. He goes downstairs and takes his shoes off and creeps into the living room. To say hello to the forgotten, the dead, the has-been, the hardly ever known, and there is something about the dark that is moving. Another step and the carpet itself is writhing beneath his toes. The drapes, the sacred sofa; they are scrawling across the slashes of the painting, now up and down his own arms. He stuffs his fist in his mouth to keep from screaming, but he's screaming screaming screaming.

Later, they found out that Seymour had left the flue open. In a room that was never used. How many years had that open chimney been waiting for those patient bugs? Who needs a gossip columnist? Decadence returns. The yuks and then some—it all comes back around to an abandoned room.

If the Bolsheviks are going to blow us up anyway, I say why not a little batta batta bing while we're waiting! You know what I mean, hey?
Oh, Seymour, even the bomb wouldn't inspire you to—
Me? Inspire me? You haven't been in the mood since Hoover.
Hey, Tony B, didn't I tell you the view from here was real?

People bleed easy. Cicadas, even when you stomp on them, don't bleed. You can't violate their corpses short of plucking out their beady eyes and ripping off their wings. And even then they don't care. Why should they? *We've had all the fun that's to be had on earth. Do what you want with us. You think you can take away our ecstasy just by murdering us?*

Miriam put on Seymour's gardening gloves and began dropping them all, the living and the dead, in garbage bags.

Miss Patel

Potawatomi Trail School. It was her first year teaching. She tried to love them all equally. She was like a new mother with twins, kissing one of them and then the other. Her nose didn't point straight. She didn't waste a hell of a lot of time on math. For Valentine's Day, they made decorative napkins for their mothers. They studied the insects of the Midwest: *American cockroach, earwig, periodic cicada, stinkbug.* Miss Patel's breasts were like small ant-hills that Popper's hands craved smoothing. Her hair was short, but got in her eyes anyway. She said she hated chalk, but for them she would write on the board. She said tornado drills and even tornadoes themselves were bosh. She said in Pakistan nobody ever heard of a tornado. The proper word was typhoon. She never ate anything herself, but she liked to feed the fish. Think about the way she sprinkled the food with both hands, her fingers rubbing together. Her one mistake: she taught Popper how to read. Other days her breasts were more like upside-down cereal bowls.

Also, you were kind to him when he crapped in his purple corduroys.

Miss Patel.

Wilmot Mountain

There they froze their gonads off. Not a mountain, or a hill either. Wilmot was a blump of old trash mounded on the prairie. Up the chairlift, down the treacherous ice. There must have been a ski school instructor around somewhere whose job it was to instruct them on how to widen their snowplows. *Pinch in your knees. Don't drag your poles. Try and go down the hill a little, not just across it.* Someone must have told them how to manage the rope tow without hanging themselves. But this, all for show. Miriam must have paid somebody for something. She thought they should learn to ski because it was something that she herself never experienced, and above everything, Miriam wanted them to have experiences. From the chairlift, slumped, they look out across the fields, the tall grass poking up out of the Wisconsin snow like scattered pepper. And they muttered to each other through frozen spit-encrusted ski masks. Leo wondered what unknown sin they must have committed in some previous life to deserve this. The answer came the same way their feet later shocked to life in the warming hut after being so numb for hours — you think you'll never feel your toes again, and then all of a sudden life, damaged, stiffened, clammy, but life, dog-eat-dog life! *We have done not a single thing to deserve this.* Ski boots like lead weights, the lacerating wind; the two of them half-blind snowsuited nomads.

"I feel like Doctor Zhivago wandering the steppe," Leo said.

This Midwestern gulag their birthright. Their frigid hands, their frigid feet.

HOLLIS

For his sixth birthday, Hollis bought Popper a subscription to *Sports Illustrated*, and he remembers stretching out on the kitchen floor while Hollis was trying to mop it and flipping through the magazine, hoping to prove how much he loved baseball and Willie Stargell.

"Get out of here."

"Mop me, why should I care?"

Hollis shadowing over him. "I'll wash you to Cuba. Who's raising you?"

"You are."

"All right, then. Let's start with your toenails. Never have I seen anything so foul in my—Go get the clippers—"

"Adopt me, then. No one will notice. I could come back here with you on Tuesdays. Where do you go on weekends and Mondays, anyway?"

"Where do I go?" Hollis stepped away, surprised, thinks about a west side apartment where he came and went, never much stayed, never much thought about. "Interesting question. On weekends and Mondays, I, allegedly, go home."

"Home?"

"2323 West Monroe. Apartment D."

Hollis in his room in the basement listening to his radio in his sleep. He never seemed to get into bed; he always slept on top of the sheets. And he never seemed to really sleep, either. You could go to Hollis at any time of the night and say, "Hollis?"

His head hidden by the mound of his stomach. "What do you need, Zander?"

"Cough medicine."

"In the kitchen cabinet above the spices. I'll get it. Don't wake your mother. Or him. Wait for me."

Pharaoh Drawing

His boss, his alderman, his Kaiser, his Ayatollah, his Colonel
Mustard — *Okay, listen, Alexanderplatz, you be the Jews on the
run, I'm the Pharaoh. Flee! Run for your lives! Go! Take off!*

He flees to his private place in the backyard, in the left-hand
corner. A place where nobody cut down the bramble or the
stunted sun-starved trees and nobody mowed the long stalks of
prairie grass into submission. A tiny wild corner where Hollis
stored the storm windows under an old green tarp. There was an
upside-down wheelbarrow and a rusted-out jungle gym like a
mangled octopus. You got there through a gap in the azaleas, and
Popper used to dig himself a cave in the mound of raked and
forgotten leaves. Pharaoh knows where the Jews are. Pharaoh
always knows where the Jews are. What are Jews to him? No,
what this Pharaoh wants is to be left alone. No game, only the
ruse of getting rid of a brother. But wouldn't it be polite to at least
look a little? No, Pharaoh only draws; Pharaoh lies on the grass
with his notebook and his pens and he draws.

Popper, waiting, breathes up the smell of fermenting leaves, a
sweet combination of wet dirt and rot and worms. The Indians
used to bury their dead in mounds around here. In the Hoynes'
yard around the corner there's a lump in the lawn that you can see

isn't right. His father showed it to him. A mass grave, Philip said, God only knows what these dead Potawatomi think of Highland Park now. We were massacred so you greedies can have three-car garages?

Popper waits for Pharaoh. He's learned how. Waiting is different from having patience. Patience he'll never learn. But waiting. All you have to do is lie back in the rot and breathe. You can even sing a little to yourself. Chew on a leaf. He wonders if a grave, any grave, is only another place to hide in plain sight.

A second-floor window shoves open. Hollis leans out and booms to the neighborhood: "I have in my possession an item of soiled underwear that was found under a certain delinquent's bed wrapped in newspaper. Please explain this behavior. In Korea, in their little mud huts, even those people wouldn't—you want me to call my lawyer?"

"Kid," Leo says, not looking up from his drawing, "Hollis wants you."

MANNY'S HOUSE

Saturday, and Popper is riding his bike to Manny Laveneaux's house, the greatest of all houses, through the woods and across the little bridge over the ravine where he and Manny and his sisters sled in the winters, that long, snaking canal of leaves — when out of nowhere two high hippies in floppy Dr. Seuss hats jump out from the dry leaves under the little bridge and grab hold of Popper's banana seat and breathe, *Where do you think you're going, little bourgeoisie fuck?* Yanking his bike back and forth and breathing in his face, and he's staring at them, dumb and shivering in June. *I'm only going to Manny's.* Finally they get bored with scaring the hell out of him and let him go, and now Popper thinks of his bulbous-headed self, pedaling away so fast to freedom his left shoe fell off. And the way that grand old paintless house looked when he came out of the woods. An old wreck of a colonial mansion, boarded-up windows, like nailed-shut eyes. He rides up the crumbling driveway, a vision of the lake just over the lip of the bluff. He goes in the back door because the front door is also nailed shut. The way Manny's grandmother, past eighty even then, looked standing in the dark cavernous kitchen beside the long metal table Manny said was for dissecting bodies when the richest of the rich still lived there. She was taller even than Manny's father, and hadn't spoken a single word of English in the three years since she'd come from Port-au-Prince, but after Popper burst in the door—he's never burst in before, he'd always knocked—she walked over to him and knelt and said something in Creole, because she must have seen something in his eyes and understood. *Pas peur*, she said. *Pas peur.* The only time Manny's grandmother ever touched him, two long untrembling fingers pulling the bottom of his chin before he scrambled up the winding staircase with the hundred broken balusters to tell Manny and his sisters about the two Charlie Mansons under the bridge, like a couple of trolls down there waiting for anybody.

February 4, 1944

   And another thing, don't believe all this travel folder talk about how stimulating the salt air can be—Already I'm so damn sick of the rolling I could cry—You spend all your energy balancing yourself unconsciously—sitting, standing, walking, even sleeping—So far we haven't seen much outside of a school of porpoise—But last night toward sunset— the biggest shark I ever saw—a real monster, about 16 feet long, jumped out of the water about ten times just off our stern—God, I wish Sid was here to see it—His eyes would have popped out of his head—That would have given him something to write about, boy—I think he was dying though, because he kept falling on his back—

PHILIP AND SEYMOUR

In the plum, thickly carpeted, Standard Club dining room, Philip and Seymour are finishing their steaks. Philip is doing well. Just recently, he took on two new partners and moved his firm to the sixteenth floor of the Monadnock Building. Seymour is moving, inexorably, in the other direction. It's still in question how long he'll be able to hold on. Still, his slow bankruptcy has only made Seymour more Seymour. He remains free with unsolicited advice. Today, though, is different. He has news, astounding news, and he's waited patiently until after their sirloins and creamed spinach to tell it. Inhaling hugely, Seymour releases a potent cloud of meaty breath and announces, softly:

"Phil. Listen. Melvie Kaufman's been kidnapped. Ransom. A hundred thousand." Seymour pauses and awes: "Cash."

Philip slowly lifts his eyes off his plate.

"Can you believe this? An innocent man minding his own business in his own driveway. Sid called me this morning. Said he needed paper money. Small amounts. Said my boy's in a real stink this time. I said I'd talk to you. You know I'll give what I can, but you know how things are right now."

"Sid called you?"

"When a man's in trouble, a man's in trouble. Who's Sid going to call, Marlon Brando?"

"Why not?"

"Friends is friends, Phil. Sid will pay it back with five percent interest."

Philip leans backward in his chair so that for a moment he's balancing on two legs. He remains up there for a moment, a cowboy on a rearing upholstered steed, before thumping back to the carpet.

"Wait a second," he says. "Who'd want Melvie?"

"That's not funny."

"You think I'm kidding?"

"Phil."

Because for the past twenty-six years, Philip Popper has toiled in the little shadow of Sid Kaufman's puny son, Melvie. Born on third base, halfway to home. With a famous father, doors don't open, they were never closed in the first place. Come on in, Melvie. Here's a job. (What does Melvie do again, manage nightclubs?) Here's a house on the lake. Here's a wife. North Shore perfection incarnate, Rona Grubner.

Philip at Melvie's wedding at the old Moraine Hotel congratulating the blissful couple, grazing Rona Grubner's scrumptious cheeks with his own dry lips.

It isn't like Philip never had any help. He did. If it hadn't been for Jake Arvey, he might be fixing speeding tickets for a living. But now he hustles. Every day, every hour, he hustles. Melvie never had to lift a pinkie and he doesn't even know it.

"What I'd really like to know," Philip says, "is who nabbed him. Now, there's an outfit I'd invest some real capital—"

"A man's been kidnapped. And you—"

The room goes silent as forks clatter to plates and men of business and law turn to watch. Seymour Popper can't be the only one at the Standard Club who knows. By eleven o'clock that morning, Sid had phoned at least twenty potentials trying to raise the money. But he'd also begged each of them to keep the thing under wraps. *Who knows what these looney tunes are capable of, and you know my Melvin's no King Kong.* Judge Abe Lincoln Marovitz is only a couple of tables away. And isn't that Pickard from the Harris Bank at the corner table beneath the china cabinet? *For Christ's sake, I'm even more ruined than I already am.*

Philip looks past his father and stares out the window at South Wacker Drive. He sniffs his drink before gulping it down in a single swoon. He finishes off the last of his creamed spinach.

"What do you need?"

"Fifteen grand in small bills by tomorrow morning."

Melvie escaped that afternoon from the basement of a house on Cicero Avenue, out by Midway Airport. Typical of Melvie Kaufman's luck—to get nabbed by a couple of novices. They stripped him down to his boxer shorts and locked him in a bathroom with a window. Then the goofs went out for a few beers to celebrate how easy it was. So many years of night shifts, morning shifts, afternoon shifts, and all you had to do was pluck a famous man's kid out of his driveway. An easy couple hundred thousand in cash. *Tiptoe through the tulips, fellas. The next round's on us!* Philip's still haunted by the image of Melvie Kaufman scooting down the block in his underwear. The headline: COLUMNIST'S SON IN MASTERFUL ESCAPE, KIDNAPPERS NABBED IN TAVERN. Ever since, Philip has wondered if there isn't more to it, if luck itself isn't part of some grand design and you either opened yourself up to it or you closed yourself off. What's the angle? That's what he's always wanted to know.

At the moment though, it being still lunchtime, Melvie is still kidnapped. "Maybe they'll tie a brick—" Philip begins to say but there's no time left to say *around his neck and dump him in the Calumet*—because time congeals in that dining room with the long tall windows and the red-and-white-striped mints in a bowl by the elevator and Paulo, the weary headwaiter in his green coat with the black-and-gold-striped sleeves who grinned with his teeth once a year on Thanksgiving. Seymour lunges across the table, elbows in a puddle of Worcestershire sauce, tablecloth scrunching, glasses crashing.

FROM THE NAVAL LIBRARY OF SEYMOUR POPPER

Silence is the first requisite of discipline on the well-drilled ship. Unnecessary noise of any kind makes confusion. Those in authority should be the only ones whose voices should be heard. During emergency drills, every man must go to his station at once on the *double*. If it so happens that a man is assigned no specific duties, he shall fall into his quarters and keep silent.

— *Bluejackets Manual* (1940), page 216

In the Garage

He'd go out to the garage and crawl under Miriam's Bug. He'd stick his nose into the rust and breathe. In the garage, with the winter-wrinkled boots, the ski poles, the deflated basketballs, the shovels, the spindly-fingered rakes, the vague stack of flat planks and 2 × 4s stacked in a pile in the corner. His father had a notion, for years, of building a rowboat from scratch. Why didn't Popper take off out the back door and wander the ravine?

Why didn't he bike down to Manny's? He and Manny Laveneaux would slog through the dead leaves and look for beer cans and license plates and corpses and gold. Or go alone to the place where the ravine ended. His favorite place, where the leaves met open beach, where the slow creek trickled out a small cement pipe, and he would sit on a pile of rocks and watch the water pool in a groove of sand, as if the last thing it wanted was to join the lake it had no choice but to join.

Popper under his mother's car, the motor oil–stained cement listening. The garage door clamped shut like a mouth. He rarely ever knew what it was about. He only picked up bits and pieces. Miriam had a few friends, sometimes she had lunch with them, sometimes these friends invited Philip and Miriam to parties. Philip didn't like any of the friends. He called them little mincy suburban gossips. *The friends,* he'd spit, *the friends, the friends. I grew up with that. It was all my parents cared about, the friends. Now look at them. Where are their fucking friends?*

Don't shout at me.

Shout at you? How can I shout at you if we never even speak, if you never even talk to me?

Cold in the garage, and he liked it.

MR. POMERANTZ

He was an odd lonely fat man, and when he met them at the door the boys would have to kiss his ring. He'd hold out his hairy knuckles, and they had no choice but to bow and do it. He wasn't the Pope. He was just someone who Miriam called "a real character." A friend of Philip's, he lived around the corner. He must be dead twenty-five years now. Philip said Mr. Pomerantz was a child survivor of Buchenwald and that they needed to be respectful and listen to his stories. Mr. Pomerantz talked; he talked incessantly from the moment they walked in his door.

Leo said that Mr. Pomerantz survived because the Nazis didn't believe that a starving Jew could be so fat. For the sake of novelty, they let him live. This, of course, didn't stop them from murdering his mother with a pitchfork. Talking protects him, Leo said. Get it? Babbling stomps the memories.

If anybody else spoke, usually Popper, to ask when they were going to leave, Mr. Pomerantz would suddenly be deaf, cup his ear and shout, what's that? One of the elfin say something?

The ring was huge and made of green glass. It was like kissing a bulbous insect eye. Mr. Pomerantz said it was the gift of a pasha. Popper remembers how smooth it felt against his lips. He remembers wondering how many other people over the years had been forced to smooch it. Like most lonely people, Mr. Pomerantz never dared look anyone in the eye. He considered himself jolly and entertaining, and he must have waited long hours so he could prove this. So he could regale, first with his exquisite ring, and then with stories of his remarkable life. If all else failed, there was always the car. Mr. Pomerantz owned a '57 MG with a polished walnut steering wheel, a car Philip loved.

His stories must have been dull or overly complicated, because Popper remembers not a shred of them.

He will never know why certain faces come back to him on certain days. He is looking out his office window at the few people roving up and down the street. The weekend Loop in winter. Bodies are scarce. Popper's alone in the office. A lone fly walks slowly across the rim of his desk lamp. Lost? Wondering where all the other flies have gone? *And I only am escaped alone to tell thee.* Tell thee what?

Mr. Pomerantz lived in a house surrounded by trophies collected during the endlessly fascinating life he could not tell them enough about. One thing Popper does remember is that Mr. Pomerantz owned Stonewall Jackson's saddle. *His actual saddle, boys. Feel free to touch the leather. Feel free to touch everything here. This isn't a museum! This is my life! Touch it! Touch away!*

The man sits in his house as the noon sun holds steady and refuses to droop into afternoon. He doesn't read one of his thousands of books. *Every day I buy ten books! Twenty books! Thirty books!* Because he's long since learned that words on a page aren't much of an audience. Words on a page can't be wowed. Popper hears his sighlike farts. Mr. Pomerantz avoids mirrors. He waits for visitors. It's a Sunday afternoon in the spring of 1975. He worries Phil Popper and his boys won't drop by today. He worries that all he needs to say will sink back down his throat and be lost for good. One day, a weekday, he goes out to the garage, stuffs himself in the front seat of the MG, and turns on the little engine.

He wasn't the only one in their neighborhood to do it this way. There were two others. Mrs. Mueller, with her two kids watching cartoons in the house, and Mr. Bloom, the indicted stockbroker.

In the Garden

This lovely garden was once part of the grand estate of Robert C. Shafner, CEO of A. G. Becker. It included a home designed and built by Howard Van Doren Shaw in 1909. Acquired by the Park District in 1969, the home was demolished in 1986. The garden was restored by the Junior League in the spirit of historic preservation.

—The Junior League of the North Shore

All you people saw was ruin. What about other people's historic preservation? Don't you know that when you restore you also ruin? Now Popper doesn't recognize the place at all. Ladies of the Junior League, would you put this in your annals?

Affidavit of Alexander Popper, Serial Nostalgist (JD, John Marshall, '99):

In the State of Illinois, County of Cook, Alexander Popper, being duly sworn, deposes and says that he is of full cognizance and generally sound mind and that he remembers this: That he always heard, from his father, that Mr. Shafner was a very rich guy back in the day, and that, apparently, he died without heirs, or they'd all gone to greener pastures, or Palm Beach, or they just simply weren't interested in granddaddy's old falling-down place on the bluffs of Lake Michigan. So the house and the property, arguably the most beautiful property in the City of Highland Park, was given to the Park District, which at the time did not have the resources to knock it down. Consequently, the place was condemned, but one portion of the mansion remained habitable, and so the Park District allowed its chief of maintenance, a man named Emmanuel Laveneaux, originally from Haiti, an engineer chased out of the country by Papa Doc, to live there with his family. Whereupon Laveneaux's oldest son, Manny Jr., made a friend, Alexander Popper, the affiant. In fact, they were each other's first friend. For a number of years, Manny was the affiant's only *friend. A considerable amount of the affiant's childhood was spent, as his own home wasn't what one might define as especially happy, in Manny's house, that white colossus rising above the lake, with boards on the windows, potholes in the floor, and bats in the attic. To the affiant, there was no more remarkable place on earth. Behind the house were the remains of Mrs. Shafner's formal garden, a bizarre tangle, a maze of vegetation, and Manny and the affiant and Manny's twin sisters used to play a game Manny made up — Manny always created their games — called* Mr. *Shafner's Gone Psycho, in the overgrown brambles, amid the killer thorns and giant milkweed stalks and Mrs. Shafner's hibiscus gone amuck. Manny would take a rusted pitchfork out of the round and crumbling shed (now annoyingly, lovingly, restored, also) and chase his sisters and the affiant around that lunatic forest, and the sisters would shriek, because Manny always went after them first. That was Manny's deal with the affiant. It was boys against girls, even though there could be only one insane Mr. Shafner. Manny's sisters: Claudette had a birthmark on her head like a small caterpillar; Sabine wore her hair as short as Manny did. Still, to the affiant, the sisters were hard to tell apart because they shrieked the same way, laughed the same way, ran through the garden the same way, the milkweed stalks bursting, spermy milk oozing — ran the same way, with their heads thrown back and their arms spread wide. They wore old sundresses of their mother's, and those dresses sometimes tore on the sharp horny thorns, and the affiant would spy on them from his foxhole at the bottom of one of Mrs. Shafner's dead frog ponds. He'd watch Manny's sisters in their ripped dresses as Manny raged* — I tell you once, I tell you a thousand times — no Jews or Negroes on my property!

But, ladies of the Junior League, listen, it was almost as if Manny Laveneaux and the affiant were playing one game and the sisters another, because when Manny did catch one of them and threaten to skewer her head like a melon, she'd — either Claudette or Sabine — only chew her gum and laugh in his face like she knew something Manny and the affiant didn't know, would never know, that you can't catch what isn't catchable, and that even the memory of a girl in a ripped sundress will always be just out of grasp (the affiant still watching from his foxhole, spermy milkweed hands).

Dead Alewives

6

STOWAWAYS

CARY AVENUE BEACH

That year the alewives began washing up on the shores of the lake and their stench rose from the beaches so that even when you couldn't smell them anymore they stank up your memory. Newly dead, they were a silvery blue. In the sun they looked like hundreds of mirrors. They yellowed as they dried up. And the smell changed, too, from freshly dead to something slightly less pungent but more permanent. A sweet pickled rot. Alewives swim in schools. They die together, as it should be. That year the tide delivered them up by the bucketful. One beach needed a dump truck to haul them away. He thinks of their small open mouths. What kind of god allows for the massacre of fish that even fishermen spare? Non-indigenous to Lake Michigan. The newspapers called them a nuisance fish, in life and in death. They rode in on ships from the Saint Lawrence Seaway. Popper liked the idea of fish as stowaways. He'd go down to Cary Avenue after school and take his shoes off and walk on them, crack the thin bones of their backs.

In the Basement

I f Hollis was needed, Hollis was there. If Hollis was called for
and not needed, he would make that judgment and stay in the
basement. Call him all you want, he won't answer. He'd retreat
below at about 9:30, to his reading and his whiskey, and would
only re-emerge on deck, as he called upstairs, before everybody
was awake the next morning. When she was through with the
dishes — Miriam always insisted on doing the dishes — some
nights she'd go down to the basement and sit with him for a while.
He'd pour her a drink and the two would sit in silence in front of
the pale light of the silent TV. Johnny Carson's guffaw never
reached them. Neither said much. She'd ask about his daughter.
He had some Polaroids of her. His daughter was twelve in the
pictures, but Hollis said she'd be sixteen by now, in Cleveland.
Hollis never asked Miriam why she stayed. He wasn't one to
underestimate the power of a roof, any roof.

February 10, 1944

    Please tell me you're not still bitter—that you're waiting for me with the openest of arms—that you really want to find happiness with me—You know, sweetheart, I was telling the men the other day you were the most luscious piece in Sigma Delta Tau, and how no one could hold a candle to you—especially in the shadow dance—My goodness, you were so gorgeous then—and even then you showed promise of developing into the delightfully voluptuous creature that you have since become—

Bingo in the den at Bernice and Seymour's. The bison-sized Zenith in the corner, the single bay window, the one tall tree in the yard, the rusty swingless swing set. Seymour throned on his La-Z-Boy with the footrest extended, calling out letters like a crazed auctioneer: *B-26? B-26? Who's got it now? B-26! Going, going, gone!* Between rounds he cranked the letters in the little metal hamster cage and discoursed on the history of bingo. *You know it was illegal in the state of Illinois until 1967. Before that enlightened year, little old ladies in church basements across the land of Lincoln were akin to brave bootleggers in the age of Prohibition, blue-haired pioneers we should salute, for it was they who cleared the way for recognition of our inalienable right to gamble away our livelihoods...*

Passing through the den to drop off popcorn in a big bowl, Bernice said, "Seymour, call out a number already."

When she reappeared forty-five minutes later with store-bought cookies, Popper said, "Granbean, put a marker on your card. D-12 got called already."

Bernice smiled over her shoulder at him. "Alex dear, by now you should be old enough to know that it doesn't matter if you put a marker on the letter or not."

"Stop making cameos, Beanie," Seymour said. "It's irritating. Either stay or go, would you?"

"Don't fuss, Seymour. I'm on my way out." Bernice was always on her way out. To luncheon, to bridge, or to the ballet classes she taught three days a week back in the city for almost fifty years. Into her eighties, she was still teaching. Not luck, work.

"C-3? Anybody got C-3?"

LEO AND ALEXANDER

Okay. Mayor Daley trivia. Ready? Concentrate now, Alexanderplatz. True or false? *His Honor's dentist has only one arm.* Please get out of my life. I don't care. I will never care. As long as I live, I will never care—

CLAUDETTE AND SABINE

Manny's sisters, Manny's sisters, Manny's sisters, Manny's sisters, Manny's sisters, Manny's sisters, Manny's sisters — locked in the bathroom, Manny and Popper pummeling the door and the two of them in there laughing and then not laughing, getting down to whatever business they had going in there. (Even now Popper can only imagine, he can't even imagine. He imagines.) Manny tried to pick the lock with a safety pin, no dice. They waited in the dark hall of that ghost-ridden mansion, a hall lined with suitcases. Manny's family always on the verge of moving away. That massive, peculiar non-home was supposed to be only temporary. *We're packed and ready to go,* Manny's mother would say. Manny's mother, her tired eyes. Popper rarely saw her. She worked as a private nurse seven days a week, left early, came home late — nonetheless she was one of the few people in Popper's early life who always seemed genuinely happy to see him. She'd smile through her exhaustion.

"Now, Alexander, please thank your parents for allowing you to come and see us." *Allowing me? I'm on the run, Mrs. Laveneaux.* Maybe for this reason he was afraid to look her in the face.

Once, Popper overheard her through the wall telling Manny's father, an even less-seen man who worked even longer hours:

"Michael, I don't want to live in a shipwreck, I want to live in a house."

On the other side of the wall, Popper waited for a response, but Manny's father didn't answer. Or maybe he did answer, Popper just didn't hear him. *Show me a house, Phelicia, that isn't a shipwreck, one way or another.*

The long driveway that went from the bottom of Ravine Drive up to the top of the bluff where the house sat on the edge. The view of the lake from the massive living room windows, no trees in the way.

"Do you know how much a view like this costs?" Popper once asked Manny.

"Yes," Manny said. "More than you even think."

Think of the bees in the attic. The stacks of storm windows in the basement they spent one afternoon smashing with their moon boots. Remember the back staircase that led to a bricked-in doorway. Remember the frames without pictures on the walls of the living room. Temporary; but for years the Laveneaux family stayed. Only Manny's sisters ever seemed content there, as if they knew they were only biding their time, that this bizarre old place was as good as any other, and that they'd be long gone soon enough.

Manny and Popper waiting outside in the hall with those suitcases and the glowing orange space heater.

"What if we need to take a piss?" Manny asked the door. "This is the only bathroom that works in the whole place."

"Piss in the lake." Claudette or Sabine?

February 16, 1945

Oh baby, I feel like a dishrag—to top it off, I've got some kind of fungus growth on my ass—Don't laugh, it itches like hell—The minute I get a little warm it feels like I'm sitting on a thousand tiny nettles—I spend half my day rubbing against an upright like some kind of insane cat—Aside from this, I'm getting very fat—

GREAT-GRANDMOTHER WASSERKRUEG

Leo said Great-grandmother Wasserkrueg was buried alive in the paneling of the cedar closet of the house on Sylvester Place, the closet where Seymour kept his old naval uniforms and enough Hudson Bay blankets to keep the French Army warm in Russia. She wasn't even dead. Seymour's mother would never die. She still lived in the city, on the seventeenth floor of a residential hotel on South Lake Shore Drive called the Flamingo, and survived on yogurt and wrath. Great-grandmother Wasserkrueg, née Popper née Katzinger, the queen mother, a tormented old woman with fluffed Martin Van Buren sideburns.

After the death of her first husband, Seymour's father, she married a man named Wasserkrueg, a man with older money and a lot more of it. He died soon after, but she wore her new name like a badge that separated her from the riffraff of the rest of the family. It was August. Great-grandmother Wasserkrueg sat beneath many shawls in a high chair with wings amid the clutter and dust. The apartment was hot and sticky. Every available surface was covered with a doily, a web of decrepit lace. Great-grandmother Wasserkrueg had dull but perpetually white hair that looked as if it had been shellacked. Seymour doted on her, offered her Lipton's and Fannie May nonpareils and Canada Dry, and Popper thought, I'm on another planet where Seymour's the maid. Her in that big chair. Her little socked feet. Her voice was hoarse and she swallowed two or three times between every word. For the occasion, Popper wore his sailor suit. Great-grandmother Wasserkrueg asked him where he lived. *I live at home. Where else would I live?* But for some reason he knew she was asking for the exact address. So he told her 105 Riparian Lane, Highland Park, Illinois, 60035. She closed her eyes for a while, but didn't go to sleep. Her tongue moved under her lips.

"What!"

"Did you forget to insert your ear trumpets, Mother?"

Popper repeated it: "Number 105 Riparian Lane, Highland Park, Illinois, 60035."

She opened her eyes and beckoned him. He got up off the ottoman and took a tiny step forward. *Closer, child. Closer.* He bumped up against her cushiony lap and did his best to hug her. She smelled like the fug of the rotting squirrel his mother ran over, the one nobody moved from the end of the driveway. Great-grandmother Wasserkrueg didn't hug back; she only watched him, watched him long, too long, her eyes buried deep in the gulch of her face. They say when she was younger she was ravishing, so ravishing that being ravishing was the only thing she ever was. And they say that since Great-grandfather Leopold never really thrived—he sold insurance on Garfield Boulevard, the family lived above the office—all that ravishing was wasted on a poorish man. Leopold died in the fifties. Everybody thought she'd follow him soon to the grave. Instead, she found Mr. Wasserkrueg and moved from four and a half rooms on Garfield Boulevard to South Lake Shore Drive.

Above her head, to mark the alcove, two babies, naked cherubs, held up the molding.

A blast of hot breath pelted Popper in the eyes.

"And how do you like number 105 Riparian Lane, Highland Park?"

Before he could say anything, she began to shake with a furious, quiet laughter.

Then, still looking straight at him, Great-grandmother Wasserkrueg said, "What's this boy's name?"

"Mother, you know his name is Alexander."

"After who? Alexander the Great? Hamilton? Graham Bell? That halfwit Haig? Who?"

"Nobody," Popper said. "I think nobody."

"And why the get-up, Seymour?"

"He's going to go to Annapolis. This boy's going to be an admiral."

She shook one withered hand loose from the folds of her blanket and, with a backward wave, dismissed him as if scattering flies. "Go away, Seymour. And take Little Lord Fauntleroy with you. Say hello to your chorus girl."

His grandfather began to plead, to blubber. "Ballet dancer, Mother, you know Bernice is a ballet dancer."

Seymour. His titanic head round as a plate, his colossal feet. "And this is your great-grandson, see how he loves you. Look at him, Mother. Look at him."

Loves me? She said it so soft no words actually came out. Then she opened her mouth as if to laugh, but instantly fell asleep. Popper could tell by the way her nose whistled. For a moment, she woke up. "Where are my cats, Seymour?"

"All your cats died, Mother."

In the elevator, Seymour loosened his tie and said, Why don't we go to the Cape Cod Room and have some shrimp cocktails and ketchup. When they reached the lobby, he got out of the elevator, but his grandfather didn't. The doors closed. He waited there in the lobby in his sailor suit and white sailor hat and watched the numbers rise. They stopped at the seventeenth floor. He pushed the down button and held his finger there. After a while the elevator came back and opened empty.

LOG CABIN LADY

For decades the oldest structure in Highland Park was used as a storage shed on the golf course at Migweth* Country Club (*founded 1860, no blacks, no Jews, Mexicans work in the kitchen*).

In 1976, in honor of the bicentennial, the storage shed was loaded onto a flatbed truck, driven uptown, dropped on the lawn between City Hall and the library, and declared a treasure of historic preservation: the Stupey Log Cabin.

Miriam was hired to play Mrs. Stupey, otherwise known as the Log Cabin Lady. From April to October she stood — Tuesdays and Fridays, 10 to 4 — in the cabin doorway dressed like a pioneer housewife. She didn't get many visitors. Highland Park, like the great city that gave birth to it, does not dwell on the past. If the city council wants to plop a log cabin in the center of town, what of it? Occasionally school groups would come by, but mostly, if it was anybody, it was one of the lonely wanderers from the mental health center on Laurel Avenue. They came in sympathy. They knew what it was like to be ignored in broad daylight. One man in particular, Billy, was the most frequent visitor. He was

---

* Bastardization of a Potawatomi word meaning to give thanks, as in thanks for all the nice acreage, Chief Winamac.

hunchbacked and walked around Highland Park as if heading down a full-force gale, a silently groaning man, and Miriam would give him the tour. She would tell Billy about the hardship of life on the prairie, about the long foodless winters and humid summers. The tour didn't last long; the cabin was small, the history scripted. *My simple, honest house was built in 1847 of hand-hewn virgin white oak timbers cut by my husband...* Inside, a butter churn, a loom, a candlemaker, and a wood-burning stove. Each was the subject of a brief demonstration, except for the wood-burning stove, which was left to the imagination due to fire regulations. The dirt floor constantly needed raking. "The work those women did," she would say. "It really is inspiring to think about." Miriam in her bonnet and layers and layers of petticoats and white nurse's shoes she wore because she wasn't allowed to sit on the period furniture. Popper and Manny Laveneaux would ride over on their bikes and wave. "Even when she's Amish," Manny said, "your mom's a babe."

At cocktail parties when people asked her what she did, Miriam would say, At the moment, I'm an actress.

Mrs. Stupey's husband, Mr. Stupey, was the local blacksmith, a character the town didn't have enough in the budget to hire. To prove his existence, Miriam would demonstrate an iron pot he'd made at his forge just up the road, where Larson's Stationery is now. Her talk was written by a historical society subcommittee and was patriotic, as befitted the bicentennial, full of struggle and rugged endurance. Also, it included recipes for snap beans and onion butter and molasses muffins. And the fact that Abe Lincoln himself, who grew up in a cabin not unlike this one, enjoyed fried apple and salt pork for breakfast. Miriam would give the talk in character, but when Billy came by she'd go off-script and tell him about Indians, which were explicitly not part of the talk except around Thanksgiving. She'd say that most of them from around these parts are friendly but some of the Potawatomi don't exactly come in peace and so it is true, Billy, that there are days and nights when Mr. Stupey and myself live in fear of rape and pillage. Nights we lie awake just waiting. And yet, Miriam would ask Billy, who'd be watching her with his busy eyes, what can we expect? I mean ask yourself, and this isn't a rhetorical question, whose land is this? I'm not saying Mr. Stupey and I deserve to be scalped and tortured and murdered, oh no, we are good people, but this doesn't mean we don't do things like loot and plunder land that isn't ours and pretend we didn't. We do a lot of pretending, don't we, Billy? Billy listening, his eyes going and going, his out-front head, his big sad ears, his shirt with all the missing buttons. (He was run over by a drunk, no joke, named Saul Paradise in 1980.) But don't shed any tears for us, ye people of future generations. I speak for Mr. Stupey also. Settling the West has its price and I'm not going to stand here and complain. Look at what we've built. Any questions, Billy? Comments? Concerns? Things of this nature? Oh, Billy, you're such a good odd bird.

February 20, 1945

    Gosh, now that's more like it—I was a little surprised and tickled too at the way you've developed a real vehemence for the Germans and Japs—you're really fightin' mad—and you're right too—You're giving me such strength now—You're finally giving me what I want—Some of the things you wrote really make me proud of you—Perhaps you don't know it, but you're developing—Beanie, your mind is growing—

The Hunters

They are Jewish hunters in northern Illinois, and the birds come out and party. Even Hollis, even with his experience in the Korean Emergency, wasn't a very good shot. They'd wear big yellow safety goggles and fondle their guns and trudge the frozen November fields. Philip had given the boys a choice: spend Sunday at Sunday school at their Reform Reform temple, Lakeside Synagogue—learning Hindu, Buddhist, Islamic, and Cherokee, and, periodically, even Jewish precepts—or head up to the North Country to become a man.

…The four of them, a platoon of meandering unkillers marching, silently marching, marching. The land never rose in their eyes, but to call the prairie flat isn't to know it with your feet. To your feet the November fields are fathomless—the more you walk, the more you never get anywhere. Above: the great mayonnaise sky. Popper liked to put his fingers in the little bullet holders of his hunting coat and walk with his eyes closed. But those hunt-club fields were so stocked with game that even hunting with a Lhasa apso, they couldn't avoid some action. Sir Edmund, in spite of his pampered backyard life, turned out to be pretty good at flushing birds. (Even one of the old regulars at the hunt club, a one-eyed man named Ky, said of Sir Edmund, "Now, that little hound has talent.") Pheasants aren't very hard to shoot. First, there's that hysterical nuthouse cackling. And then the running start, followed by a slow rise, like a fat, wide-bodied plane taking off. Occasionally, with their volley of shots, somebody would hit a bird. Sir Edmund would retrieve the body. It was Popper's job to ferry the deceased, and he liked that part. He was a backward kangaroo, the pheasant against his back, warm, bleeding, heavy with the puttylike inertness of the newly murdered. Every third field or so there was a rack and a row of nails. Birds would be hanging there like spent rags, their eyes as if pried open. Later, a man would come in a pickup and throw the birds into the bed of the truck and drive them to the lodge, where they'd be made into pheasant burgers, pheasant stew, pheasant casserole, and frozen pheasant to go. So he would have to give up his bleeding child and squeeze another little neck between the nails. And Philip would say, with near-reverence, These birds were raised to be killed, so we're only doing our part, playing our role in nature's great cycle of life and death and food on the table. Besides, if we don't shoot them, the next barbarian will, and then what? Isn't that right, Hollis?

COMISKEY

Hollis took Popper and Manny to a Sox game at old Comiskey. They sat in the left-field bleachers. When he was out of the domain of 105 Riparian, Hollis was a lot quieter. He left all his booming in the house. At Comiskey, with all that razzing, bellowing, spitting, guzzling, Hollis mostly watched the pigeons stab the popcorn at his feet. Popper and Manny gaped at the girls strutting up and down the bleacher steps. A broiling summer night in Chicago and Comiskey's bleachers were a scantily clad place. Flesh, beer guts, and tits all over. Manny whispered, *Screw Wrigley Field, this is life.* These were the Bill Veeck years of the exploding pinwheel scoreboard, and when Jorge Orta hit one out in the sixth, the fireworks started going off. Popper and Manny went nuts because everybody else was going nuts. Hollis stood up also, but refused to hoot or yahoo. He sat down long before anybody else.

Hollis bought them more hot dogs and doughy pretzels than they knew what to do with. Popper and Manny bopped each other on the head with their churros.

Think of the urinals, those giant metal troughs, the sound like pounding rain. And what the light was like at Comiskey, not a total blinding brightness like you see today. The light at Comiskey was spotty. There were always bulbs that needed to be replaced. The bleachers lived in blue darkness. If you dropped a quarter under your seat, you'd have to grope around as if you were at the movies. Amazing some of the things he and Manny found. A half-eaten candy bar with a label they didn't recognize. A petrified roach. From within that darkness, Popper watched the light. Dust particles were visible in the streams that separated the bleachers from the rest of the park like a shroud.

Hollis sat beside them without speaking, his eyes not on the batter or the pitcher but the second baseman. He didn't say anything. His face said it. He loved only the quiet of the game. All the yelling and screaming had nothing to do with it. A barely foul ball, a check swing, a pick-off move — these things. It was about possibility, not fruition. Not the false pizzazz but the shush between innings. If something happens, it goes from dream to gone. *Don't you people know this?*

They tore Comiskey down. In this city we tear everything down, eventually.

After the game Hollis commented on the score out of obligation, Sox 3, Cleveland 5, the dirty white colossus rising behind them as they walked across the parking lot. He didn't mention current players' names. Jorge Orta was nobody to him. The only player he mentioned was Swede Risberg from 1919. "If Risberg and the rest of them had only been paid a fair wage," Hollis said, "they'd never have even been tempted by the gamblers in the first place. Purity of the game? You boys think Charlie Comiskey himself ever cared about the purity of the game?"

They lost Miriam's car in the vast parking lot. For an hour the three of them wandered row after row. Eventually Manny found it. He climbed on top of the car and called out to them, "I'm on the Bug!"

Miriam was grateful to Hollis for providing them with a new perspective. "It's important," she said, "that these boys from the suburbs see the South Side." Now Popper wonders if Hollis was grateful, too, that he had an excuse to go to Comiskey. Of course, he was working. He had to take a couple of nine-year-olds on a field trip. He was working. And he must have known that his and Manny's excitement over Orta's home run was a sham, that for them it was all about the exposed flesh. Even so, for Hollis the night seemed not to go slow enough.

Local Nazis

Miriam said that although she personally supported the efforts of the American Civil Liberties Union to protect free speech, you boys are, of course, free to draw your own conclusions. These particular Nazis were a Chicago-born band of undergrown twenty-year-olds. They heard some Jews lived in Skokie. So they applied for a permit to march. First the court said yes. Another court said no. A third court said yes. It was very confusing. On the appointed day, the Nazis were late. As they waited with the rest of the crowd, Miriam extolled the virtues of civic democracy. *Look at this turnout! It's the First Amendment in action.* Cops in riot gear lined Touhy Avenue as the Skokie elderlies shouted and waved the hard Polish sausages they'd brought to plunk on the heads of the little pimpled Hitlers. Not that anyone got a glimpse of them over the heads of the shields and helmets. Nobody could even hear them saying, "Heil Hitler," they were saying it so quietly. An old man shouted, "Speak up! I can't hear anything. Florence, can you hear what they're saying?"

Another woman screeched, "Manslaughter them. I'll do it with my own hands. I'll manslaughter each and every one of them."

"Now there's a new verb," Miriam said. "You don't hear verbs like that every day."

"Let's go throw rocks at their heads," Popper said.

"Honey, these poor misguided loons wouldn't know a Jew from Jehovah. Have some more grapes."

"But they'd know me," Manny said.

"That's true, Manny, they would," Miriam said. "But here's my thought. Everybody's worst nightmare is to be ignored. Try it sometime, boys. Ignore somebody. You'll drive them bananas. I say, Let the loons lark. I'm not saying this works every time or in every circumstance."

EARLY FROST

The Des Plaines River flooded the golf course at Migweth Country Club, and then there was an early frost and the whole place was like the hugest skating rink ever created, acres and acres of ice, except that if you wore skates you'd cut through it too easily. So they bandaged their socks with garbage bags and slid across eighteen holes. All the time screaming their heads off to the trees: *No blacks, no Jews, Mexicans work in the kitchen!* The frozen green goose shit they threw at each other like bullets. The clubhouse, a mock castle with turrets and battlements rising in the distance. Someday, Manny said, we'll storm that dumbass fortress.

The Mayor

They have vilified me, they have crucified me, yes, they have even criticized me.

—Richard J. Daley, 48th mayor of Chicago

It turned out he was mortal.

In December of 1976, Philip came home and bowed his head at dinner and said, "There will be no other mayor like the mayor." He paused, looked around the table in case anybody had a challenge to that. Popper started to eat. They were having chicken and corn on the cob from the Kentucky Fried Chicken that is no longer on Central Avenue across from Jewel. Popper always ate the chicken after the corn. He took his buttered bread in one hand and his corn cob in the other and rolled the cob around in the butter. Buttered bread is always better than the corn and the corn is always better than the chicken. Nobody else was eating. That big striped bucket plump in the middle of the table.

"Daley's been dead since he ordered the cops to shoot to kill looters in '68," Leo said. Popper kept mowing his corn, being sadly finished now with the buttered bread.

"Looters?" Philip said. "You want to tell me about looters? Tonight?"

"Humpty Dumpty," Leo said. "A boss, a dictator."

"I remember that night," Miriam said. "I watched it from the window."

"Look at your food, Leo," Philip said. "This chicken, Mayor Daley raised it. He fried it up. That piece of corn. Mayor Daley grew it. The bread, he milled it. He brewed this beer. Your shoes—look at your shoes. The mayor cobbled them. Everything we have—What, Miriam, you've stopped cooking?"

"And all the king's horses," Leo said.

"What about the Colonel?" Popper said.

"The whole city was dark," Miriam said. "But there was this pulsing glow, like the sun was rising at the wrong time of day—"

7

FIE, FIE, FIE! PAH, PAH!

WUNDERKINDS

Chicago, 1977

The Rosencrantz kids were gifted. They played flute, cello, harpsichord, electric guitar. At meals one of them was liable to break into an aria.

"Wildly gifted," Martha Rosencrantz would say. "I honestly don't know where they come by it. Hal and I are only just above average intelligence ourselves."

And gifted, Leo and Alexander were given to understand, is a far cry from clever. Leo was clever. Eli, Leah, and Jacob Rosencrantz had left clever in the dust as soon as they'd learned to walk, which was four to six months earlier than average children.

In the basement of their Lincoln Park townhouse they painted elaborate Diego Rivera–style murals, putting their own faces on the bodies of peasant beasts of burden to show their solidarity with the poor.

Hal Rosencrantz was a partner in a venerated white-shoe law firm. He and Philip had done some business together. One day Hal said, "Phil, why not bring the wife and kids into the city next Saturday?"

And so it began. The Saturday trips to the Rosencrantzes' townhouse on Cleveland Avenue in Lincoln Park.

The Rosencrantz kids only mingled with the Poppers because

their parents had *decreed* it. Yet the arrival of these country cousins from the suburbs was an opportunity for the Rosencrantz kids to demonstrate their latest expressions of genius. Walking along the dark upstairs corridor of the townhouse was like being swallowed down a long throat. To see: a hand-written draft of Eli's second novel. Or his 3-D model, built to scale, of Jupiter and its sixty-one moons.

Another time, Leah explained, in detail, the eating habits of her tropical fish.

This one eats this one and that one eats that one—and her— see her? The one with the beard?—she eats them all."

As they stared into that green gloom, Jacob, the kinder one, the only Rosencrantz incapable of looking down on anybody, including Poppers, waltzed into Leah's room on his hands and proceeded to conduct a ventriloquized conversation between his feet.

Ah, Sir Barnaby! What a surprise, I didn't expect to see you on that leg!

Simon, old boy, the shoe must be on the other foot today! I can't think of any other plausible explanation.

Ah, I see the young Poppers have arrived! How fortuitous! I was just beginning to think I'd be marooned—stuck in the mire if you will—with La Famiglia Rosencrantzia for the rest of my days.

Books! They didn't merely have books on their bookshelves. The Rosencrantzes didn't merely *read* books. The Rosencrantz townhouse itself was built of books, open books, scattered books, living books. To a Rosencrantz, a shelved book was a defunct book was a dead book. A book was something that you ought to be in the middle of, so as to be able to say, such as when the situation arose after Popper puked on the floor of Eli's bedroom, "How

PETER ORNER

ironic, just yesterday I was reading *The Anatomy of Melancholy* and there's that part where Burton talks about the spleen being a greater indication of character than the brain…"

"Wait," Leo said. "What's a spleen?"

"Don't you even go to school?" Eli said.

"Anyway, Burton is wrong," Leah said. "If character is fate, the spleen is only incidental."

There was always a book tented on the banister, halfway up. Cervantes was in the upstairs bathroom for longer stays; Emily Dickinson in the powder room for quicker ones. Not only were there no televisions at the Rosencrantzes', they were constantly reminding you that there were no televisions at the Rosencrantzes'. *The rectangle of imbecility,* Eli once intoned, quoting a family friend, *is a vast wasteland.*

"I'll bet you have a TV in every room in Highland Park," Leah said.

"One in the kitchen," Popper said, "another in the basement, one upstairs, one in our mom and dad's —"

"See?" Leah said. "See? That's civilization? That's progress?"

If it all sounds like hell on earth, it must be said that it was and it wasn't. Saturdays at the Rosencrantzes' had a way of transforming the Poppers. It all seems so ridiculous now, but then it was serious, deadly serious. Saturday was the day the Poppers would come together to shore up what was left.

Class

The Rosencrantzes were classier than the Poppers. At least the Poppers thought so. The Rosencrantzes were more educated, more cultured, more sophisticated conversationally. It wasn't about money. This may be because class is so often defined not by those who have it but by the people who are worried sick they don't. How can you buy it if the whole point is you can't buy it?

The Rosencrantzes had deep Chicago roots. They were part of the migration of German Jews who'd come to the city before the Civil War. A Rosencrantz was a captain in the 83rd Illinois Infantry and fell at Chancellorsville. Hal's father was once a law partner of Abraham Lincoln's son, Robert. Family lore even had it that one brave member of the illustrious family perished battling the Great Chicago Fire while the Rosencrantz survivors stood ready, alongside legendary men like Potter Palmer, to re-raise greatness out of the ashes. *I will rebuild my buildings at once,* Palmer shouted. *Put on an extra force, and hurry up the hotel!*

Philip and Miriam Popper, on the other hand, considered themselves Russian Jews, although they were descended from Polish/Hungarian Jews on Philip's side and Lithuanian/Polish Jews on Miriam's. Only a generation or two out of the shtetl, they were the grandchildren of bookbinders, junkmen, small-time salesmen, decandants of the great hoards of Eastern European Jews who settled in Chicago in the twenties and thirties. Give us your poor, your dirty, your needy, the German Jews said, and we will help them (with a vast array of charity programs), and also we will condescend to them. For years and years, we will condescend to them.

By the 1970s the distinction was hardly noticed, and this is trod ground. Hardly noticed but noticed. A sense of superiority dies hard, a sense of inferiority even harder. So the residue of the distinction remained, if unspoken.

Yet worse than what their grandfathers may or may not have done for a living was the fact that Philip and Miriam Popper had moved to the suburbs. The first chance they could, they up and moved north while people like the Rosencrantzes had, gallantly, in spite of everything—the crime, the terrible public schools, the black people (shhhhhhh)—chosen to remain steadfast in their city. Now that's class. So part of the motivation for these new Saturday trips was the fact that Philip and Miriam were seeking a kind of penance for having abandoned the city. Of Highland Park, Philip would say something like, "Talk about Dullsville. We keep waiting for something to happen, anything, and nothing ever does…"

And Miriam: "Yet just the other day, Judy Dombrowski got her purse snatched in Hubbard Woods. Hubbard Woods! And everybody goes on about how there's no crime on the North Shore."

Once, on the way home from the Rosencrantzes', Leo asked, "So why don't we move back if you guys hate Highland Park so much?"

"Oh, honey," Miriam said. "We're just making conversation."

March 13, 1945

You know I've been thinking—There really are only two great emotions out here—fear and loneliness—Fear of course is always present, although after a while you learn to shrug it off or rationalize it—except occasionally when it grips you in spite of everything you can do—then you sweat—but for most of us, our fear is in anticipation—although the other day when one of those bastards came over us so low we could have touched him—we didn't have a chance to be afraid—It happened too quickly—He was over and gone— But loneliness—that's with us constantly—day and night— and, oh, you can't know how it hurts—

THE MUSIC OF THE LANGUAGE

Her small face hidden behind giant sunglasses, Miriam liked to watch people watch her, because she was never sure she was as beautiful as people were always falling all over themselves insisting. An unlit cigarette between her fingers, red-tipped from her lipstick. Philip, hearty, ruddy-faced, windblown even when he was inside. And the two boys in their scratchy gray wool shorts and clip-on ties. They always had to dress up when they went into the city. Weren't they little wild-haired clones of their jaunty father?

Each of the Rosencrantzes had a large, impressive head mounted on a less significant body. Hence, to the Poppers, they were walking talking human embodiments of the life of the mind. Physically, Hal Rosencrantz was the least assuming of them all. He had the big head, yes, but also extremely narrow eyes and appropriately tiny glasses. He seemed to be going bald only on one side of his head. Miriam once said on the way home that Hal was poetic-looking. Philip asked what she meant by that, and Miriam couldn't explain, except to say that Hal looked like a person who might write poems.

"Hal's a partner at Abramson and Smoot, Miriam. A senior partner. He represents General Electric and the Continental Bank."

Martha was stockier than her husband and had a heavier face. Leo said she looked like Henry Kissinger.

"Try to have a little sense of decency, Leo," Miriam said. "Just try. If for nothing at all, then for me."

Long after Saturdays at the Rosencrantzes ended, Popper would think of Martha's hugs, how when they arrived at the door she would mash him and Leo together and coo, *Oh, my minikins. Oh, my lambs.*

Jacob and Leah took after their father, though Leah had much bigger eyes and more hair. Jacob wore huge Coke-bottle glasses that were always falling off his face. He also had a set of braces that gleamed in his mouth when he smiled, like a miniature power station. Eli looked like his mother, only more pompous in the eyes.

So it's possible that, in spite of their intellectual superiority, there may have been times, fleeting moments, when the Rosencrantzes envied the Poppers. Their healthy suburban glow, their simple familial bonds. Because there was always turmoil in the townhouse. Eli was jealous of Jacob. He couldn't understand how his brother could elicit both awe *and* admiration. Didn't the two cancel each other out? Leah often felt rejected by her mother. She once confided to Miriam (people were always confiding to Miriam) that Martha didn't consider her a committed enough feminist. *What am I supposed to do? Burn down Soldier Field? Run for Congress? I'm only twelve and a half.* Miriam, laughing quietly, soothing: *Oh, you're fine, Leah, you're just fine.* Martha herself seemed to mostly ignore Hal, who sometimes seemed to mind and other times seemed relieved. His eyes would roam up to the ceiling while Martha was talking, and Martha was usually talking.

Philip would take long walks with Hal. They'd talk politics. Or they'd play chess in Hal's study. Once, on the drive home—

Leo and Popper slumped against each other, worn out by the three-ring circus of Rosencrantzian brilliance — Philip wondered out loud if Hal was letting him win.

"He nearly always castles late. This is a man who does algebra for fun in his spare time. You think he's throwing the games?"

Miriam yawned. "Maybe you're just good at chess, Phil."

Her own time with Martha was a whirlwind of lectures, meetings, volunteer work, self-improvement. There were betterment association meetings, garden clubs. Martha and Miriam delivered books and pencils to the needy children of Cabrini Green. They cheered for Bella Abzug at the Civic Auditorium. They attended monthly gatherings of the Alliance Française, where Chicago women discussed all things French in French. This excluded Miriam from understanding much of what they were saying, but did not prevent her, as she put it, from enjoying the music of the language.

Martha asking, "From where, Miriam, did you say you were from again? Boston?"

"No, not Boston. I'm from Fall River, Textile Capital of the World."

"When was that, darling?"

"The 1870s."

Miriam, who had not yet graduated college (she was finishing classes toward her degree at DePaul and working on her teaching certificate). Miriam, the poor misinformed woman from the hinterlands who'd come to Chicago to marry a lawyer. Marrying up, for heaven's sake! Dear dear girl, don't you know that's all behind us now?

FIGHTING JANE

She used to be one of the wonderful people.
>—Michael Bilandic (forty-ninth mayor of Chicago) on
Jane Byrne (fiftieth mayor of Chicago)

All over now, and this not much of a secret, anyway. Still, it's never been told before. In the '78 campaign, Jane Byrne's enemies couldn't use it against her because they weren't sure whether the story would help her or hurt her. In politics you can't run the risk that embarrassing someone might actually make them look more human. Voters like a human being once in a while. And that's why everybody loved Jane — at first. After a while, she got a little too human.

If Mayor Daley was the Popper family's benevolent deity, then Jane Byrne was their nutty fairy godmother. (Not to mention that Mayor Byrne, too, like the old man, steered city business to Philip's law firm.)

Miriam said she was a great role model for not just girls but boys, too! Chicago's own Margaret Thatcher.

One night, Miriam was making herself a martini. Philip burst in the house door, breathless. He growled low, "I got something juicy."

"What is it, Phil?"

"Visualize this: Marina City, opposite apartments. Jane Byrne — in the buff, she's only got on her heels — standing on her West Tower balcony. Jay McMullen's on his balcony in the East Tower. And he's watching her with binoculars while she puts on a little show. I heard it from a guy in the Corporation Council's office. Apparently, these two do this all the time."

"I love it," Miriam said.

Byrne and her husband-to-be, the grizzled ex-reporter, McMullen. Those two unbeautifuls on their respective balconies, in the cold, checking each other out with binoculars. By then they'd both been knocked around enough, not a sight to see for most people, but what a thrill it must have been for them. Like two grunts poking out of their foxholes on Christmas morning. Luxury apartments, but that didn't make a Democratic primary battle any less the blood sport of chattering gladiators. Brothers killing brothers. But they were going to be in this thing to win. Together they'd conquer that simp Michael Bilandic — or die. They were the Romeo and Juliet of municipal government. The Bonnie and Clyde of Streets and Sanitation. Jay once said he'd slept with every girl in City Hall. He'd roll over in the morning and get a scoop. *So tell me, baby, is Sewers Eddie Quigley on the take or what?* But now even McMullen's going to behave. Because he's in love with the next mayor of Chicago...

Remember Jane Byrne? Fighting Jane, Mike Royko called her Mayor Bossy. She ran against the Democratic machine and squashed it, the whole goddamned machine. The machine that gave birth to her, the machine—what was left of it—that she re-embraced practically the day after she sent Bilandic, that seat warmer, packing. First you beat something up, then you make it all yours. Winning was one thing, running this city another. So long, you reformers, take your Goody Two-shoes and run, Marty Oberman! Operator, get me Alderman Vrdolyak on the phone, and quick—

She couldn't be bought off. That wasn't the problem. Jane Byrne loved power, the pure idea of it, not what you did with it. And what she did with it was tell people off. Oh, how gloriously did Jane Byrne tell people off. Bless her, nobody had done it that well since Big Bill Thompson threatened to thump the King of England on the snoot. She told off Jimmy Carter. She told off Princess Margaret when she came to visit and tried to put on airs. She told off the firefighters of Chicago. She even told off the old man's son, Richie. The old man had taught her about timing, and in the end that's what was so off. She punched and she punched, and finally the only person she hit was herself. And when she aimed at her foot, it was Jay McMullen who pulled the trigger. But of all the scraps of what's been long forgotten, there's this: One night Philip came home and told his wife Miriam a story. They'd always have politics. Leo and Popper reconnoitering, standing outside the kitchen, ears to the swinging door, listened to her laugh.

"Good for her," Miriam said. "I can see them."

Just the two of them against the crowded, polluted night. Jane does a little come-hither dance in her famous white heels. Stay there, Jay. Don't move. Stay right there and watch me.

Bernice, Seymour, Leo, and Alexander. Four Poppers in a boat. Chain O'Lakes, Fox Lake, Illinois vacation wonderland. Leo brought 25-pound dumbbells with him and sat in the middle of the boat and did curls. Seymour manned the helm in fatigues, a militarized Buddha revving the outboard.

Bernice wore her mink coat.

"What are you all waiting for?" Seymour bellowed. "Cast! Why doesn't anybody cast?"

Nothing else to do but fish, and so they fished. Leo held his rod in one hand and a dumbbell in the other, breathed, counted, exhaled—then felt his biceps for progress. The boat floated aimlessly. The laughter of the people in the RV park carried across the water. The grind of the trucks shifting gears on Route 41. By late afternoon nobody'd had a single bite. Seymour blamed environmentalists.

"Wouldn't environmentalists mean there'd be more fish?" Leo said. "This place is so full of toxins, if there are any fish left, they've got thumbs."

"You think you can solve everything with your government noodling? Cast! Cast!"

The sun faded away like a sad pink eye. Leo held his weight on his thigh. They shivered. The lake weeds waved beneath the surface of the water. Bernice made peanut-butter sandwiches on her knees. "I'm a woman in a mink making peanut-butter sandwiches," she said. "Seymour, take a picture. I'm finally domesticated."

Lazy sandwich in hand, Popper flicked a silver lure in the water. The line plunked. The tug was immediate, but at the same time halfhearted, a bite with resignation. It hardly bent the rod. At first Popper wanted to be alone with it for a while, to caress his bite in private. This clutch of life, my only own. But Seymour spotted it and leaned forward and said, quietly, as if the fish might overhear:

"Reel her in with all the fight in your very soul."

Time passes, you swim, you spawn, sometimes you move around in schools, other times on your own, deloop, deloop, bop, bop, it's all a murky blur. But it's yours. You down there in your dark, the Chain O'Lakes the only home you've ever known, and then one day you take a bored little nip at something shiny. You don't even think about it, you're not even hungry at this time of day; it was just there, dangling in front of your mouth.

It was a four-inch-long yellow perch. It did not flop on the line, only made a couple of halfhearted twitches and went limp. "Avast," Leo said under his breath as the little head peeped out of the water. "It's the fucking white whale."

Popper reeled and the fish swung out of the water toward him. He cradled it in his bare hand, its underbelly like sandpaper. He ripped the hook out of its mouth and looked closely into its mouth—a delicate little oval membrane of a mouth—before dropping it into the boat at his feet. The fish lay bleeding in the bilge water, gills panting slowly. A lone lidless pupil stared up at him. Maybe a minute passed. Everybody in the boat just watched.

It was Bernice who finally said, "Aren't you forgetting something, Alexander?"

"What?"

"The rock, it's under your seat."

It wasn't as if he'd never caught a fish before. Who knows? Maybe he was only mesmerized. Maybe he only wanted to watch it die slowly in the dirty puddle of water, gills silently working.

In the Driveway

Seymour was finally forced to sell. His company had been losing money for years. It wasn't a big company, but it wasn't a small one either, and it had made him rich, for a time, rich. The story of how it all unraveled is convoluted, and every time Popper used to ask about it, he'd get a different version. It had something to do with the fact that Seymour's company (allegedly) began writing more insurance policies than they could possibly cover with their cash reserves. When business improved, went the rationale (allegedly), there would be more cash to cover the increase in policies.... Somehow the state got wind of it and was launching an investigation. In the meantime, a group of investors put an offer on the table and Seymour accepted. But to demonstrate his good faith, he then turned around and invested all his proceeds from the sale back into minority stock. When the price fell after the state went public with the investigation, Seymour didn't sell. The price kept falling. Seymour, who'd put his soul into that company, who'd built it up from a two-man storefront office on Garfield Boulevard (*POPPER* is still chiseled above the doorway of that building, now a hair salon), stood by. He held on and he held on. Philip begged him not to be a fool, to sell off while there was still something left.

Father and son had it out in front of the house on Sylvester Place.

Seymour was washing his Fleetwood. *A man should always wash his own car, boys. You don't need to import a Mexican to wash your car.* It was eight o'clock in the morning. Philip, on his way to work, stopped at his father's house.

"Don't be a goddamn coot," Philip said. "Your theoretical goodwill and your integrity don't mean a thing to the stock price. Sell. Sell it all tomorrow, and at least come out of it with your toenails."

Seymour in an undershirt, his stomach wagging, wielded his hose. "What good are principles if they are so easily cashed? Do I not have honor? When the ship is sinking, do I leap?"

"You're drowned already."

"What do you know about loyalty? I am an honorable man."

"Wasn't Brutus also? And you're lucky you're not going to jail. You knew you weren't holding enough in reserve. The only reason they've stopped chasing you is you've got nothing left to chase."

"Are you impugning me?"

"Dad, at least think about Mother."

"That woman hasn't said boo to me in years."

Father and son stood in the driveway and eyed each other over the hood of the car. Seymour laughed and wagged his hose, and the water cascaded down on the windshield, the light—pink, yellow, green—sharding in all directions.

"Dad," Philip says. "Dad—"

HOLLIS

Philip and Miriam were at the Lyric Opera that night with Hal and Martha Rosencrantz. The boys were upstairs watching a TV movie about a blind man accused of murder. The blind man had white hair and pink eyes and looked to Popper as if he could have done the murder, though even he knew that the point of the movie was the fact that the blind man was a *falsely accused innocent man.*

Earlier, Hollis had said he felt a little sick and so had gone to bed early. During the blind man's trial, where it was being shown that a blind man could commit murder as easily as the next guy, Leo decided they ought to take Hollis some tomato juice. Together, they went down to the kitchen. Leo poured the juice. Popper carried the glass with both hands, trying not to spill, and followed Leo down the basement stairs. The light was on in Hollis's room, his door open. Hollis was on his back, half in bed, half on the floor. In his left hand he held a novel. The radio was on.

Popper dropped the tomato juice on the carpet.

One of the paramedics told Leo that Hollis was probably already gone when they found him. A heart attack so massive, he said, bringing him the V8 earlier wouldn't have made any difference.

"Who was he?" the paramedic asked.

———

His Alabama brothers drove up for the funeral. Three men who looked much like Hollis. What did they see when they saw the Poppers? Little Alexander was still wearing that fucking sailor suit as his formal attire. He worried his face didn't look sorry enough.

Hollis, I came dressed as a sailor to your funeral, and all I wanted was to sprint into your brother's stomachs and bounce off. Your Cleveland daughter didn't show up. My mother wept. She said, We didn't know you. Four days a week you lived in our house and still we didn't— What book was in your hand? The last sentence you read said what?

Hollis Osgood is buried in a Jewish cemetery in Skokie, Illinois. One of his brothers said it was all right. *Isn't he from here now, anyway? He moved up here for the wages.* He lies across the road from the Popper family plot, in a narrow rim of grass along the outer fence, bordering Gross Point Road. There is no birth date, no death date.

The Sulphurous Pit

The Rosencrantzes present *The Tragedy of King Lear*... With sock puppets! Jacob played the King. Leah played all the daughters, but was least convincing as the nice one. Eli played everybody else and directed and collected the tickets, 75 cents per bumpkin; Leo shelled it out for both of them.

And Lear wailed:

> *Down from the waist they are Centaurs,*
> *Though women all above;*
> *But to the girdle do the gods inherit,*
> *Beneath is all the fiends';*
> *There's hell, there's darkness, there's the sulphurous pit,*
> *Burning, scalding,*
> *Stench, consumption, fie, fie, fie! pah, pah!*

The story has always been told that it was the second *pah!* that sent Popper over. And nothing Leo whispered could make him stop bawling. "Have some pride, Alex. You want to confirm everything these smugglers already think about us? That we're so far beneath them we can't even sit through Shakespeare?"

They stopped the show.

From behind the curtain, a voice asked, "What's wrong?"

"Listen," Leo said, "he doesn't give a shit about your Punch and Judy show. Someone died."

"Who?"

"Our houseman."

"Your who?"

Jacob, King Lear drooping from his hand, came out from behind the bedsheet and sat down beside Popper.

In his gravely Lear voice he asked, "Your first raw wound, you whoreson dog?"

Popper went on screeching.

"Inconsolable? And so green in revolutions of the sun? 'Tis an unlikely torrent in such an early knave."

Popper leapt up and bit him in the leg.

Jacob tossed the puppet on the carpet and said in his ordinary voice, Popper's teeth still clinging to his shin, "It's a wrap, everybody. Seems to me the kid gets the play."

Morning Orders
March 2, 1945
Follow Plan of Day

    0450 Wake duty cooks
    0620 Reveille
    0635 Chow down. Wake officers.
                          S. Popper
                          Exec. Off.

Note to O.O.D. Keep the helmsman alert and on course. No lights are expected tonight—but call me if any are seen.
                    SP

8

THE DISINFECTANT POOL

March 28, 1945

This morning at 0530 a report came in that there was an unidentified ship astern of us about four miles closing rapidly—Well, the old heart jumped a little, and I looked to see if my life jacket was in order—I went up to the bridge, where the captain was already—and we started peering through the darkness with glasses—We waited—Finally a touch of gray came into the sky, and then I picked up a shadow in my glasses and so did the captain—What an eerie sight—Just a lot of gray swirling mists and then a long shadow that comes and goes until you're not sure whether you see it or not—Now that it's lights-out, it's all forgotten—How are you feeling, angel? And how are the children? How is darling Esther? I miss her so much it's just like a physical pain—

THE BASEMENT STAIRS

Once more into the house on Sylvester Place, open the basement door. Go halfway down the basement stairs and stop.
The huge framed collage Bernice made for Seymour on the occasion of his sixtieth birthday. Newspaper clippings, postcards, war
dispatches, a Western Union telegram:

12/27/45

HAPPY NEW YEAR FROM YOKOHAMA WAR NOT
CAKE ONLY EATABLE CAKE YOU — SEYMOUR

In the center of it all, a photograph of Seymour in his captain's
uniform. Below him two quotes:

*In the naval service, there are customs and usages that are peculiar to the
personnel serving in the Navy. The origin of many of these is obscure, but they
have the power of full authority and are conscientiously observed.*

And: *My country—may she always be right, but right or wrong—my
country.*

Ringing Seymour's head like a halo are snapshot cutouts of
the heads of his loyal crew, his family.

And along the right margin of the collage: DON'T GIVE UP THE
SHIP!!!

Another story of that house. It has to do with Popper's Aunt Esther, Philip's sister. In the late 1970s, Esther divorced her husband Lloyd and moved back home with Bernice and Seymour. Sometime during her first year back home she scratched out her ex-husband's face on Seymour's birthday collage. She also scratched out herself. Maybe it was the fact that his aunt and ex-uncle's face were part of a larger whole that made their obliteration so fascinating. Sometimes, when Popper was over at Sylvester Place, he'd go down there and look at the collage. The rest of them, all smiling patriotically around Seymour's bulbous head. There was something about the proximity of Popper's own intact face to Esther and Lloyd's scratched-out faces that intrigued him. It was as if he'd survived the onslaught. Because Esther had scratched herself and Lloyd out hard. She'd really hacked that collage.

Of course she had her reasons, good ones. Who could blame her for not wanting to look at her face and his face every time she went up and down the basement stairs?

One late summer day he'd been heading for the basement when he paused and looked for a while at the collage. For some reason he decided to take the frame down in order to inspect the wall behind it. His grandmother opened the door and stood at the top of the stairs. Behind her, the kitchen window and the yellow August light. She breathed a sigh, held it in her shoulders.

"What are you doing?"

"I'm just looking at the hole."

"What hole?"

"The hole she made in the wall when she scratched out the faces."

"What are you talking about?"

She was lying. Everyone had seen it and pretended they hadn't. The basement stairs were well traveled. The laundry was down there, and so was the Ping-Pong table, as well as the filing cabinets full of the letters Seymour wrote Bernice during the war. He once told Popper he wrote her a letter a day for the entire war.

Everybody paused to look at the birthday collage on their way up and down the basement stairs.

Bernice standing at the top of the stairs with the light behind her, almost like snow, Popper thought, outlining her still beautiful body—lying. His Aunt Esther was at work then. Through it all—the being back home, the hardly talking to Bernice and Seymour, the cutting herself off from her friends, stories about her circling around Highland Park and Chicago. *Hear about it? At forty-odd something, Esther Popper moved back in with her parents.* Through it all, she went to work in an office. But Esther, Esther Popper a receptionist? All the hopes Bernice had for her. *At fifteen she was a better ballerina than I ever was. And, my God, so smart, she could have been anything at all.* Aren't our expectations a form of love also?

But this daughter will never be ashamed. And she couldn't give a damn what people said about her. Esther, who left a rich husband to stew in his own juice. Esther, who eats TV dinners in her old room and reads *Middlemarch* all night long.

Within three years, she will be dead of a cancer that struck so fast and so decisively it would have been merciful if it hadn't been so terrifying.

Popper never knew her that well. Philip and Esther had never been close. Since the war, it was said. Brother and sister had been at odds with each other since as long ago as the war. Bernice, Philip would occasionally mutter, paid no attention to him from Pearl Harbor to V-J Day. It was always *Esther, Esther, Esther.*

After Esther's death, Seymour and Bernice finally sold the house at 38 Sylvester Place. They moved into a small rented ranch house on the west side of the expressway, a place with yellow wall-to-wall indoor/outdoor carpeting and colossal toilets. Even though he was in hock to the tune of tens of thousands, Seymour still had to have certain things huge.

Bernice standing at the top of the basement stairs, her love for a daughter at its most fierce, and Popper down there holding that old collage, fingering the hole she made in the wall. Is it possible to have a single moment back? Why this one? Bernice and Popper watching each other? In the shambling house on Sylvester Place? Bernice at the top of the stairs, the August light? A sigh trapped in her shoulders?

"Alexander, put that idiot thing back on the wall where you found it."

A BROTHER AND SISTER

No cathartic goodbye for these siblings. Toward the very end of her life, Esther refused to let Philip come by her hospital room. There's a Saul Bellow story with a similar subject matter. A decades-long rift, a dying sister, an imploring brother. In "The Old System" the sister finally writes to the brother, *All right already. You can come and say so long, but it will cost you a grand.*

Esther, on the other hand, wasn't interested in Philip's money. Nor did he ever offer any. And she didn't respond to the notes delivered to the hospital by Miriam. *In spite of everything, you are still my sister and I am still your brother,* Philip wrote. She didn't crumple the letters up. She set them on the table, thanked Miriam for coming, and went on reading. The story pretty much ends there. At least the end of the story does. Of course, the ending wouldn't have come about were it not for a lifetime's worth of enmity. Why the hate, a brother and a sister? No one thing. Esther's difficult personality. Philip's difficult personality. And always the old explanation: Esther got all the attention. A simple lack of love between them feels like a better answer. But who can say? Popper remembers family dinners at 38 Sylvester Place after Esther moved back home. At that time, Bernice and Seymour were mostly silent. So was Miriam. It was all she could do to endure these Popper family dinners. Even Leo didn't have much to say. Philip would dominate the conversation, holding forth (not because he had anything in particular to say either, but because somebody had to fill up all that quiet), until Esther, invariably, would throw her napkin down on her plate.

"Now, Esther, please," Bernice would say.

She never bolted from the dining room. She'd slide back her chair slowly, as if in some odd way even she would never understand or acknowledge she didn't want to part from her brother's company now that he was finally silent and watching her.

You Can't Say Dallas

Eli played the President. Jacob was Jackie. Leah, naturally, Oswald. Leah Harvey Oswald. And because it had to do with politics — and if the uncultured Poppers knew about anything at all, they knew something about politics — the Rosencrantzes let the rabble in on it as footnotes. Leo doubled as both the Kennedy's chauffeur *and* Texas governor John Connally. Popper was given a bonnet and told to play Connally's wife, Nellie. A brief speaking part for the kid Jacob always called Señor Quietus, which meant, according to him, that Popper was a kind of holy mystic/idiot.

The game was mobile. They started at the corner of Fullerton and North Cleveland and moved gradually down Cleveland toward the townhouse. Leo welcomed the President and Mrs. Kennedy to Texas. He apologized for being the driver and the governor, but this being Texas, a man does like to drive. This was Leo's own unscripted joke, and the Rosencrantzes, even Jacob, refused to laugh. Then Eli pucked out his chin and waved at the crowds. Jacob needled him. "Now, Jack, I won't ask you again, please stop trying to stare up Nellie's skirt. It's not polite." Jacob was always playing a different game than Eli. They moved slowly, but closer and closer, ominously closer, to Leah, who was standing in the upstairs balcony of the book depository with Hal's hat stand mounted on her shoulder. Maybe Popper was too busy watching and listening to the others. Unlike all the other games, for some reason this game he liked. How they all moved so slowly, unnaturally, up the street. Parades are freakish things. To be watched, watched by thousands of rapturous, cheering people who only want to see a glimpse of your face, your actual face. And that's it. Then you move on. And the people who lined the streets remember you later, talk about having seen you, for years. He got so caught up in it he forgot to say his one and only line, Nellie's line. Kennedy was worried about Dallas. Why wouldn't he have been? Even with Johnson vice president, Texas didn't love Democrats. And the election wasn't that far off. But they lined the streets and cheered and cheered, and Nellie Connally told him not to worry a thing about Dallas. The last words he heard before it all went dark or numb or whatever happens in your brain when you are shot point-blank in the head. Dazed and wandery, Popper bonked the line, and Leah had to stand there and wait for him to say it. Jacob congratulated him: *See? Señor Quietus is a just and humble God. He lets a man live merely by remaining silent.* But Eli ripped Popper's bonnet off and shouted, "Say the line, dwarf!" And then, bonnetless, he did. Except he whispered it: "Oh, Mr. President, you can't say Dallas doesn't love you," and still Leah fired and fired her hat stand, and Eli fell, and Jacob fell on top of him, saying, *I give bloody bloody kisses to my bloody bloody brother,* and Eli belted Jacob in the stomach, and that was it, the game was done.

Leo Discoursing

But really, in some ways Bobby's murder was actually the more mysterious of the two. Certainly any guy with the same first and last names intrigues. Was there ever a better assassin's name than Sirhan Sirhan? No other name would have done. That was a big part of it. Also, his motives have never been very clear. Something to do with RFK's position on Israel. The point is, watch your left flank, always. A shot can always come from that direction. Lee Harvey Oswald was, at one time, a Communist, I think, wasn't he? Spent some time in Moscow? My point is that more often than not, you're going to take a bullet from someone who should love you—but doesn't. Booth and Lincoln both hated tyrants. They might have been allies in another life. Of course, there are always practical considerations. Garfield's assassin? He never even has a name. He is always "a demented office-seeker." All he wanted was a job, any job. Garfield could have made him a messenger and the guy would have put a picture of Garfield up on his mantel. Instead—bam. I guess what I'm saying is, never let your guard down. And where you think it's safest, it never is. Are you even listening to me, Alexanderov? Do you ever?

APPLE PICKING

Popper's eleventh birthday party. Apple picking in Oconomowoc, Wisconsin—a windless drowsy early October day, the sunlight a honeyed pink, the rows of graggled trees, the propped ladders, boys among the boughs, the plunk of apples into the little baskets. Philip took pictures, photographs that in spite of Popper's best efforts to destroy, always seem to turn up. Alexander's famous apple picking birthday party.

A slow day, nothing happening, just that plunk of apples into baskets and some bored kids on ladders. Miriam wandered off down the row of trees. Philip fell asleep holding his camera. At one point that afternoon Popper began throwing his apples at his friends. The version he tells himself is that his friends, Manny and everybody else who'd come to his apple picking party, Barkus and Moose and Samnick, threw apples also, back at him and at each other. That it was one big, joyous Wisconsin apple war. This has never been true. The others, even Manny, were too startled to fight back, and they knew immediately it wasn't a game. The birthday boy threw apples at his friends because they'd come to his party. His father asleep, his mother gone. The light like honey, the ladders propped against the trees, the sleepy day.

TUESDAYS IN THE CITY

That Hal Rosencrantz loved Miriam Popper shouldn't have come as much of a shock to anyone. Who didn't love Miriam? The evidence: Hal and Miriam would meet at the Belden Coffee Shop on certain Tuesday afternoons when Miriam wasn't substitute teaching. Hal would take off work, Martha ensconced somewhere in a meeting.

The evidence reached Martha only after an acquaintance of hers spotted them on more than one Tuesday. *I saw your husband the other day with your young protégée.* In broad daylight, just a few blocks from the townhouse, at the Belden, having coffee. Maybe they wanted to be caught. But for Miriam, the truth was, it was less the Tuesdays in Martha and Hal's extra bedroom (the old maid's room at the back of the townhouse)—fumbling and graceless but somehow untiring, years since it had been untiring—than the coffee after. Hal asked her things. Miriam was in her early thirties by then, and up to then nobody had ever asked her much about her life.

"Tell me more."

"My father was an odd duck. He collected phone books."

"Interesting. I wonder why."

"Names. He liked to read all the names. I think he thought

there was something almost biblical about the lists. Like those
long lists of names in the Old Testament. Maybe knowing there
were so many people he'd never know, never meet, somehow
made him feel less alone."

"Tell me something else."

"I used to go skating on Watupa Pond."

"Watupa?"

"Local Indians. They were long gone by my time. They only
left the name."

"Always how it goes, isn't it? Names again—"

For Martha, it was less Hal's betrayal than Miriam's insult. She
had clearly taken advantage of what everybody knew was Hal's
weakness. The man's an utterly ridiculous romantic. Who didn't
know that? Drop your glove on the sidewalk and the man swoons
for weeks. Even so, for good measure, she threw Hal out of the
townhouse. *Love, Hal?* Maybe like most people Martha was more
than a little bit afraid of it. Could be she'd felt its terrible warping
once or twice herself. A week later she took him back. Because we
Rosencrantzes are builders. Lyric Opera houses don't get built on
daydreams. You don't lick poverty on whispered nonsenses over
coffee. Not in this city or anywhere else. Progress takes brick and
labor and tenacity and money. Get over her, Hal, we've still got
work to do. Anyway, she's charmless. Isn't she charmless? Isn't
she? Hal? Hal?

The Green Couch

After dinner—was it after dinner?

It must have been after dinner. Miriam must have come upstairs to the TV room to be with them after dinner. She'd never done it before. She'd always stayed downstairs with him and the dishes, and that's usually when—

But Philip followed her upstairs and pushed her onto the green couch and then fell on top of her, punching: *I don't give a damn who you—but to humiliate me in front of every two-bit lawyer in Chicago?* And Leo jumped on his back and started biting him in the neck and yelled to Alexander to call 911, and Alexander did. There was a phone on top of the television, the old Zenith that was more like a cabinet than a TV. But when the woman answered, he didn't really know what to say, and he would later remember imagining her on the other end of the phone listening to some kid pant into her ear. *Can you speak slow and tell me what the problem is?* Him holding the phone and the three others silent—even his father not saying anything at all, not even shouting—and then all of them sliding off the couch onto the floor, which seemed to wake everybody up out of a daze. Popper breathing harder and harder into the phone and the woman's soothing voice coaxing him, asking him for the address, and him finally saying, whisper-

ing, "105 Riparian Lane. R-I-P-A-R-I-A-N. It means by the water."
Philip began weeping and yelping apologies, and Miriam, without
a word, stood up and went to the guest room and closed but didn't
lock the door.

When the police showed up, the car crept lightless, slowly, up
the gravel so as not to alarm the neighbors. The two hulks standing there sheepish, too big for the front hall, Philip and Miriam
saying, We are so sorry for the misunderstanding. Saying—but
not with words—we are not the kind of people who would ever
need the police. In fact, we would be pillars of this community if
there was a community to be a pillar of. We are terribly sorry. One
of those things. Only one of those things.

The two cops shy, looking at their big feet, wanting to look at
Miriam, too shy to look at Miriam.

"Injuries? It's procedure that we ask if there's been any—"

Miriam and Philip chorused at the same time: "No, no
injuries!"

April 2, 1945

Well, I finally have set foot on some formerly held enemy territory — All I can say is that the whole country should see the lousy strips of sand and stone that men have died for — The American plan of conquest is to blast the hell out of a place so that not even a blade of grass is alive — Move in and set up a bar, an ice machine, and then start importing whiskey, beer, and Coca-Cola — Build a post office — Open the Chamber of Commerce — Dig graves —

The Green Couch

O r maybe it was Popper who leaped on Philip's back and Popper who teethed him in the neck, and it was Leo who called 911? Popper and his father and his mother gumbling off the couch to the hardwood floor, the floor waking them up, and his mother standing and his father on his knees, hoarse and half-crying. Then, not long after, all of them, the whole tattered family, in the front hall, the two blue oafs, shifting their weight from foot to foot, hands fidgeting, looking at the floor, not looking at Miriam, trying not to look at Miriam, staring at Miriam. We are not the kind of people who—

Nurse Kellner

No white uniform for Nurse Kellner, fuzzy sweater and blue jeans, glasses on a string riding her chest; she sits behind a metal desk in her office and waits—for you. *You want to tell me where it hurts? What do you need? How about an an ice pack?* Not much on the face of the earth that can't be cured with a few kind words and some ice. Your pain was her pain and the answer always: ice. Bloody nose, ice; stomach trouble, prune juice and a little ice; complete mental freak-out, ice. She didn't even have to stand up. The little freezer was behind her desk and the panacea pre-wrapped in napkins. Every hour of every day, you went to her, stood before her desk, years of you, decades of you. *Don't you have a brother? You look like him. Leon? Where's the pain?* All over and nowhere at the same time, Nurse Kellner. *How about two packs, one for your head and one for your soul? Lie down a while?* That little bed in her office, orange bedspread matched the carpet. *Don't worry, leave your shoes on.* Peaches and Herb low on the radio. Nurse Kellner would sleep with her head cradled in her hands, her elbows tri-angled out, so that if the principal walked by her open door, it looked as if she was contemplating some serious medical prob-lem. And maybe she was, maybe she was dreaming of pain— hers, yours, numb it, the best you can do, the only thing, numb it.

THE GUEST ROOM

Not one quiet in the guest room but many, building on themselves, multiplying like cells. Miriam's silences spread to every corner of the house, to the space behind the furnace where sick, wheezing Sir Edmund sleeps beside the blue flame.

They'd never had many guests.

A closed-door room in a house of closed doors. Two closets, one locked. This is where the silver is kept. Always the threat that no matter how much a part of the family the help, they still one day might be tempted to run off with the silver. Two windows, one looking out at the backyard, the other at Mrs. McLendon's garage next door. The bureau is empty. Most of Miriam's clothes are still in Philip's room. But Popper, spying, knew that mostly she changed in the laundry room in the basement. There is a night table with nothing on it, no clock. The big guest bed. The four posts are topped with pineapples that look to Popper like grenades, and sometimes before she comes home from work and he's alone in the house, he stands on that bed and pulls one out of its socket and throws it on the floor to blow the place up to blow it up.

IN THE BACKYARD

L eo reading Ayn Rand. Late fall, the dead leaves already hard and crinkled, the old brown grass, Leo on his back in a blue-and-black-checked lumberman's coat, holding *The Fountainhead* over his head with both hands, reading, imbibing. It's a phase, Miriam looking out the kitchen window, prays. Please, God, let that fascist bitch be a phase.

Sir Edmund beside him, gnawing on his paws.

Popper wanders outside munching a double-stuff.

"You're in my sun."

"There is no sun."

"That's what you think. You're the kind of person who waits for the sun to come to you instead of creating your own energy."

"Mom says if we're looking for something to do, we could rake the leaves."

"What about the Mexicans?"

"Dad fired them. He says they did something to the roses."

"Go away. Stop being superfluous."

"What are you reading?"

"What'd I say? Vámanos."

"What is it?"

"The Bible."

"Oh, got a different cover."

Popper stands there licking the cream off his cookie.

"What are you reading?" Leo says.

"Nothing. I'm talking to you."

"See, there's your problem. You don't engage your mind. You lack initiative. You're a useless loaf taking up space. How are you going to have any impact if you never do anything?"

Popper sits down next to the dog and gives him the last of the cookie. Sir Edmund, more out of obligation than interest, takes it in his mouth. Even the dog today.

Leo tosses the book in the grass and gets up, struts out the back gate toward the bluff at the end of the block. Popper looks at the trees, the old grass; at the McLendons' sagging fence, at the dog chewing on his paws. He picks up the Bible.

> *Late at night, often, Dominique came to Roark's room. The touch of his skin against hers was not a caress, but a wave of pain, it became pain by being wanted too much, by releasing in fulfillment all the past hours of desire and denial. It was an act of clenched teeth and hatred.*

Nice.

In the trees, a bobwhite bobwhites another bobwhite who bobwhites, demurely, back.

Bob? Bobwhite?

Bobwhite, bobwhite, bobwhite.

Bob White...?

Bobwhite!

Bobwhite, bobwhite, bob white bob whitebob bobwhite, bobwhite, bobwhite...

LOVE AND SHAME AND LOVE

Bob, Bob, Bob, Bob, Bob, White, Bobwhite, Bobwhite, Bobwhite, Bob-
white, Bobwhite, Bobwhite!
Whitebob, Bob! White! Bobwhite! Bobwhite!
Bobwhite.
Bobwhite.

Popper checks the window for lack of his mother and works his hand down his pants and waits. Above, the sky is a white lake with flecks of raining ash.

WALKER BROTHERS

When Allen Dorfman was gunned down in the parking lot of the purple Hyatt in Lincolnwood, Seymour took pride in the fact that one of their own was still high enough in the mob to rub out. See, he said, not all the Jews have moved to the North Shore and become dentists.

He'd been indicted again. Dorfman was the syndicate's chief accountant. He ran the Teamsters' pension fund, the mightiest unregulated bank on earth. Dorfman seeded the clouds that rained mob money on sunny Vegas. The other clouds he bought off. Or had deposed of by other means. But above all, Allen Dorfman was a keeper of secrets. Five, six, seven federal indictments, and still he hadn't sung. The eighth was the charm. Dorfman was looking at twenty-five years in the pen and he wasn't a young guy anymore. The FBI had wiretaps. Why take chances? The boss, Joey the Clown Lombardo, decreed it. Joey the Clown, whose children Dorfman had bounced on his knees — they loved each other like brothers, Cain and Abel, the Dago and the Kike. *Nothing personal, Allen. You and I both know this is nothing personal. For the good of the body, sometimes a neck has to go. Your neck, my neck, a neck is a neck. Anyway, I'm doing you a favor. You want to spend your golden years in Joliet?*

In the parking lot, they shot Allen Dorfman seven times in the back of the head.

Philip knew him from summer camp. They'd gone to Ojibwa together. He said Dorfman used to steal the tennis balls and sell them back to the counselors at a markup. One time, he ransomed the camp dog.

And they used to catch glimpses of the man himself, in the flesh, at Walker Brothers, sitting in his corner booth. Seymour and Bernice would take Alexander and Leo there for breakfast Sunday mornings. Dorfman wasn't a big man, but his deep tan radiated influence, glitz — his rings, his English suits, his pomaded hair. Everybody pretended to love their omelets and waffles and time with the grandkids, and the whole time watched the man over the lips of their coffee cups. For a man with so many secrets, he talked like a megaphone. "Hey, Howie? You don't come by? We're cousins and you don't come by?" And cousin Howard, befuddled, shrugs and says, "Allen, you know how it goes, the wife, the kids" — pausing, pausing — "the day job."

"You know what you are, Howard?"

"Allen, look, I'm sorry, I —"

Quiet at first. Dorfman's eyes water a little. This is all about family, about loyalty, about the ties that bind. "Howard," Dorfman says, slowly dragging it out. H-o-w-a-r-d. Then he wiggles a little in his seat. "Howard Pincus, you're a wart on my ass. I should have strangled you in your crib in '38."

Dorfman was four booths away. When the din of forks and blather rose again, Seymour said, "You can't say that the man doesn't have a certain style. Every day the man works side by side the scum of the earth, yet he breakfasts with his own kind. I'd call that class."

Popper scooted up and over the ledge of the booth to get a

better look, the leather under his sweaty thighs, that fartish rip. Dorfman was chewing, a bit of powdered sugar on his nose.

"He's a bagman for the scum of the earth," Leo said.

"Now you're a Maoist? What happened to rational self-interest?"

"And he makes his dough off the backs of the little people."

"Exactly," Seymour practically shouted. "At last the boy shows some sense. It's the way of the world." With his knife, he harpooned an egg yolk and brought it to his mouth.

"The man shoots people." Bernice yawned.

"He doesn't shoot people," Seymour said. "His people shoot people. There's a difference. If I say go out and shoot somebody and you go out and do it, you're going to blame me? Allen Dorfman's got charisma. You're going to blame a man for having charisma? Show me a man with charisma and I'll show you—"

"Seymour," Bernice said, "there's egg on your shirt." She took a napkin and dipped it in her water glass, reached across the table, and pressed it against his chest as if she were staunching a wound. And in a way she was. Seymour's despair would manifest itself at the oddest times. Even here, even now, at Walker Brothers, in the presence of Allen Dorfman. His wife doesn't love him. She's never loved him. Even his grandkids don't love him. Sometimes feared, sometimes worshipped, more often ridiculed, but loved, never.

"You see, charisma's rare. It's got to be stamped out the moment it rears its ugly head. Isn't that right, Bernice?"

Bernice blew her nose.

"How come Dorfman doesn't have a nickname?" Popper asked as he carved a leery mouth in his last pancake.

"Jews don't have nicknames," Bernice said.

"What about Hymie Weiss?" Leo said.

"Not Jewish," Seymour said. "But good try."

"Dopey Fein?"

"There's a bingo."

"Seymour, the check," Bernice said.

Seymour, vanquished, returned to the dregs of his breakfast. If Popper had his way, though, Dorfman would have been finished off at Walker Brothers. There was so much glorious plate glass to come crashing down. So much beautiful chaos to be had during breakfast on a Sunday morning. Seymour saying, "This is it, my boys, this is what we've been waiting for."

The gunfire, the overturned tables, the whimpering aftermath. And they were there. They nearly got knocked off by Joey the Clown when he did in Allen Dorfman at Walker Brothers. For the good of the body, sometimes the accountant has got to go. Can't you see it? Dorfman bleeding among his own people, his bold, pomaded head in a pool of maple syrup?

And Bernice, double-checking her hair, tsking. What absolute nonsense. Even a mob hit would bore her. Allen Dorfman bored her. Seymour especially bored her. Popper keeps an old picture of her from the twenties on his desk: Bernice dressed in feathers, her right leg raised parallel to her body, her slim bare foot rising above her head like an arrow. People say, That's your grandmother?

TWIN POOLS

They called them the Twin Toilets. Popper indulged more than once himself. There are few things more satisfying than pissing in a pool. It's hard to pinpoint why it's so great—something about the engulfment of the water and becoming one with the chlorine. *Just let it go, brother. Let it go. Who will ever know?*

Two overcrowded public swimming pools, side by side. How many hours of his life did he spend in its pleasantly urine-warmed waters? But it isn't the toilets Popper wants right now. It's the disinfectant pool, the shallow rectangular bath of chemicals you had to step in as soon as you came out of the locker room showers, where you'd just pretended to take a shower. The water was frigid, colder even than the showers. Yet if you dared to side-step the disinfectant pool, the lifeguards would throw you out. For the season. No first warning. No appeal. They'd watch that little pool like hawks. They would rather somebody drowned.

NO DIVING
NO RUNNING
NO SPLASHING
NO KICKBOARDS AFTER 3:00
PERSONS WITH COMMUNICABLE DISEASES NOT ALLOWED
ALL SWIMMERS MUST USE DISINFECTANT POOL

You went in quick. Try it with one foot. Step in, step out. Both feet! I said both feet!

Call this a vision of nothing much. Popper at twelve, his big bowl of hair, his ill-fitting nylon Speedo clinging to his thighs and drooping in the middle. Fat belly protruding. Unclipped toenails. Chubbled knees.

It was around this time that Miriam sent him to see a psychologist. The psychologist insisted that Popper call him Jack. Not Dr. Jack, just Jack. *I'm only a guy you can talk to, Alexander, and you don't even have to talk.*

Jack fed him Jay's potato chips and Cokes.

Popper didn't mind going to see Jack. He loved the alternating tastes of salty chips and Coke. He'd conduct science experiments in his mouth. There was this frizzle he could create if he ate and drank fast enough. Frizzle followed by operatic burps.

So you're sad? Your mother tells me you have been feeling sad. She says you have good reasons.

She said that?

She did. Yes. So are you? Are you sad, Alexander?

I guess so.

Why do you think you're sad?

I don't know. (Burp.)

You don't know?

I guess I feel guilty.

Guilty? Guilty about what?

I hate my family.

You know, I don't know you very well, Alexander, but I'm going to go out on a limb here and say you don't hate your family. Maybe you get annoyed with them. Maybe things aren't going very well at home right now. I understand this. But—

Also about things I've done.

Ah —

Yeah. And things I will do.

Things you will do?

I guess so. (Burp.)

Hmmmm. That's an awfully advanced stage of guilt for someone your age. I'd say that's to be commended. What sorts of things will you do to feel guilty about down the line?

I'm going to maybe betray them.

Really? Your family?

Yes.

When you say betray, what exactly do you mean?

I mean betray. I mean I'm a liar. (Burp.) Ask me something and I'll look you straight in the face and lie my ass —

More chips, Alexander? We're running low on time today.

Yes, Jack, please. More chips.

And from Jack's to his bike locked in the alley. And then riding down Central Avenue past the Clark Station, the new Style Shop, past the Jewel, the Rec Center, past the fire station, past Manny's new house, where his family finally moved just before they knocked down the Shafner house, past the little houses by the highway where the Mexicans live, up and over the overpass to the Twin Toilets.

He's just faked a shower. A little trickle of water on his shoulders. He comes out and steps into the little pool. Except that's it. He doesn't move. He stays in the disinfectant pool. The cold stiffs his ankles. Chemicals kill the fungi on his feet. I'm going to stay here — right here with both feet.

———

(Echoes, voices)
    Marco!
    Polo!
    Marco!
    Hey, green shorts — off the ropes!

Right here like a statue, like a monument, like a gift from his old lying self to his present lying self. It's 1979. Popper, don't move. Hold your ground. You're a strange alone kid being pushed from behind. Before you the great blue sewers.

    Move, idiot! What are you doing?

    Get the fuck out of the way!

April 7, 1944

Mine darling, my river perch, my swordfish — Saw some white women for the first time out here — army nurses — and what a tough-looking bunch — Of course most of them are pushing forty-five and shouldn't be allowed to wear pants — Still you should see the heads turn when one of them walks by — C'est la guerre — C'est la guerre —

CHOPIN IN HIGHLAND PARK

Taking recorder was allegedly a precursor to learning the violin. Music, Miriam said, is a lifelong vocation, like golf and tennis. It will provide you with a social outlet when you're older.

"Golf and tennis are for assholes."

"Oh, Alex, don't be like your father and revel in despising where you come from while at the same time remaining happily part of it. If your father hated this world he was born into so much he could have moved away from here years ago, but no, here's a man who lives a mile away from his parents."

"What are you talking about?"

"Just give the recorder a try, honey."

Her name was Mrs. Gerstadt and she lived in a gingerbread house on Dale Avenue. In this puny troll of a house, she gave music lessons. Popper would stand before the music stand in a sunroom filled with dusty plants she never watered. He'd tootle on his recorder, and Mrs. Gerstadt would watch him as if in pain. Sometimes she'd lean toward him and absentmindedly correct his fingering, her breasts bumping his shoulder. Mrs. Gerstadt's breasts were nothing like fruit. They were more like small fists punching out of her shirt, not in anger, casually. This occasional contact kept him going to recorder lessons, violin in his future or no violin in his future.

His hours with Mrs. Gerstadt may also have been Popper's first lesson in the truth that what you must do to get by in this world is often tedious and mind-numbing and even humiliating, but that if you didn't expend too much mental effort, it was possible to make it through the day. So Mrs. Gerstadt taught recorder and (he assumed) violin to Highland Park's Zimbalists and Heifetzes who actually made it that far. If there was a husband or children in that tiny house, they have been expunged from the record. Popper's memory is an increasingly emptier room. The less furniture, the more he gropes around.

He never touched a violin.

Mrs. Gerstadt had tangled, prematurely gray hair and vague, distant eyes. At the end of the lesson she'd sit him down in the old kitchen chair in the corner and put on a record as if to cleanse them both—and the violated air itself—of the tooty abominations he'd been blowing out the last forty-five minutes.

As the music played, she'd whisper facts about the composers. Who went insane. Who mourned his too many dead children. Who got chased away by Nazis. Who jumped into the icy waters of the Moldau and flowed down the river with the current. *And Chopin? You know what they did to him? When he died in Paris, they sliced his heart out and mailed it home to Poland. The French held on to his brain and fingers.*

One day she put on Bach's cello suites and wept without tears. Popper watched her, gripping his recorder. She trembled. He couldn't feel what she was feeling. He squinted and hummed a little, tried to follow some notes. Mrs. Gerstadt reached for him and dug her fingers into his shoulder blade as if to say, Don't twitch, listen, just listen, you little oaf, listen. And the sound in the room got deeper and more terrible, a long dire moaning, and he tried to feel it, in his gut he tried to feel it—

———

A forgotten afternoon in a too hot room and Mrs. Gerstadt has just taken her hand from his shoulder and given up on him completely. Not only doesn't he have talent, he doesn't even have ears. Bach, and to him it could be the toilet flushing. And then—as now, this minute—all he wants is to jump on Mrs. Gerstadt and crush her sadness with his confusion and his sick sick wants, in the sunroom with the dead plants.

PHILIP AND MIRIAM

They don't speak. They sit listening to a Dionne Warwick record on the stereo, and these days are getting longer and these nights are lasting decades, and Miriam puts her hand slowly to her mouth and breathes into her fingers. Between them, on the low table, is Philip's chessboard. Dionne sings, *What's it all about when you sort it out, Alfie?* The light outside is a thick, dark green. Philip thinks of seaweed, of trying to see through seaweed. The people who owned this house before them left a tall flagpole on the lawn. Philip didn't get rid of it; that pole represented a permanence, a rootedness, *This is our place.* When Popper was seven, playing running bases with Manny, he ran into the flagpole and conked himself out. Does a lawn retain its histories? Do living rooms? Chairs? Philip watches the flagpole. He no longer hoists the flag every morning, but the rope that runs the flag up the pole remains and so does the heavy metal clasp that continues, even on a night with so little wind, to clang like a halyard against a mast, a faraway sound Miriam likes.

"You did something different to your hair," Philip says.

"Did I?"

Philip coughs, but he doesn't say anything else. Tonight he

will not knock on the guest room door. He will not try to turn the knob without knocking, either. Miriam looks past him at the wall behind his head, the blank space to the right of the window, where she had always meant to hang something.

CENSUS, 1980

M iriam dressed up as the Easter bunny for Easter Seals. That bulbous-headed costume, those big floppy feet. She volunteered for the March of Dimes. She sold magazine subscriptions. She trained to be a docent at the Oriental Institute at the University of Chicago and could speak at length about mummification and hieroglyphics. She worked as a substitute high school teacher, Gordon Tech, Lane Tech, Maine West, Glenbrook South. She also worked as a census taker. In 1980, the year the Second City was demoted to third and Jane Byrne was so livid she threatened to sue the federal government for defaming Chicago's character, Miriam tromped the streets of the city to count the people.

Popper would go door to door with her and listen to the song and dance. *Yes, I'm with the government, but the Census Bureau is an independent agency under the auspices of the Commerce Department charged solely with the collection of numerical and demographical data. We're not interested in, for instance, your criminal record, tax history, immigration status . . .*

Slam.

Knock again.

All information is strictly confidential. It is against federal law to share information collected by the census. The government merely wants to —

Slam.

Knock, knock again.

The census is a constitutional mandate. The Founding Fathers believed that the lifeblood of democracy itself was dependent on an accurate —

Slam.

On the first day of the second month, the Lord said to Moses, take a census of the whole —

Slam.

Banging on the door, Look, do me a favor and just throw out a number, any number —

Miriam in a trench coat, sunglasses on her head, carrying a bundle of questionnaires and booklets. Anything to get out of the suburbs. On the Kennedy Expressway — the city rising — she would say, Look around, observe! And Popper would call out the sights: Morton Salt, Aabbitt Adhesives, the Polish Catholic Union, Ukrainian National Bank, Magikist lips...

She loved construction, she loved muggings. She loved traffic. She loved traffic reports: *14 minutes to the Circle Exchange. Kennedy, 19 minutes to Montrose, the Ryan outbound 28 minutes to 95th, Lake Shore Drive free and clear from Monroe to Hollywood, fender bender on the inbound Ike, gapers' block from Manheim to the post office — Traffic sponsored by Ray Hara's King Datsun, home of king-sized discounts.*

"That's us. Nineteen minutes to Montrose. We're flying in today. Careful, Honey —"

That move she used to make, that all mothers used to make,

gone now in this dull age of seatbelts. Miriam slashing her arm across Popper's chest at the hint of any danger.

A Fall River girl in Chicago and she couldn't get enough. New England was stale, complacent. Chicago was about the new. Knock it down, big boy, and build me something bigger. The City That Works won't be slowed by sentimental nostalgia. And Miriam, census taker, counter of souls, was now a cog in this unstoppable wheel of action. This remarkable place where a woman—a woman!—was elected Himself.

But census taking, the act itself, is its own special hell. Popper began, even then, to understand how hard it can be to confront even the most basic questions about your life. *Who do you live with? Who don't you live with?*

In his census memories it is always raining and they are always drenched. And Miriam would say, "Enough of this already, let's have a drink." And so together they'd flee to the nearest bar, never more than a block or two away, and she'd plunk down her papers and say to the bartender, usually a sloe-eyed man emerging out of a corner of darkness, "Give me a martini. Very *very* dry."

To Popper: "Cola or Uncola?"

"Uncola. No, wait. A Coke. No, Uncola. No, wait, a Coke."

Always that unlit red-tipped cigarette between her fingers. She'd practice on him.

"Who do you live with?"

"You, Leo, and Dad."

"Immediate family?"

"What do you mean?"

"Are all the persons you named members of your immediate family?"

"I'm confused."

"Occupation?"

"Archaeologist."

"Highest degree attained?"

"Huh?"

"What grade are you in?"

"Fifth."

"Years in the state of Illinois, not excluding terms of military service?"

"Whole life."

"Religion?"

"I know, Mom, I know. We're Jewish, but I don't have to be. I can be anything—"

He remembers. They were on the 1800 block of South Pulaski and the door of a basement apartment was immediately opened by an alarmingly tall woman with a wild mass of orange hair. She swatted away the speech. "Come on in, Commerce Department."

The woman lived in a single room, a kitchen and a living room. Rain was banging on the little rectangular windows. She lived eye-level with the wet feet going by on the sidewalk. One lamp hung from a chain, a single bulb behind a tattered red shade. The light in the room was the color of washed-out blood. You could tell where the border between the kitchen and the living room was supposed to be by where the linoleum ended and the worn, gnarled carpet began, but her stuff didn't seem to care what was the kitchen and what wasn't. In the red shadows, he could see scattered piles of newspapers, old mail, coupon books, clothes, and unwashed dishes. Spent Kleenex were strewn across the apartment like little crumplets of flowers. On the single chair in the room was a plant the size of a man. Shoved into one corner was an upright piano that doubled as a bookshelf and a place for shoes. On the sofa, memory swears, a small load of lumber.

"Make yourselves at home!"

"Oh no, I wouldn't want to trouble you. I only have a few very brief—"

"Sit."

For a few moments they stood there confused. Sit where? The woman motioned toward the chairless kitchen table. As they got closer, they saw that on the other side of the table, wedged against the wall, was another, lower, couch. On it were crumpled sheets and a pillow. They sat. The orange-haired woman might have been tall enough for the couch to double as a bed *and* a kitchen chair, but Miriam and her kid were smallish people. Miriam scooted forward, so that at least her head and arm were above the table. Popper did his best to do the same, shoving his chin just over the edge.

"No! Sit back! Make yourselves comfortable!"

Miriam propped her papers up on her knees and poised her pencil. The woman joined them on the couch bed.

"Move over a bit, honey," Miriam said.

"So, what was it you wanted to ask me, Commerce Department?"

"How many people in your household?"

The orange-haired woman swayed backward and laughed. She stopped and abruptly stood up. The effect was like a trampoline, the two of them flung upward.

The woman looked around the apartment as if she were looking for somebody who'd been hiding.

"You know, I used to have a lot of men," she said, and reached down and set her large hand on the top of Popper's head. "Cute when they're little. They ought to snip it off early."

"Age," Miriam said. "You can be approximate."

"Are you married? You must be married. Petite, pretty. Although, I notice, no ring. It's in your pocket? Men talk easier that way. Answer your questions?"

"Source of monthly income?"

"Happy in that matrimony?"

Miriam changed her grip on her pencil and sank deeper into the half couch.

"Disability," the orange-haired woman said to buoy her a little. "I'm on disability, $160 a week. Monthly, that's — You're not from here."

"Massachusetts," Miriam said. "I'm from Massachusetts. Alternate source of income? Stock dividends, bond yields, interest on long-term savings accounts —"

"Would you two like some pretzels? I'm sure the little monkey eats pretzels." From the front pocket of her blue jeans she yanked out a crumpled bag of pretzels and handed it to Popper. He took one pretzel and listened to himself chomp in his own ears.

"Doesn't talk much, does he, Commerce Department?"

"I've only got a few more —"

"Oh, don't be shy. Ask away."

"Would you consider yourself white, black, Hispanic, Asian, American Indian, or Aleutian Islander and/or Eskimo?"

The rain went on banging on the windows. Miriam was diligent. She soldiered on. The training manual had said expect certain countees to be resistant. *Remember the three Ps: Patience, Persistence, Politeness.*

"And my hair's not really red."

"It's not?"

"I dye it. Out of vanity. I'm not saying I was ever beautiful. Not like you. I was never as beautiful as someone like you. I can only imagine what you must have looked like as a child."

"Highest degree attained?" Miriam whispered.

"I'm not lonely. You can think what you want."

He watched his mother write this down. She'd begun to write it all down, everything. But he remembers thinking this was true. The orange-haired woman wasn't lonely. It was the two of them who had come to her out of the rain.

"Occupation?"

"Insomniac."

"Is this your primary residence?"

"What's he do?"

"Who?"

"Your other monkey. The bigger monkey."

"He's an attorney."

Miriam wrote this down also. Popper read it. My other monkey is an attorney.

"Religious affiliation?"

The orange-haired woman watched his mother so intently and for so long that the afternoon collapsed. The patterns of wrinkles radiating from her eyes were like fresh cobwebs. She reached for Miriam's throat with her big fingers and held them there, as if she were taking her pulse.

Popper spoke then for the first time all afternoon, nearly shrieking, "It's not required!"

The last shred of outside light now gone, only that blood light, but the rain still banging on the little windows. He doesn't remember leaving. He doesn't remember the walk back to the car, South Pulaski reaching flat for uncountable miles, or even the rain, the rain beading on his mother's coat, the rain in his shoes, the rain in his eyes, the silence between the two of them on the drive home, none of it, he remembers none of it.

THE BLUFF

He follows Leo out to the bluff. The lake down below rasping in the dark. They never even need to listen to it, because it is always there. The bluff is a scoop of land above the lake, as if God's mouth took a bite out of the middle of an apple and left the top part, and they sit up there and pluck weeds and kick the scrawny trees that barely hang on to the ground. Erosion will send these trees off the cliff sooner or later. Over the edge are carcasses of newly fallen trees, uptorn roots like festoons of pubic hair. Every year the bluff shrinks more. Two brothers on their backs looking up through the trees at the scrumble of clouds in the purple dark, not listening to the lake.

Leo?

Yeah?

What's taking her so long?

He wants the house. Think about it, Alex. Mom doesn't have a dime.

Leo?

Yeah?

It's late

So?

Back Porch

You aren't going to be a kid without a father. My own father, by the way, who you only knew in the very last years of his life, was a wonderful father, ineffective in many ways, he spent most of his life dreaming, but he couldn't have been more loving. That's neither here nor there. The point is, you can't choose your father any more than you can choose the weather or how tall you are or how straight your teeth are—and your father loves you, never think for a minute that—

"But you chose him."

They were on the back porch. Leo, being older and more independent, and pretty much mayor of his own life, was exempt from this speech. On the patio the fountain gurgled, the little naked boy with the leaf over his dick was still holding his turtle, and out of the turtle's mouth water was still drooling and collecting in the pool at his feet.

Miriam shrugged. "Oh, honey, you know your father can, on occasion, be extraordinarily charming. I used to think of him as a short Warren Beatty. I admit there are times when I forget this myself and want nothing at all to do—Also, he's quite a good dancer. Beanie taught him. And he says she never paid attention to him. Well, at some point she must have—Not that he and I have danced in—"

Vanished Scene

I t's stopped, but still the trees keep on raining. The loud plops
amid the leaves. Philip and Leo took turns digging a shallow
ditch. Popper held Sir Edmund to his chest. The grass wet, the
new dirt blue and wormy. The dog fit snug in the hole. Philip held
Lord Byron under his arm. He had planned to read: *Oh could I feel
as I have I felt, or be what I have been,/Or weep as I could once have wept,
o'er many a vanished scene...* But he didn't. Instead, he paraphrased:
"It never started. It ends." Miriam watched from the rain-fogged
kitchen window—her breath and the steam of the rain.

9

SO LONG, WALTER MONDALE

White Cedar Apartments

You want the house, Phil, take it. I'll take the kids, some furniture, a few wedding dishes, and the cat nobody ever mentions. And they did, they took Louise with them, a cat that spent her life avoiding the Poppers as if she knew too much about them. Louise emerged from the shadows only in the deadest part of the night for her chicken-flavored kiblets.

They left on a weekday afternoon while Philip was downtown. The three of them in the gravel driveway packing up his mother's convertible VW Bug with the last of their clothes and junk and pillows that would fit. Leo put the top down, so there'd be more room, and the two of them sprawled on top of their stuff, trying to keep socks from blowing away in the wind. It was November. Miriam drove, cigarette between her lips and the cat in her lap. Mom as Steve McQueen. They vagabonded seven blocks to an unfurnished apartment in a small complex called White Cedar Apartments. There weren't any white cedar trees anywhere. They must have chopped them down to build the place.

December 1980. The new place smelled of plastic. It came with a built-in bar. The day after they moved in, Miriam picked up some stools at a restaurant supply place in the city. It was mercifully quiet. His father's raging hurts a few miles away; they heard only an echo. Miriam had left him the phone number. He called and he called and he called. *Nothing's been finalized. My lawyer says you have zero right. You can't just pack up; you think this is some hotel you can just check out of?*

Finally, Leo took the phone off the hook and put it in a drawer. They weren't poor, but the illusion that they might become so was thrilling.

Strange, they celebrated Hanukah in that empty apartment. Some years Miriam remembered this holiday, other years she forgot all about it. They'd always been proud Christmas-tree Jews. *Take away America's greatest celebration of unfettered consumerism from us? Not a chance.* But that year she put her father's, Grandpa Walt's, menorah on a folding chair and lit the candles and sang the prayer. Miriam sang. She so rarely ever sang. Her prayer was like a low hum, and very beautiful, and they listened and watched her face in the light of the candles. She was still so young then. She was their mother. How could they have known? A time of happy exile. They'd moved down in the world. Miriam's voice. An empty apartment that smells of plastic. Her voice like a hum, rising, rising.

Charlie Beinlich's

Popper picks up a single fry and tries to eat exactly half of it, gnawing off the ridges but leaving the essence of the fry itself.

"Stop that, will you."

The remains of the fry cling like a worm to his finger.

"What?"

He eats the fry.

"Talk to me."

"About what?"

"About yourself, something."

Charlie Beinlich's is supposed to look like a Lake of the Woods fishing cabin with the pine paneling, except that it's on Skokie Highway across from the movie theaters, Eden I and Eden II. Popper looks at the mounted sturgeon above Philip's head. Its bulgy glass eyes, fat scaly body. The monster of Lake Michigan stuffed and nailed to the wall.

He starts working on another half fry. The ridges are where the best grease gets trapped. This is distinct from the actual potato part of the fry, so you want to try to separate it out. It isn't easy. It's a surgical operation.

Just Popper and Philip. Leo is exempt from the divorce

decree's stipulations. He sees his father when he feels like seeing his father, which is hardly ever.

Philip watches him, chewing his fish slowly, searching for the bones with his tongue. Wednesday night. Dad's night. Charlie B's. *Best damn burger on the whole North Shore!*

"There's nothing you can tell me?"

"What?"

"Oh, I get it. Already you've seen all there is to see. You've seen peace, you've seen war. You've been on the goddamn moon with Buzz Aldrin."

"What are you talking about?"

"You think this is all some joke?"

"What?"

"Being someone's son. Being someone's father. I'm trying to have a conversation with you."

"Can't we just eat?"

"So they've poisoned the well for good?"

"Who?"

"Who. Ha. Your mother and brother indoctrinated you against me when you were six months old."

Time for more ketchup. He whacks the bottom of the bottle and gets lucky on the first try. The ketchup throbs, spurts, pooling thickly onto his plate, and the fries poke out like the heads of drowning people. Like when the Eastland tipped over in the sewage of the Chicago River. Seymour told him all about it. Hundreds flailing in the city's shit. And he was there. Seymour is always on the scene. He said he missed half a day's work pulling women and children out of the smelly muck. *The only day in my entire life—but for the war—I ever missed a half-minute of work.*

He rescues a drowning Chicagoan, eats the fry whole.

"Look at me once in a while, will you."

"I've seen you."

Philip laughs. He pulls a bone out of his mouth. "All right. You win." His head turns just slightly to watch the skirt of a waitress fling by. Popper watches the side of his father's scrubbed, ruddy face. His father is the cleanest, most scrubbed man on the face of the earth. Dogs would be in heaven shitting on the snow-white carpet of his bedroom. In fact, Sir Edmund, just before he died, once took that gorgeous liberty.

The wreckage on his plate, the half-eaten burger, flooded fries, avoided garnishes.

Popper thinks of Sir Edmund. One day he was lying on the kitchen floor breathing, but he couldn't stand up anymore. For a week he was like that. Breathing heavy on the kitchen floor and not standing up. Here was a dog that loved Milk Bones, but that last week he wouldn't have eaten a Milk Bone if you shoved it down his throat. Popper knew. He'd tried to jam one into his panting mouth.

The Catcher

Plumper than ever that summer. Baloney slices in bed. Entire packages of Oscar Mayer blissfully consumed. At first practice Coach Cameron throws him a catcher's mitt and a mask.

Mr. Popper, won't you catch for us?

Fattish kids catch. He plays for Lake Car Wash. Red hats, red shirts, red stirrup socks that hook under the bottom of your foot. Coach Cameron has a bushy mustache and teaches English at the College of Lake County. He's nobody's dad. He tells Popper that the catcher has the odd and not unimportant role of being not in the game exactly but at the same time *is the game*. Coach Cameron asks if this makes sense, and at first he just nods his head as if he's got a clue what the man's talking about, but after a few games he thinks he sees what it all means. He stands literally outside of the action, the only player, as Coach Cameron says, for whom foul territory is actually home. A catcher is a kind of bystander God. But you couldn't have a battery without him. *Thurman Munson, Carlton Fisk, Johnny Bench, Steve Swisher.* He gets the ball back to the pitcher—Manny—who puts everything in motion. Then he sits back on his hams and watches the world—his world—which is now free to fuck up however it feels like fucking up. His job is simply to deliver back the ball. Stolen bases, plays at the plate, things that directly involve him are rare. Frequent wild pitches an exception, but even so. It's the day-in, day-out, pitch after pitch. He catches the ball. He tries to catch the ball. He throws it back to Manny. The attrition of back and forth. And maybe it's not even about the ball. Maybe it's only the gesture of return. He crouches. The ump's knee in his back. The tensing of his hams. Tense those hams, Coach Cameron says. Popper alone in foul territory. The ump is only a prop. There is no honest judge in Lil' Pony League or anywhere else. His mitt like a fat waiting mouth. And a world no longer his seen through the bars of a cage.

April 14, 1945

    *Sweetheart, I started this letter a few days ago but have
not had a chance to finish it—We received the news of the
President's death and of course we were all shocked—It was
certainly a cruel twist of fate that he should be taken on the
eve of the victory—I guess there is no doubt he gave his life
for his country—Would you send a copy of the Chicago Sun?
I'm starving for more news—They only tell us things in thin
little trickles—Your box of Fannie Mays arrived yesterday—
and it was swell and came in good condition—very well
wrapped! Except that there were no creams—just caramels
and nougats—*

Churchillian Scene

Seymour took a position in a suburban bank as a vice president. There were many vice presidents, but Seymour insisted he was the true second in command, a heartbeat away from honcho. One day he took Popper with him to Downers Grove to repossess a car. Seymour was of the opinion that a vice president shouldn't always hide behind the almighty desk but must also go out among the people.

A woman answered the door. She was tall and wore glasses and was holding a piece of toast.

"Well, hello."

"Mrs. Charlotte Anders?"

"Is this for the Cub Scouts? You're not in uniform."

"We're from the bank. We're here for your Cutlass."

Mrs. Anders was sexy in a teachery Rosalynn Carter sort of way. Popper imagined she'd just come from reading a book and had set the book on the table, facedown. Now the book was waiting for her like a small house with a small peaked roof. A tall woman, her dress was short, at least it seemed that way to him. Her knees were bare and bunchy. It was an afternoon in August. The mail had come, but she hadn't retrieved it. It was sticking out of the box. She was the kind of person who could wait for days to retrieve the mail. Popper liked that about her.

The woman went away for a moment and came back without the toast. There was no car in the driveway.

"Your payments, Mrs. Anders. Our records show they're fourteen weeks overdue."

"You seem a bit young."

"But not too young," Seymour said. "There's nothing in the statute that prohibits minors from repossession cases so long as they, of course, don't drive the vehicle!"

The woman looked up at the trees. "My husband has the car."

Popper kept his eyes on her knees. They were not so much fat as bunched up from all that sitting and reading and grading papers and waiting while her students took quizzes. Cheated on quizzes. Popper often cheated on quizzes. Seymour cleared his throat.

She stood there, holding open the screen door. Then she looked at the drab, bleached sky and smiled mournfully. Maybe she thought the kid was going to let her off. He felt the heat of his grandfather's breath on his neck. *What would Churchill do? "We shall not fail or falter; we shall not weaken or tire." Make the choice, are you a bulldog or are you Neville Chamberlain?*

"Mrs. Anders, I'm sorry, but we have other cases."

"Other cars to take away?"

"One van and a boat, actually."

"My husband's dead. And he took the car with him."

"Would it be all right, Mrs. Anders, if we had a quick look in your garage?"

She held her ground. He waited. He'd been trained to wait. Finally, she pulled him inside her house, murmuring, "Little banker, come here, little banker..."

You want there to be an end to moments like this, but they go on. Upon moments like these, time never stops gnawing its little beaver teeth. And the dialogue never stops, even after we stop listening. Now Popper talks in his head, and even he hardly hears it. He'd gone on a mission with his grandfather to Downers Grove. *People have to pay for their cars, their boats, Alexander. If they take out bank loans, they have to pay the bank back. Otherwise, don't you see, all would be anarchy. The entire system would collapse. You think we're talking about just one lady in Downers Grove? I'd love to give her the car, hell, I'd love to give her a boat, too, why not, but don't you see? Capitalism needs broke people. How else would anybody know they were rich?* A Mrs. Charlotte Anders once pulled him inside her house, a house as dark as the inside of a shoe. Or maybe it's only that she pulled him closer, closer, and smothered his head. People's troubles, death, eternal sadness, even love, yes, love for your sad reading eyes. He will think of you, so many years later, he will think of you and your eyes tired from reading and the way your body smelled like soap and fresh-torn leaves, but first and foremost, above all, business is business. Do what you want with me, Mrs. Charlotte Anders — haunt me — it won't change the bottom line. No sentimentalists us. And, also, we'll be needing the keys to the Oldsmobile.

BOMBARDMENT

Bombardment, the art of it, the raising the ball above your head and aiming at one person, Stu Bortz, when the person you really intend to nail, Brian Dombrowski, is just on the edge of your vision, last-minute pivot and throw and bango, Dombrowski gets it in the neck—is akin to the art of enduring the seventh grade, which is akin to the art of enduring our lives period, because isn't it all about hitting people before they can hit you? Remember the squeak of rubber and all the laughing and the threatening and the acrobatic avoidance and even when somebody buys it in the eye—play must go on. In this game, we stop for no man or crying Fiona Nardini. It is true, though, that there are a few who are savvy enough to understand that to truly survive it's a lot less about the hitting than the evading. Let everybody else kill each other. Just play it cool, non-aggressive, Swiss, Manny Laveneaux–style. Lurk around the outskirts of the game, maybe pick up a stray ball and toss it at somebody halfheartedly, but always keep your eye on your own back. Yet we're talking here only about a chosen few, the rare ones, the graceful ones left standing in the end. Definitely not Popper. He's happily part of the rabble, and anyway, he never wanted to win. Like everybody else he just wanted to kill.

Jacob Rosencrantz

O f Jacob's funeral itself he remembers the shocked silence. A
thing like this wasn't supposed to happen. Jacob died, the
doctors said, of a concave heart. He had had it all along. He was a
junior in high school when he suddenly slumped over in the middle of class. Popper remembers sitting in the funeral home,
stuffed like a sausage into one of Leo's old blazers. They didn't
come in as a family, but they sat together as one. Philip and Miriam next to each other, stiff, occasionally bumping shoulders.

I hear you've found a friend.

Phil, we're at a funeral.

He remembers that his mother's head didn't seem to move for
the entire service, and yet in a weird way, to him, it was moving,
as if Miriam was getting farther and farther away from this place,
this scene. He sat silent, sometimes standing up, trying to get a
glimpse of Leah and Eli, Martha and Hal. It occurred to him that
the Rosencrantzes were even easier to hate now that Jacob was
out of the picture for good. It also occurred to him, *I'm not dead, I
may be a fattish little stupid pig, but at least I am not dead.*

In the middle of the service, the rabbi still speaking, Martha
stood up, looked around in bewilderment at the enormous crowd

of mourners. Then she slowly walked down the aisle and out the banging double doors.

After, in the foyer, Martha was sitting on a lone folding chair. An impromptu receiving line formed, and one by one people went to her, stooped to her. She seemed not to recognize anybody, but when it came Miriam's turn, her eyes focused and she nearly fell off the chair into Miriam's arms. They had not spoken in years, but it was to Miriam that she had words to say, words that Leo, Popper, and Miriam still repeat, words that sometimes overshadow Jacob's death itself. Or maybe they help him live on? Sometimes they repeat the line out of cruelty. Other times out of something opposite.

"Oh, Miriam, I feel like I'm in a Fellini movie."

Miriam said, "I know, I know."

MAYOR REGRETS

Bernie Epton comes to him like other dead. Out of a crack in the day, out of the anarchy of his awake dreams. Popper at his desk, crafting a plea agreement—isn't one way or another our whole life made up of plea agreements? *Okay, okay, I did it. Now don't I deserve a lesser sentence for saying so*—and suddenly, deep in his ears, another guilty voice murmurs: *Shut up, shut up, shut up.*

Election night, 1983. He and Leo are watching the returns on TV in the White Cedar apartment. Maybe it was exhaustion. Or maybe the campaign had, finally, driven Epton as bonkers as some Harold Washington partisans claimed he'd been all along. On paper the man was a living miracle. He'd just won 48.6 percent of the vote, a hangnail short of being elected mayor of Chicago.

Even Popper knew that Bernie Epton was a wild-eyed Republican from another planet. And a Jew no less. Not to put too fine a point on it, but Miriam once told them, Remember, we're Democrats before we're Jews. It's the only thing that's nonnegotiable. We believe in social programs and hate war unless it's absolutely necessary.

Leo kept flipping the channels, from Harold Washington's raucous victory party to Bernie Epton's concession speech.

"Wait," Popper said. "Turn back to Channel 2. Let's watch Bernie a little longer."

"Why?"

"It looks like his head is going to explode."

"By jove, you're right. You're getting perceptive, Alexanderilyich."

His people were still cheering him on, and finally Bernie couldn't take it anymore. From the podium, he began shouting at his own supporters. *Please, would you all just shut up!*

Because Bernie Epton wanted to speak. He wanted to say something profound. He had wisdom to dispense. *I'm an intellectual, a lakefront liberal, for God's sake. I'm a Republican because I believe in fiscal restraint and I'm against sweetheart deals for the unions. Mayors don't go to war, dumbo. Unless they're Richard Daley—who was a Democrat. I never meant for things to get so out of hand. I'm no monster. I'm only a human being. Who wouldn't have been seduced by the possibility? God grants you how many chances at immortality? And if there's somebody somewhere who holds a title more glorious than His Honor Mayor of the City of Chicago, we never heard of him in Illinois. And, hear me, hear me loud and clear, I didn't play the race card; other people snatched it out of my hand and laid it down for me. Blame a man for going along for the ride for the good of the city? If the people in the streets have to call Harold Washington a child molester to stop him from getting elected, then they've got to call him a child molester. Cicero accused Cataline of bestiality with donkeys, all kinds of unspeakable things. That's politics.*

Win first, heal later. Is that your plea, Bernie?

Now wait, Bernie says to Popper from beyond the grave. *Hold it right there, partner, I only said tax cheat, I never said child molester. I deplored child molester. Get your facts straight. The truth is bad enough without some snotnose ex-suburbanite lying about it, even in his random, private meanderings. And I always said, "This election is not about colors. If I thought for one moment that this election was about colors, I wouldn't be standing before you today…My fellow Chicagoans, I will lead you from the desert to the city of hope, to the golden city of your dreams…"*

The choice between a sheeny and a shine? What's a Chicagoan to do? And *Newsweek* shouted to the country, to the world: WHAT'S GOING ON IN CHICAGO?

Tax cheat? Child molester? What's the difference? A con's a con. Go get 'em, Jew boy. Italians for Eptonini. Irish for Mac-Epton. Poles for Eptonizinski. Mexicans for Bernie Cruz. Wait, what? (Never mind, just pull the lever for the white guy.) Bernie! Bernie! Bernie!

And Popper thinks of you now, delusions thumping down on your head like wet March snow. Jesus? Moses? You weren't even a good Judas. You're a footnote, Bernie. The real story is Jane Byrne and Richie Daley and how Harold Washington made them both look like the hacks they were. It was Harold who had the class, the elocution, the ideas. It was Harold who kept sending the reporters to their dictionaries. *Mayor Contretemps. Mayor Hoisted by Your Own Petard.*

You, Bernie, were Mayor Almost. Mayor Not Quite. Mayor Already Forgotten.

But tell the truth. Who gets remembered? And for once, Popper understands something fundamental about politics without Leo having to explain it to him. The loser's party is always more interesting than the victor's. That spirit of chin up, all those dumb balloons hanging up there dreaming of release, of that slow victorious float to the floor. Is there anything so beautifully democratic as a concession speech, even when the conceder's having a total meltdown?

Shut up and listen, Bernie pleaded.

Popper thinks now, I know what you were trying to say, Bernie. That your heart was broken, and not only because you lost. The world's an ugly, ruthless place, you wanted to say. There isn't nearly enough love. Love, you wanted to sermonize into the microphone, in front of the cameras, in front of the city, what this city needs is love —

But how to explain this? Who'd believe it? Popper believes you, Mayor Regrets. In this, you speak for all of us. They should put your name on a plaque somewhere. Rest well in purgatory, Bernie. Your bones in Oak Woods Cemetery, 1035 E. 67th Street, in the Jewish section, just across the road from Harold Washington's sad, grand mausoleum.

D inner at home. Home? What is he supposed to call this place now? Wednesday, again. Philip's not back from work. Still got a little time to himself—

Above the toilet in the downstairs bathroom (they always called it the "Powder Room," mocking the Rosencrantzes) is a small framed picture of a young pinkish girl. Under her chest are the words: *A Tribute to My Pretty Star*. Her porcelain face, her fat delicious cheeks. As far as he knows, she's still hanging above the toilet, wondering where Popper disappeared to. Where has he disappeared to?

And there was something else about the powder room other than his Pretty Star. If you stood on the toilet itself, you could see out a small window that had a good view of the Krawchecks' driveway next door to the east. Unlike the McLendons, the Krawchecks had always been almost invisible neighbors. They lived behind a wall and line of tall trees and rarely came out in the street. It was generally thought that because the Krawchecks had a direct lake view out their back windows, they considered themselves above everybody else on Riparian Lane. But they had a daughter about Popper's age. He'd never known her very well. Her name was Daphne. He'd never known her very well, because she went to private school. (Now, that's some serious class, to send your kid to private school when you live in the suburbs.)

Consequently, like her parents, Daphne also held herself aloof from the neighborhood. Further adding to her mystique was the fact that she'd been adopted. Popper, who was saddled with the knowledge that whatever was missing between his mother and father had created him, had always been a little jealous of her. That Daphne could, with a flip of her hand, say, "Hey, you see those two over there masquerading as my parents? No relation, none." To be able to cast off this town, this neighborhood, Riparian Lane itself—it was an awesome power. Even her name was incongruent. It was a made-up country, like Yugoslavia. There was no such person as Daphne Krawcheck. Daphne Krawcheck was a fiction. And some days in spring she'd come home from her private school in Lake Forest and lie in the driveway, in her tweed private-school field hockey–looking dress, and stare at the sky, and Popper would stand on the toilet waiting for her skirt to crawl higher, higher, exposing milk-white private-school thighs.

Daphne Krawcheck composes poems in her head on the asphalt driveway, and Popper is a scumbag.

Why is it that shame never stops bleeding? Even now, he's still standing on that toilet? Even now, the whole world knows he's up on that toilet aching himself to a vision of Daphne Krawcheck? A girl he'd once said hey to while riding past her driveway, nothing more, ever.

That emptied house, his furious hysterical loneliness, his nose against the pane, fogging it up. Only our disgraces are permanent? Once—only once, and he'll never forget it as long as he lives— Daphne grabbed her ankle and raised her leg so that her foot was directly above her head, and he was so stunned he stopped breathing. That tweed dress collapsed over her face like a parachute.

April 30, 1945

I imagine everyone must be happy now—But as Truman said—It should be a solemn celebration—because there's still a tough, fanatical, and desperate enemy out here—I tell you this to give you a little ammunition to take care of some of the loose talk I know is probably spouting from a lot of our friends—Speaking of, did you see the March 5th issue of Time *magazine where some spies were implicated? One of them was a Phillip Jaffe from Chicago in the greeting card business—Isn't that Irma B.'s brother? It seems they are all Communist sympathizers—Do you remember that parlor-pink harangue Irma gave us a few years ago when she was at our house—I'd like to kick her teeth in—*

THE ROBBERY

He comes home from school and the front door of the apartment is slightly ajar. Nobody home. Miriam at work. Leo rarely home these days. Hello, Popper says, *Louise?* Not a sound. No sign of that cat. Popper creeps in slow, Columbos around a little, peeps around corners, opens closed closet doors. Skulks backward into a bar stool and knocks it over, and leaps, screams, hides behind the couch. Breathes, waits, crawls on knees and elbows into the kitchen. Ah ha. The refrigerator is open. Wide open. Quite interesting. Make a note of this. Said thief may have been out of margarine. Continue the investigation. His room all amiss, therefore nothing amiss. Leo's room perfect order, therefore nothing amiss. His mother's — holy fucking shit — the tackle box Miriam uses to store her jewelry is open on the bed, and rings, earrings, bracelets, lockets are strewn around — strewn!

"Good afternoon, Koenig and Stray. May I —"

"Mom?"

That year she was working part-time for a realtor.

"Yes, honey."

"Somebody broke into the apartment and stole your jewelry."

"What?"

"And the refrigerator's open."

"The refrigerator? Why don't you go over to Manny's? I'll be home after six."

When Miriam came home, he was waiting for her under the bed. The cakes of dust, the lint, the missing slipper, a shoebox of old letters, cat hair. She came into her room and sat down on the bed. The bottom of the mattress pressed closer to his face. It took her awhile. She must have been examining each piece before dropping it back into the tackle box. Under the bed, Popper, holding his breath, listened to each sad plink. At one point, she began laughing. *Why didn't you just ask me?* She was silent for a long time after. When he finally sneezed, Miriam didn't say anything, didn't move, didn't seem to even hear him.

RAVINIA

Jackson Browne played Ravinia Park, even the cops were stoned out of their gourds. After the concert, a friend of Leo's, Samantha Levinson, lay down on the Chicago and Northwestern tracks and waited for the southbound train, its light already visible in the short distance.

Earlier, Samantha had wandered away from the group and disappeared into the trees on the edge of the park. Samantha wandered away as Samantha often wandered away.

"Where's Sam?" somebody said.

He was always listening for him then. Leo never much acknowledged that he existed anymore. Sometimes he introduced Popper to his cavalry of friends as a distant cousin visiting from Muncie. After three, he heard the apartment door open. He got out of bed and spied down the hall. The light was on, and Leo was standing and gazing at a bowl of pears on the kitchen table. He took one and had a bite of it, looked at it, had another bite. Leaving the light on, he walked down the hall toward the dark bedrooms. There was mud on his shoes and his feet left tracks. Leo stopped at Miriam's door.

"Mom?"

Miriam, like Leo, the lightest of sleepers. She got up almost immediately and opened her door wider. His mother, nightdress, bare feet. Popper watched them in the box of light breathing down the hall from the kitchen. Leo leaned toward her as if he meant to whisper, but he didn't whisper.

"Mom!"

Miriam looked down the hall at the muddy footprints. There's no crisis unless there's blood flowing and even then no reason to get excited. (Popper remembers being about four or so and squatting under the glass table on the patio of the house on Riparian. He was looking up at his mother. She was writing in her address book. At one point she looked down at him, and he stood up so fast to go to her his head cracked the glass. As he wailed, she kept saying, "Look, Alex, just a little bit of blood, not even a thimbleful.")

She looked at Leo as if she already knew without needing to be told any facts. *A dead girl, Leo? You poor kid, the world is full to the hilt with dead girls.*

"You're still high, honey," Miriam said. "Go to sleep, we'll talk in the morning."

She never minded mud on any carpet, either. Leo was still holding the bitten pear. Later, days later, he told them what he'd seen by the light of the cop's flashlights. That Samantha was just torn-up clothes, no body. That night Leo went to sleep right where he was. He slumped and dropped to the carpet. At noon the next day, he was still there in the hall in front of their mother's door, crumpled, snoring.

DR. RALPH

I tell you the one about the female urologist? Terminal case of penis envy.

His mother's new boyfriend, the urologist Ralph Fishman. Six feet tall, enormous hands, tells jokes. Poppers don't tell jokes. Poppers tell themselves that Poppers tell stories. *Jokes are beneath us.*

Come on, Alexander, live a little! That's humor, that's comedy. Not everything's got to be a drama. Miriam, what the hell's wrong with this kid?

She comes and sits on his bed, rubs his head. "And now, honey, don't be scandalized if Ralph stays over one or two nights a week. What you need to understand is that Ralph absolutely understands what you're going through. Plus, he really likes you, not only because you're my son, but also he likes you as a person. He has kids himself, you know, and we all acknowledge that this is a challenging situation. In the long run, this is good for me, good for you, good for your brother, even good for your father. Because it might force him to move on, to get over his bitterness —"

"Who said anything about him?"

"Won't you try, sometimes, darling, for me, to not be so sullen all the time?"

Mr. Vice President

It is by politics that the work of redemption must be
wrought.

— William Stead, *If Christ Came to Chicago!*

Miriam hosted a coffee for Walter Mondale in '84. He stood
in their living room, in front of the fake fireplace. Like the
candidate, the plastic logs lit up but gave off no heat. Mondale,
mournful and apologetic, smiled wanly as Leo said, Nice to meet
you, Mr. Vice President, Nice to meet you, Mr. Vice President,
Nice to meet you, Mr. Vice, as if a record had skipped in his head.
Mondale nodded at him as if to say, It is me, my son, but if you
truly knew me, you would not be so impressed. Popper wants it
all to mean more now. Still, it was the former VP in the flesh. And
his mother could not have been prouder or more radiant in
her optimism about a future led by this man who would beat
Reagan. Walter Mondale as past life. The three of them, Miriam,
Leo, and Alexander, were a part of, let's say, the 35 percent (maybe
38 percent on a good day), of the country who believed in
Walter Mondale—not only as a man but as an idea of human
decency.

Miriam, serving platter after platter of mini-pizzas, exclaimed to her new, unawestruck neighbors from the apartment complex, a few retirees, a smattering of teachers: "Isn't he sensational? Isn't he?"

Who needs Gary Hart? His ruggedness, his good hair?

No, plod we must.

Miriam's mother (on a visit from Fall River) just beamed and beamed—*Look at my Miriam now. Look at her now. The leader of the free world is standing in her living room.*

Ralph Fishman sidled up to Mondale and said, *I got one in your sweet spot, Fritz: Jimmy Carter, the Shah, and the Ayatollah walk into the Kasbah, and the Shah says to the Ayatollah, Let me at least buy you a drink, and Carter says, I thought A-rabs didn't drink, and the Ayatollah says, who you calling an A-rab, and the Shah says, Khomeini, what if I bought you the whole Kasbah? And Khomeini says, Off with your head, and Carter says, Why don't we all have milk? and the Shah says, How about a couple of royal palaces? No? An oil well? An oil field?*

Miriam shooed him back into the kitchen. "Ralph! Check the oven for the rest of the mini-pizzas!"

"Alex," Leo said.

"He looks about the same as he does on television," someone whispered. "A little smaller maybe."

"Alex—"

"Yeah?"

"Outside. The honking—"

"Shit. Wednesday. You think he'll come inside?"

"No. He'll just honk. Maybe the Secret Service guys will go out there and shut him up."

"Should I go out there?"

"No, make him wait. This is Mom's time. Leave him be."

And Walter Mondale, hapless before the fireplace, the little red lights flickering under the false logs. He spoke about the importance of a living wage, as the neighbors, politely, trickled out the door. As background music, Philip honking his horn. The Secret Service didn't seem to notice.

Yes to job training. Yes to education. Yes to a nuclear arms freeze. A resounding and unequivocal NO to the MX missile! And a big Yes to Geraldine Ferraro!

Time for him to go. Mondale took a sip of coffee. He thanked Miriam not once but four times. Go forth from our humble home, sir, and lose—it's all right, lose. We no longer aspire to anything so crass as actually winning. We cashed that dream in ages ago. Our peace-loving friend of labor and the workingman. Our soldier of the Old Guard liberalism. Our warrior of nonconfrontation. You were an era that was over before you even started. But this doesn't mean you didn't have integrity by the Minnesotaful. You were a man who would have absolutely raised our taxes, but is this so terrible if for the common good?

So long, Mr. Vice President. You were once us. He blew Miriam a last ineffectual kiss, spittle flying, and was gone.

Walter

Mondale

was

gone.

10

SOPHOMORE

The sin of impurity may not be cured in a day, a year,
or perhaps in generations.

—The Vice Commission of Chicago, 1911

May 3, 1945

This Johnston I told you about, in the engine room, remember, the one who writes poetry? Well, for a guy who only went through high school and has practically no education, he does remarkably well—He is quite a toughy and loves his engines better than books or things like that—He was ashamed to admit it to me, but since I found out, I keep encouraging him—He has a peculiar talent—He cannot write a lucid letter to save his life, but he can sit down and write something like this—

No Performance Today

A guy woke up one morning feeling rough and ready and reached over for his wife. She was already up and in the kitchen fixing breakfast. He didn't want to get up for fear of spoiling everything, so he wrote a note and sent it to her by his small son. He said,

> The tent pole is up
> The Canvas is spread
> To hell with breakfast
> Come back to bed.
> She in return sent her answer by the boy, saying
> Take down the tent pole
> Tear up the canvas without delay
> The monkey has a hemorrhage
> There'll be no performance today.

TIME PRESENT

Winter: no beginning, no end. And so. And so. April, and still there will be no gym outside. They descend again to the gloom of the indoor track, where they will run walk run walk, loop after loop, like trapped hamsters. Popper, Mooch, Manny, Pampkin, and Sal Marcello. They're an arbitrary grouping known as a "fitness squad." Round and round and round, they walk together. The only respite is the occasional glimpse of the pom-pom squad — Julia Horowitz and friends — practicing their yowls and splay-legged leaps on the handball court. Few things make Popper sweatier than jumping girls in sweatpants, but even this, thirty times round, is enough already.

Now, mercifully, the fitness squad is getting dressed again. They've taken their showers, fast cold showers, in the shouting bedlam of white tile and fungus, and now they're shivering, trying to unlock their lockers. Popper can't remember his combination — again. What the fuck is my combination? And Sal Marcello, standing on the bench above him, drops his towel and shouts, "Hey, Popper, I got a boner!" And Popper looks. An announcement like that? Didn't Mooch, Manny, and Pampkin look? And then Marcello, he was a strong little fat-thighed guy with an incredibly squeaky voice, shrieks: "Hey, Popper! *Whatayoulookingat?*"

T. S. Eliot. Snob, casual anti-Semite, etc. Born in the Midwest, St. Louis, though he got to be so British he acted as if he never heard of Missouri from the Canterbury Cathedral. Wife went crazy, probably from having to live with him. Anyway, *famous* poet, he wrote:

> *What might have been and what has been*
> *Point to one end, which is always present.*

What might have been: *What if I was looking at your little dick, you gym class fascist?*

What was: "I was looking at the fucking clock, Sal."

Sal: "Mooch, was Popper looking or was he not looking?"

"Pretty much," Mooch says. Mooch, freckled and kind; he can't tell a lie, but he won't rub it in, either. "Pretty much looking."

"Laveneaux?"

"Well, look at this way. The clock is right above your head, Sal. Popper likes to be on time to English. It's the only class he's ever on time for. I'm going to throw my support behind his denial."

"Fuck off, Manny. Pampkin?"

Pampkin. Benji Pampkin would turn his mother in to the Gestapo. "Absolutely totally looking."

Footfalls echo in memory

Down the passage we did not take

I found my thrill on Liberty Mill. Most sophomores lead lives of quiet masturbation.

The uniforms they wore, reversible shirt and shorts. Their

LOVE AND SHAME AND LOVE

names written in permanent ink on the blank white stripe on the left thigh. All their names. All their mothers' handwriting. *Laveneaux, Pampkin, Marcello, Popper, Boobus, Gordon, Deutch, Newton, Moritz, Lund, Mueller, Moncada, Rudman, Cahill, Tiziano, Frankel, Edelstein, Meyers, Palandri, Bortz, Stenzler.*

The little man in the cage who threw them towels. His name was Mr. Carl, and he'd throw a kid a towel only if he could prove that he'd at least got his hair wet, and so they would shake their heads at him like Labradors just out of the lake, him saying, Not on me, spazolas, not on me. Mr. Carl lived and probably died in the stench of that locker room. Their shoes, their sweat, the crotch rot of their never-washed shorts. Mr. Carl in his cage with his tiny black-and-white TV, watching *General Hospital.* Those were the days of the wedding of Luke and Laura, and Mr. Carl would periodically shout updates.

She said no!

She said yes!

She's fucking his friend!

He knows!

The wedding's off!

Reconciled! The wedding's on! Luke and Laura, everybody! Who says there's no such thing as romance?

So Mr. Carl. So those towels. Washrags, really. So small you couldn't tie one of them around your waist, and so they'd have to hold it there to make it stay. Again, Sal on the bench.

Hey, I gotta—

Marcello's dick littler even than his own, but since it's uncircumcised, it actually looks bigger. This is something Popper wasn't prepared for. A hooded sausage doomed to lurk for all time as part of his permanent record. Not a day goes by. Who said, you don't choose what haunts you? He will die not with beautiful conjurations of home, family, a long record of contribution, of achievement, but instead with an image of Sal Marcello's dick in his head. And yet it seems now, after all these years of re-enduring this moment, that Sal's poor dick itself, independent of Sal, is now, in Popper's head, trying to apologize. As if Sal Marcello's unsheathed shlong is whispering: What choice did *I* have? You think anybody would willingly choose to be an appendage of Sal Marcello? You can't choose your family, either.

All is always now.

Fine, fine, but shouldn't he also be able to hold on to the moment before? Aren't there synapses in the space/time continuum between when Sal says "Hey, I gotta—" and he, Popper, pops his eyes up to see what once seen he will always see? Shouldn't there be a way to reverse things and hold the moment before? But he never can slow it down. There's always this slippage from the boner to the looking.

> *the bench Sal stood on*
> *beneath his unclipped horny toes*
> *the combinations of dead locks etched*
> *other echoes*
> *shouts, reverberations of*
> *slams*
> *all sound once heard is heard again*
> *here is a place of disaffection*
> *us in the thick brown shit-stained light*
> *hey I gotta*
> *whatayou?*

PEEPER

It's not a question of whether or not you're guilty.

—Horace

Alight in the window upstairs. A hand moves slowly down the pane. *So long, sucker.* Burton Avenue. Bedroom. Popper's on the grass, Stan Smiths in hand, socks in his pockets hanging out like little rabbits. The light darks. He slips his shoes on and gets on his bike and begins to drift home no-handed. Takes a right on Roger Williams. Now Roger Williams was also a man. He wanted to be pope of his own religion, so he left Massachusetts and rowed his boat to Rhode Island, where he created his own 5 by 7 kingdom. Why we honor him in Illinois, who the hell knows. Now the great man connects Sheridan Road, named after a boozy Civil War general, to Green Bay Road, named after a football team. Left onto St. Johns. Down the hill and up again. A soft right onto Forest. Two blocks. *And here, ladies and gentlemen, behold the mute houses of Highland Park's notorious white-collar-criminal element. Three homes in a row, three indictments. The Blotners, Missy Blotner's father (insider trading). The Sterns, Dr. Stern (Medicare fraud, embez-*

zlement). The Gordons, Judge Gordon (bribery, racketeering, witness tampering, extortion, influence peddling, Operation Greylord).

The bridge connecting Forest to Hazel Avenue. And down there below the deep ravine, his own personal abyss.

She fended him off for hours. She'd make a great goalie, Joanna Frankel. Popper on her bed. In her pink pink room. And now his hard-on is so cemented he imagines wistful that it aims out his pants and reaches out to his handlebars and drives this bike. Which makes no sense. What he means, ladies and gentlemen, is that he is unrequited and thus heroic. This mindless throb has to count for something. Muffled battle hours. Joanna's parents across the hall. Mr. Frankel snoring like a garage door opening and closing. Pink her room, Joanna's room so pink. Everything pink. Carpet, wallpaper, door. Stuffed pink billy goat, stuffed pink banana. He choked the goat and whispered, Next I'll off the banana, and Joanna breathed, Hurt my banana, Popper, and I'll kick you in the balls. Wait, you'll touch my balls? *Never, Popper, never will even my cold dead fingers*—Silent lights stripe the houses. He turns. Amid his inglorious emanations he's being pulled over. Weird, it's actually happening. A bullhorned voice: "Stop the bike."

He stands in the dusty heat of the headlights and waits. The cop takes his time. Popper will die alone, untouched, his once-proud manhood fast shriveled. To top it off, he's under arrest. The car door cracks open and the cop walks over to him, slowly. He is young and hatless and biting his lip to show he isn't bored. No. Ensuring the public good sometimes involves innocent-seeming cases just like these.

"Your laces are untied," the cop says. "Dangerous. Laces get caught in the chain and a kid goes flying."

He holds the bike while Popper stoops and ties his shoes.

"I'm out past curfew."

"That, too," the cop says.

"What else?"

The cop looks away, at the tall trees, at the dark houses of the not-yet-indicted. The dizzy light swings.

"Who are you?"

"A sophomore."

"You have ID?"

"You mean like a bike license?"

The cop sighs. He chews his lip. His face isn't unkind or even that officious. Only curious. His wife thinks he's just a suburban cop, but things aren't always as they seem along these quiet trees. The rampant criminality here could churn your stomach. *Don't you read the papers, Diane? These people are completely out of control.*

"We've had a complaint," the cop says. "A face in a window."

"Huh?"

The cop's head doesn't move an inch, but still Popper gets the impression that he's sadly shaking his head. "A peeping Tom. You'd think they'd be obsolete. Not quite. Know anything about this? An apartment building across the street from the train station. A window. A face."

Whenever he's accused of anything, Popper immediately assumes he must be guilty. A buzzer goes off as he leaves a store and he throws up his hands. Someone screams in the night in his dreams and his hands are on someone's throat. Why is it that the truth is always a lie in these situations?

"I was over at Joanna Frankel's," he says. "Studying."

"Righto," the cop says.

He picks up the bike and sticks it in the trunk of the car. He looks around for a Bunjee cord but ends up not finding one, so the trunk bangs against the bike frame as they creep slowly back up Linden, Walnut, St. Johns.

Back of the squad car. That smooth trampoline seat. That

trapped-animal stench of stagnant crime. The no-door-handle doors make him feel dangerous to himself. The smudged windows. He thinks of all the other bravehearts who have tried to claw their way out of here to exquisite freedom.

As she opened the door, the woman had the surprised and joyful look of someone about to sneeze. Her eyes were closed. She opened them by slow degrees. The cop stepped helpfully aside to give her a better view. The light above the door was a shallow yellow. She tilted her head left a little to look at Popper from a different angle. That didn't work, either.

Her features, her eyes, her nose, her mouth, all went into free fall.

"Is this him?"

She laughed, not a real laugh, a forced, stage laugh. "Not even close."

A small doughy-faced woman wearing a purple kimono and, over it, a housecoat. On her feet, slippers with the tips pointing up. They looked like little gondolas. She was maybe forty, with exhausted eyes. Like Popper, she'd clearly had a long night. There were tear streaks in her makeup. Or she'd clawed her face with her fingers.

"Which window was the perpetrator standing at, if you don't mind my asking?"

She pointed to the window to the right of the front door.

"Why don't you go back in the house? I'll have this individual go stand—"

"The face—It isn't his face."

Popper tried to seem, what, disappointed? He wanted to tell her he wasn't getting any, either. You want a peeper, lady, I'll peep. We just got to get rid of this cop. I'll look right in the window at whatever you want me to see. Except Popper wasn't the right him. He was no one, brought to her door out of the dead night.

Joanna Frankel. Popper dials her phone number sometimes. Her mother still lives in Highland Park. He hangs up. Her mother calls him back. Hang-up calls have gone the way of blacksmiths and Indians. Who are you? Joanna Frankel's mother says. And what on earth do you want?

They tore down the apartment building across the street from the train station years ago. It's where the new Walgreens is now. Whoever she was, she's long gone. He thinks of her eyes, how they were fissured with tiny bloody twists. One sleepless night she thought she saw a face, a certain face (out of the past?), in the window and called the cops.

Won't be long now before the doorbell bleats. Who's there? What are the chances? How much potential in such a stupid tinny noise? Snatch a look in the hallway mirror, shoot back the dead-bolt, hand turns a knob, pull the door open. Open it. Remarkable how fast it all happens. We fling from expectation to failure — to relief in how long?

Is this him?

Because that's finally what she was, relieved. Relieved Popper was Popper, whoever in the hell he even was. He's always wondered what might have become of either of them had he been that other face.

AP English

Mrs. Engerman says that the Stranger is animalistic because he eats standing up, that Camus meant for him to be a symbol of modern dehumanization. The tragedy, of course, is that even frogs fall in love. As the Stranger loses his humanity, his love for Marie (that vixen) begins to confuse him, weakening him in his own eyes, so that love itself becomes a sickness he must overcome.

LEADER OF MEN

#4 Fighting Spirit: You know what this is. Without it, you are only a human biped with pants. With it, you are a live, red-blooded go-getter — one who will succeed. Have you the grit to *stay with* a hard job? Never say "I can't." Forget there is such a phrase. Don't be a quitter. "A man may be down but never out" until he admits it.

— *Bluejackets Manual*, page 7

The Hill

Late September and panting up the long hill up from Park Avenue Beach. Coach Piefke sent them to do the hill. Do the hill, Coach Piefke said, and come back. And so they ran. First down Vine and across on Linden, and then the steep descent to the lake via Park Avenue. Going down, it's all Chariots of Fire, baby. At the bottom, the lake, blue and innocent, the light catching the white lips of the waves as they lap up the beach, bringing their tide of beer cans and detergent bottles and raw sewage. But the lake is no respite, because there will be no pausing, no moment to take in its vast transporting waters. How far could he have fled from Coach Piefke if he dove in? A man once did it off Glencoe Beach. He started to swim into the sweet endlessness and just kept going and going. Maybe he was heading for the coast of Holland, Michigan, where all the fake Dutch hotties shod their feet in wooden shoes. Somebody called the Coast Guard, but it was too late. His body washed up in Waukegan two days later.

Whoever built the road up from Park Avenue Beach had little imagination. It shoots straight, no meandering; it has no respect for the unique moraine landscape of the North Shore. They started back up, leaning into the hill as Coach Piefke had taught them, letting the rise of the road pull them toward the top. If any of them cramped up, they bit their lower lips. Exchange one pain for another pain, Coach Piefke said. That's courage. Courage, for some, is as infinite as the lake itself. Popper cramped up. He bit his lip. Coach Piefke said, Love the blood of your pain. He bit his lip till it bled, and he loved the blood. He loved it, and still the cramp crushed his gut until he could hardly breathe. He tried composing a ditty, which is what Manny taught him to do when nothing else worked. Martina, Martina Navratilova / Won't you let me come ovah? This didn't work either. He slowed to a little run that was more of a chicken walk with flapping arms. The other guys ran on. Manny looked back, offered to stay. Popper waved him on. *I'll catch you later.* He stopped and stood there in the wind halfway up the hill and watched the others' shoes disappear over the rise. He knelt by the side of the ravine and yacked.

Alone with the squirrels in the trees, the looming lake below. He was calm. He half-whistled through the residual puke in his mouth and loafed onward.

By the time he got back, everyone else had gone home. Coach Piefke was waiting for him behind his desk in his office, the fluorescent light buzzing ferociously. There was a chair to sit down in, but Popper didn't sit.

It was said that Coach Piefke—somewhere deep inside—was a human being. This theory was based on the fact that his infant son was sick, with what nobody knew, but many nights Coach and his wife had to run the kid to the hospital. Mrs. Coach Piefke would sometimes come to the track with that sick baby wrapped around her stomach and watch them do middle-distance drills. *Run, walk, run, walk, run, walk.* She had hair that reached down to her butt and swished like a curtain when she walked. It was also said Mrs. Coach Piefke was a hippie and that the baby wasn't even Coach's. Once, when she came to watch them, Manny said, "Damn, her Rapunzeled hair makes my loins ache."

"What are loins exactly?"

"They're dormant needles in your scrotum. Arousal makes them suddenly pointy."

Nobody gave Manny any shit about being smart. Nobody gave him shit about his French name anymore, either. Because Manny was so big now, he could pop you if he wanted to. All those years Popper and Manny were practically the same size. They tried to recruit him for football, but Manny chose to run cross-country instead. In part to be with Popper. Also, he said, running fanatical distances cleared his head.

"You can't hack the hill," Coach Piefke said.

"You got it, Coach. I can't."

Coach Piefke raised his small eyes. His eyes didn't go with his large head, and this gave them even more power. Twin gulags floated in those tiny orbs. The extra miles on your weekly totals, the early-morning practices, laps until your heels bled, being ordered to do the hill again. Coach Piefke, another of the false-father figures who have roamed across Popper's life. Bad enough to fail your own father, but legions? To Coach Piefke it had nothing to do with talent. Or stamina. Or having strong legs. It was about will. You either had it or you didn't. But it wasn't entirely Popper's fault. It was Coach's, too. This was by far the worst punishment he could muster, the torture of him assuming responsibility for your lack of will.

Popper used to wonder what a coach needed an office for. Now he understood. Coach Piefke's office was a harbor for disappointment. *You may rest, my son, from your futile labors here.* Those pale walls. It was almost a relief to be standing there in his cold sweat and skimpy shorts. Coach Piefke closed his eyes, his unwrinkled face a lump of smooth flesh. Without his eyes, Coach Piefke looked almost benign — his skin, putty you could dig your hands into and mold. Popper wonders now how old Coach Piefke was then: twenty-nine? thirty? Mrs. Coach Piefke? Twenty-five, twenty-seven?

Their baby would die later that school year, and this also Coach Piefke seemed to accept without raising much objection. It was simple. The kid couldn't hack it. Let the mother with the long, long hair weep a lake. He was no harsher with the cross-country team than normal after he came back from the week the school gave him off for the burial.

"You stopped in the middle of the hill?"

"Yes, Coach."

"You saw the top, you saw the other guys go on ahead of you?"

"That's right, Coach."

"Glory was within your grasp and you chucked it?"

"You want me to do some laps or something, Coach? Clean out the locker room? Repair some old hurdles?"

"And you enjoyed stopping like that?"

"Absolutely."

Coach opened his little eyes only slightly. They were wet with tearlets.

"It doesn't matter," he said.

"It doesn't?"

Popper didn't know she was there until she spoke. She had the silent kid with her, tied to her chest. She poked her head inside the office, her hair hanging downward.

"Doug? What's wrong with you?"

May 8, 1945

Received two letters today—that's all—one from my mother, who said she hadn't seen you—the other from Mose—Oh, my darling—Some men get 6–7, 10–15 letters when we make port—Don't you realize that if you only write once a week or every ten days—that that letter might miss a ship or a plane and it may be delayed another two or three weeks?

APPARATCHIKS

Some of Leo's happiest days were in that period when the Soviet General Secretaries were dropping one after the other like fur-hatted dominoes. They'd wake up in the morning and another would have bitten the dust. Andropov lasted about twenty minutes. Leo said the KGB was poisoning the goulash in order to lull Americans into believing the Russians had lost their lust for world domination. And then, bam, when we're not looking, they drop a bomb on Kansas City.

Leo was already in college in Boston by the time Konstantin Chernenko croaked. He called to say that Popper should watch the funeral closely and study the pallbearers to see which apparatchik was going to get the Kremlin's nod this time.

"Apparatchik?"

"Party hack. Henchman. We've got them, too. They aren't without their purpose. You know what I mean? In a way, they're like the true pillars of any society, civilized or otherwise. Where would we be without hacks? In this Dad was right about Mayor Daley. He at least taught us this. Without blind loyalty, without obedience, nothing would get done. No higher virtue in politics. Or families. Speaking of which, always be loyal to Mom. She's our Trotsky."

"Trotsky an apparatchik?"

"No, they killed him because he wasn't. Some people get to rise above apparatchiks, but you got to earn it."

"Since when am I not loyal to Mom?"

"Sometimes you've got Dad's personality."

"What?"

"Occasional petulance, immunity issues, flashes of strange anger. Like at your birthday party when you threw apples at your—"

"I'm hanging up."

"Just think about what I'm saying—try to be happier around the house. It's not easy being Mom. It seems like it is. But it's not. She thinks you don't like Ralph."

"I like Ralph fine."

"Mom's worried you don't."

"She's wrong. I guess I just never think about him that much. Ralph's kind of like the cat."

"How is Louise, anyway?"

"We think she finally ran away."

"She was a pretty cat."

"She never liked us."

"They're getting married."

"What?"

"And you're going to be a good soldier. Don't tell her I told you. She's planning a sitdown with you soon. Act surprised. And happy. Got to go—"

Tonnio's

Let the record show: It was not Popper who scrawled *Go Fuck Yourself Tonnio* and *Viva Ché* in indelible marker on the wall above the delivery phones. It was Manny. But Popper took the heat for it, since Manny was on a delivery when Tonnio noticed it. It goes on the short list of honorable things Popper's done in his life. I got you covered, Laveneaux. Hope you get a decent tip.

They'd turned sixteen. On Tuesday, Wednesday, Friday, and Sunday nights, he and Manny delivered pizzas to the North Shore wealthy, who didn't tip with any grace, or frequently, very much money. (His father's old friend Melvie Kaufman, for instance, once tipped Popper thirty-four cents on a twenty-three-dollar order.)

Tonnio pointed to the wall. "You wrote this filth?" Tonnio was a round and hairy man given to screeching and conspiracy. Pretty awesome pizzas, deep dish and something called a stuffed that Tonnio invented, a pizza with unimaginable heaven-sent amounts of cheese.

"What if I did, Tonnio?"

The monstrous ingratitude of pizza delivery boys astonished him. *You ungrateful cahootzes, Was it not me, Tonnio de Chirico, who pulled you boys off the street and made laborers out of you? I came to this country with seven lire, a moldy piece of bufala, and a dream. Now look at me. I move pizzas, 500 a night, from Lake Bluff to Kenilworth. And to you I give and I give...*

"Why," Tonnio breathed. "Why?"

"Because you rip us off," Popper said. "Because you don't pay us for gas or for the wear and tear on our moms' cars."

Tonnio, solemnly, raised a bearlike arm, pointed to the door, and mouthed, as if he lacked the strength to say it out loud—there was only the sound of his betrayed saliva—"Go." Popper was still holding the padded vinyl pizza warmer. He'd been waiting for his own delivery to come out of the oven, a half-pepperoni, half-mushroom, going to 1881 Groveland Terrace. Popper stood there holding his warmer. He wanted to take back the gallantry. *It was Laveneaux, Tonnio, don't you even recognize his handwriting?* But Tonnio gently took the warmer out of his hands and gently pushed him out the door. The law must assert itself. Even the puniest mutiny must be quashed.

Outcasted, the suburban night, the pizzaless streets, his mother's Chevelle—he drives to the lake. Under the parking lot lights at Cary Avenue Beach, he rolled down the window and listened to the slap of waves. At dawn, he didn't wake to see the lights popping silently off like extinguished souls.

May 18, 1945

I can now tell you we have participated in the Okinawa campaign — some of the things we still can't say, others you will just have to use your imagination — It was my first taste of a shooting war and I admit I was a trifle shaky — We didn't take any fire ourselves, were about a mile offshore — but we were pursued quite smartly by some denizens of the deep so I had to do some fancy turning, and there is nothing more pathetic than an LST attempting evasive maneuvers — especially on a good black night — It's funny how our idea of a beautiful moonlit night can change — At sea, when it's so bright you can read a newspaper — that's the time you hate the moon and pray for a cloud to blot it out — The Army guys, though, they love a bright night — then they can see the bastards crawling around — Everything is relative — depending on how far your own neck happens to be sticking out at any given moment.

THE BALLOON LADY

They bought dope in Humboldt Park beneath the giant equestrian statue of Thaddeus Kosciuszko. Their supplier was a woman who pretended to sell balloons. Well, she did sell balloons. She just made more money off dope. Thaddeus Kosciuszko was a great Polish hero of the American Revolution. George Washington called him our own Rock of Gibraltar. Had it not been for Kosciuszko, the redcoats would have overrun the fort at West Point, and Americans to this day would salute a queen and say aubergine (hey, that rhymes). Thank you, Kosciuszko. Manny and Popper disrespected your memory by purchasing dope beneath your horse's raised left hoof, but considering that you and your deeds are largely forgotten by those who should remain forever grateful, maybe the fact that anybody repeats your name — Kosciuszko! — keeps you less dead a little longer.

The balloon lady? Gone now also. It's possible that she got rich enough and retired. She was abrupt with a customer. The transaction had to be done fast. The balloon lady didn't do change. If you gave her a twenty for a dime bag, she kept the ten. And you also had to buy a balloon, a couple of balloons, if you wanted to endear yourself to her. The balloon lady was of unfathomable age, not so old, maybe, but very wrinkled. She wore clown makeup and baggy pants with bells up and down the legs. Tall red boots. You could find her under Kosciuszko Tuesday through Friday. She liked a three-day weekend. She kept her dope neatly done up in Ziplocs. Homegrown, Mexican-grown, Costa Rican–grown. Panamanian Special. The balloon lady was made up like a clown, but her face never contorted into anything other than that one frozen smile, which was nothing at all like a smile. This clown was all business. Manny once said the balloon lady was an artist, that the getup, the unsmiling smile, the bells, the boots—all of it was a performance and another proof that what makes Chicago truly great is its people: Jane Addams, Sears and Roebuck, Harold Washington, Harry Porterfield, Roland Harper, Harold Baines, Reggie Theus, the weather guy who's also a pilot, the balloon lady.

"Jim Tillman."

"Who?"

"The pilot on Channel 7."

"Exactly. Very great man. Jim Tillman."

"How come you're naming only black people?"

"You think Sears and Roebuck were black? They probably didn't even let blacks in the store till—"

"So you're black now?"

"Did you just notice?"

"Remember when you said you weren't black, you were brown? Up in the attic of the mansion. You said you were more the color of wood than the color of oil."

"Popper, I was eight."

"I'm just trying to get a handle on where you're going with this."

"This is a completely dipshit conversation. Jane Addams wasn't black, either."

"What about John Belushi?"

"Okay, add Belushi."

"And Fahey Flynn. Fahey Flynn's a great Chicagoan."

"Fine, Fahey Flynn. But not Mike Ditka."

"No, never Ditka."

"Fuck Ditka," Manny said. "Anybody else you want to add?"

"Steve Dahl."

"Fine."

"And Frazier Thomas and Ray Rayner."

"You want Garfield Goose also?"

"Yes."

"Donahue?"

"That's all right. But why the balloon lady?"

"Don't you get it? She could just sell drugs. She doesn't have to go through the whole rigmarole. She's an artist. Think about it, every day she has to fill those balloons with helium. After a while even helium's not that fun anymore." Manny took his hands off the wheel and shouted, "To home, gentle steed!" Kennedy Expressway, four in the morning, driving snow streaking toward them in long white tails. "Popper, look out the back window."

And they did, they both did, they both looked out the back window, at the snow chasing them, and they scrawled across three lanes and were about to slam into the guardrail when Popper, of all people, grabbed the wheel and righted them.

The balloons bobbing against the roof, those dull thumps, and Manny said, "Don't you miss it?"

"What?"

"This. Us driving. The Kennedy merges into the Edens. Next exit, Peterson. Touhy, Dempster, Old Orchard, Tower Road… Bear right for 94 to Milwaukee. How come we never go to Milwaukee? Why doesn't anybody ever go to Milwaukee? Does it even exist? If we never go there, does Milwaukee exist?" He leaned over and drove a little while with his forehead. "But anyway, it's gone," he said. "All of it. Milwaukee, too. Gone."

"Dope's making speeches."

"Yes and no," Manny said.

Kosciuszko was a hero. After he helped win the American Revolution, he went back to Poland to lead the fight of another one there. That rebellion lasted about twenty minutes. The Russians were meaner motherfuckers than the British. They threw Kosciuszko in prison, where he wrote that he regretted being alive, having so failed his country. Now, there's a man. Chicago put up a statue of him in Humboldt Park. He rides a horse. He waves his sword. Chicago is full of such statues. Alexander Hamilton. Cervantes. Hugo. Goethe (pronounced Go-thee and don't let any highbrow tell you otherwise). Churchill. Hildago. Dr. Greene Vardiman Black, the founder of modern dentistry. Because giants once walked the earth and Chicago saluted them in stone. Manny once said, Where's Toussaint L'Ouverture, the greatest rebel since Christ? And he was right, Popper says now to himself, to nobody listening. Chicago, if Greene Vardiman Black, where's Toussaint L'Ouverture?

T onnio rehired Popper at Manny's behest. He fired him again later. But they will always have this: Late afternoon, no orders in, just him and Tonnio in the kitchen and Popper sweeping up and at the same time helping Tonnio prepare for his citizenship exam. In the kitchen with those big black ovens and the cockroaches and the toppings trays and the neatly stacked ramekins and the walk-in freezer, where Manny and Popper used to do whippets with the whipped-cream cans. That quick and perfect five-minute shot of high. If he could have a little of that high back—

Tonnio was always getting ready for the citizenship exam, although he never actually took it. The whole idea offended him. His adopted country didn't know a thing about Garibaldi—but sure, sure, they eat my pizza, they love my pizza, and then they turn around and make me answer questions about a country that the sweat of Italian immigrants like me helped build in the first place. *You know, we used to celebrate Garibaldi's birthday in this country? Now they just give us Columbus, and what kind of Italian name is Columbus? Columbo, you cretins.*

"Name the U.S. war between the North and the South."

"The World Series."

"Why did the colonists fight the British?"

"Tea."

"Right, and also high taxes, because they didn't have self-government, and because the British Army stayed in their houses, a practice known as billeting. For some reason this really pissed people off. People didn't want any soldiers crashing on their couches. Who wrote the Federalist Papers?"

"Dante."

"James Madison, Alexander Hamilton, John Jay. Or you can just say Publius."

"Who?"

"You know, like a band. The three of them, they're Publius. John Jay was Ringo. How many judges on the Supreme Court?"

"The fuck do I care."

"It's an odd number."

"A hundred and thirty-seven."

"No. Less."

"Hold on a minute," Tonnio said, and looked at Popper as if seeing him for the first time. It could almost be said that Tonnio, who had seen it all and said so, hour after hour, was, this time, floored.

"There's only nine judges," Popper said. "What's wrong? They've got more in Sicily?"

"The boy doesn't know how to sweep," Tonnio said.

Popper shrugged. He was afraid Tonnio was going to tell him another story of toil, about his grandmother in Ragusa who buried five children dead of malaria, but instead Tonnio showed him. He stood behind Popper and put his right hand toward the top of the broom and his left just slightly above the middle. *Keep this elbow loose. See? And row the boat, row. Don't be afraid to bend the bristles.* And they swayed like that for who knows how long, rowing, rowing, Tonnio's stomach like a pregnancy, like a fresh little citizen, pushing against Popper's back.

The Light at Donny's

Seymour still wears his white duck pants. Gently, he rattles his Scotch. That always round face, those few remaining strands of hair that scribble across the top of his head. They're out. They're at Donny's. Bernice, her face made up, her huge chorus girl eyes, those eyes that always got her noticed.

They're alone in a booth toward the back.

They don't talk much. It doesn't matter. All that counts is they're at Donny's. They wait for their tortellini soup. The Rhapsody Inn, Highwood. Anybody who's anybody calls it Donny's. It's not a club and Donny takes no reservations. Doesn't matter if you're a bum or Ron Santo — you wait for a table at Donny's.

That was always the beauty of the place. A real democracy. Thank God for Highwood. An oasis, for decades one of the few places to get a legal drink on the parched North Shore. And Donny presided. There was order to the universe. You waited at the bar till Donny came and tapped you on the shoulder: Follow me. Donny wasn't a big man, but his hair was — a towering froth of bouffant. Took a man with powerful friends to wear his hair like that.

Seymour! Bernice! Where have you been all my life? I haven't seen you since Tuesday. What? You cooking slop at home?

All those laughs. It used to be you could measure your life in those roaring laughs.

The soup's still to die for, and the Steak in Marsala is still thick as a radial tire. Donny had a simple notion—make the food decent and serve a lot of it. Then charge up the wazoo for drinks. They used to come here with the Pearlmutters, with Morton and Nita Bernheimer, with Richard and Doris Pinkert, with Myron and Phyllis Skulnik. And they'd hold court in one of the big semicircular booths up front and laugh and gaggle, talk business, children, politics.

Years pile up. Divorces. People fall out. People go bankrupt, to jail. Saturday nights now you stay home and watch television. And Donny's kind of swank isn't that swank anymore.

Tonight, the place is mostly empty.

Seymour! Bernice! You two still kicking around? It's a miracle. I could have sworn I dropped dead myself last month.

And Seymour raises his head and laughs at the ceiling. And Bernice reaches for Donny's beringed hands, and Donny squeezes and Bernice squeezes, and for a moment there's nothing like it. To be seen, to be known by Donny in front of a crowd even if the crowd is a decade back in your mind. She thinks of the smoky reddish light, how it used to slowly drift.

Donny always did give Bernice a second look. He liked Seymour, everybody liked Seymour, he was all hail-fellow-well-met, but with Bernice there was always something more, even secretive; Bernice Popper kept her own counsel and Donny liked that in a woman. Plus, it added to the mystery of his place.

"How come you still got your figure, Bernice?" Donny says, quiet in her ear.

Bernice pulls away and only answers with her eyes. *Because only the real talented ones ever enjoy the fun of going to seed.* And yet here was a man who could still make her feel like that one moment she'd get after hours of dancing—that brief surge in her heart. That was all she was ever after.

Seymour hollers, "For crying out loud, Donny, why don't you cash out and move to Sarasota? You don't need to stick around just for us. Bring me a Scotch."

"Fuck Sarasota," Donny says.

But it's true. Donny's worn out, too. The act has just about run its course. And he could have retired eight times over with what he's socked away. He always preferred cash. In the salad days they'd roll the tax-free paper money out the back door in a wheelbarrow. Now even the light's worn out, Bernice thinks. It sags, bloodless, across the walls. It no longer floats. Still, some nights you get in the Cadillac and you go out. You go out. What's the alternative?

Chicago and Northwestern Tracks

W aiting for the midnight train. Manny and Popper lying on their stomachs on the huge corrugated sewage pipe in the ditch between the tracks and the bike path. Sometimes they'd howl at the trains like coyotes, but that night they were quiet. It was about the light, the green gloom of the late-night trains, and how there were always a few people, bobbing heads, asleep, pale-green cheeks pressed flat against the glass.

Manny's an emergency room doctor in Seattle now. Sometimes he calls from work and leaves messages on Popper's voice mail. He saves the messages. For months and months, Popper saves the messages, listens to them, but he rarely calls back. He rarely calls anybody back. *Hey, Popper, want to hear about a broken arm?* And he'd hold up the phone so Popper could hear the chaos, the moaning. *How about a gunshot wound? Psychotic break, anybody? Listen, seriously, Popper, where have you been and why don't you ever call me back?*

"Something else just occurred to me," Manny said, though he hadn't said a word in half an hour. Neither of them had. They were waiting for the train.

"What?"

"It's apropos of nothing, really."

"What?"

"My mother thought moving here would give us a better chance, you know, being around the children of rich kids like you. Now look at me. Look at us. My feet are asleep. The 12:22's late again."

"You think we won't make good?"

"No, that's the problem, we probably will. The suburbs work, it isn't that they don't. That's what's so disgusting. What are you pondering? You look pondery."

"Gina Amalfitano."

"What about Gina Amalfitano?"

"I slept with her last Saturday. I've been holding it in, savoring it."

"Damn, Popper, even in your imagination, Gina Amalfitano's not unimpressive. Not unimpressive at all. Describe."

"Like butter. She whispered to me in Italian."

Petty Is Lord

The crowd whoops, swoons. The man himself emerges from the smoky purple light. Behind him lurk the Heartbreakers. The crowd awed into reverent silence.

Good to be back in Wisconsin, yeah—

He gazes at the crowd. With love. With respect. Has there ever been a human being more comfortable in his own skin than Tom Petty? What an amazing gift, to actually be able to stand yourself. And then he does it. Petty plays the opening notes of "The Waiting."

"The Waiting" live. Got to be the greatest moment in Popper's entire life. It's like anthemic.

Alpine Valley is an artificial bowl of grass in the middle of a cornfield. Earlier that night, during the opening act ('Til Tuesday), Popper had licked acid off a postage stamp and has spent much of his time trying to climb out of the bowl. He is as screwed up as he is lost as he is sweaty. He's a total ecstatic sweaty mess. Where's Manny? Didn't I come here with Manny? He's sweating so much he's thrown his shirt away. But when "The Waiting" begins, there is nothing but the song, and he believes in the song. Petty is lord. I will always be alone. I will always stink like a pig in my aloneness. Popper can't really see anymore. Tank-topped girls, he cross-eyed lusts. All those perfect tits jouncing to Petty as he screeches. *Oh don't let it kill you baby, don't let it get to you.* Popper picks up a half-eaten hot dog and rams it in his mouth. Raises his arms to the music — *the music* — before his tranced feet ungrip the grass for good.

May 22, 1945

Of course there are so many factors in war, so many contingencies, that it's really difficult to predict — who, 10 months ago — could have foreseen the German collapse on any other basis than wishful thinking — but the thing happened — Sometimes, nobody, not even the enemy himself, knows how close the end is —

Water Treatment Plant

The thing itself is nothing to the lies we tell about it. By the time it happened, there was nothing left to feel. She was safely from Deerfield. Deerfield only two miles away, but across the highway, another cosmos. A nonplace—the mall was in Deerfield. So was the DMV. You drove through it to get out to O'Hare. Deerfield was west, lakeless. She was shy, not fat, not unfat. She was what Popper's Massachusetts grandmother, Grandma Sarah (who was wonderfully spongy herself), would call healthy-proportioned, with kind eyes that didn't look for your flaws and exploit them, as she must have been used to people doing to her. They met at Tonnio's. Her name was Sandy. She was a cashier known for her fast fingers on the keys. She also took phone orders. She was serious about her work. She never chatted back when the takeout customers tried to talk her up. She never got change wrong. Unless you gave her your coupons before she started to ring you up, she wouldn't honor them, I'm sorry, no exceptions, Tonnio's policy, I don't make the rules. Popper took her to Bennigan's on Route 41 one night after their shifts. They ate mostly in silence, staring at each other's hands. After so many hours in the glazed light of the pizza place, the neon-green dim of Bennigan's was a place where they could both hide. They shared an order of onion rings. He'd heard stories about her from other delivery boys, all lies probably, but he wanted to believe what he wanted to believe. He tried to eat slow. She was eating normal. She said her cheeseburger was good, yours? Mine's good, too, he said.

"What does your father do?" Popper asked.

"Why do you want to know?" she said.

He didn't really know why he wanted to know. Why did he want to know?

"No reason," he said. "Good onion rings." She smiled. He smiled. After, they took her car to the abandoned water treatment plant off Cary Avenue Beach. Earlier, before his shift, he'd left an old comforter, a couple of pillows, condoms from Osco, a flashlight, a tape deck with Lionel Richie, three cans of beer. Is this your fort or something? she said. Sort of, Popper said. He kissed her. She didn't kiss him back, didn't stop him, either. She put her hands on his shoulders. He groped aimlessly, trying to avoid her eyes in the dark. Do you want to lie down? I don't care, she said.

They lay on the cement together, beached. In their August sweat. The mosquitoes found them, and they slapped and missed.

"Sandy?"

She didn't say anything. She wasn't looking at him in the moonlight but up at the rafters of the water plant.

"I think I just saw a bat," she said.

For the first time then he heard the lake, high tide slapping at the edge of the building.

"He's a teacher."

"What?"

"My father. He teaches fifth grade."

"Beer?"

"Okay," she said, and Popper reached across her for a can, opened it macho with one hand, and brought it to her mouth, poured it slow; she swallowed, some drained out the sides of her lips. He kissed it up and she laughed.

Manny?
Popper, you can't call so early, you know my mom doesn't get home till—
Guess what, baby—

He put the beer back down on the cement. He kissed her neck. I don't care, she said. He kissed her chin. Do you have to flail around so much? she said. He traced his hand down the veins of her wrist. Later, when she moaned a little, he felt like a general. I don't care, she said. I don't. The drab light woke them up, tangled and alone, the cement floor, the lake quiet, the gulls hawking and circling.

Shoe Shine, North Wabash

Philip doesn't—like other men—hold a newspaper spread wide, flex-armed, like a downtown Hercules studying battle plans as the man below works his shoes. No, Philip inspects. He watches, makes suggestions, criticizes—sniffs. It takes two minutes and thirteen seconds for a decent shine, but Philip Popper could sit here all day, being happy, being well pleased. There are, of course, different degrees of shine. He likes it a dull tint. Shine is the wrong word. You don't want it noisy.

It's late March. Morning light glints across the upper floors of the buildings. Up there, it's spring.

Always the same chair, outside his parking garage on North Wabash. He has watched this same dark head age from black to snow. He knows the head's name. *Howzit, Jackie? Oh, can't complain, no sir, Mr. Popper, can't complain*—and he always tips well, even better around Christmas, when Chicago is rivered with slush and your shine is lost to history after a block and a half of dirty rock salt, but this has never mattered. What matters is the shine's existence. And what is the difference between five years of having your shoes shined and twenty?

In 1983, Chicago elected an actual reform mayor, a *black* reform mayor, and Philip lost his city contracts. Under Daley, Bilandic, and Byrne he thrived. Now times are tougher. He thought, *Harold Washington, he too shall pass.* He hasn't. Not yet, anyway. Soon. But for the moment, even with Council Wars, Harold Washington's still up in the polls and might even win again.

On his throne above the sidewalk, Philip tries to empty his mind of all he will remember again as he walks to his office—court in the morning, a deposition in the afternoon. Now he does mostly personal injury. There's no sadness in this face unprotected by a newspaper—only the inevitability of another day of sitting up here in this red vinyl chair with tape stretched across the holes. When you sit down, it always lets out a chute of dead air, like a squeezed bloated stomach.

If it isn't sadness, what is it?

Philip isn't a tall man. Once, early in his career, during an argument in front of City Hall, an opposing counsel tapped his cigarette ash in the brim of Philip's hat. Philip went low, and like a LaSalle Street Napoleon stomped so hard on opposing counsel's foot he broke the man's toes.

His old lions, Daley and Arvey, are long gone. Only Abe Lincoln Marovitz is still kicking around. Philip thinks of the last pages of *The Radetzky March,* Commissioner Trotta at his table, ringing his little bell, the death tinkle of the Austro-Hungarian Empire.

He watches the hands that grip both ends of the rag—that exquisite movement—how could he describe it to anyone? Who would listen? A shoe coddled in the side-to-side of a chamois. He watches, inspects. Today he doesn't offer advice. *See that smudge, Jackie? Slight left of the laces.* He doesn't know why. He leaves the smudge be.

Funny, he and Miriam had always talked about going somewhere else. When they lived at 1444 North State, they used to take out an atlas and open it wide on the kitchen table. Not forever, just for a little while, a year or two, while Leo was still young. Edinburgh? Aix-en-Provence? The Pyrenees, where they say the snow never melts. The Bosphorus? Where's the Bosphorus again?

PART
TWO

11

1233 NORTH DAMEN

THE MASSACHUSETTS MIRACLE

Ann Arbor, 1988

I n literary parlance, it is referred to as a Madeleine Moment, meaning the secretions released by a certain cake-like cookie bring back haunted images of a time when you were exquisitely happy. Not that Popper ever read the book. (In college, it was beautiful, creative writing majors hardly had to read any books at all.) But the word Dukakis has this selfsame impact. All he has to do is hear it and Popper becomes fuzzy, emotionally overcome. Say it slow, stretch it out, prolong the pleasure. Give me a Du, give me a ka, give me an akis...

Dooooooooooookaaaaaaaaaaaaaaaaaaaaaakiiiiiiiiiiiiiiiiiiiiis.

And so Alexander Popper would like to take this opportunity to thank Michael Dukakis, not only for his contributions to the Democratic Party,* but also for presiding over a brief, happy period known only to himself as *Popper in Love*. Long live the Massachusetts Miracle. You, Governor, will always be my Commander in Chief. Kitty is one lucky lady.

---

*As Leo says, Mike Dukakis is not the hapless helmet-headed goof he's made out to be. That ungrateful Democrats should acknowledge that Dukakis (a) reunited the party—remember he won ten states to Mondale's one (Minnesota!) and (b) he began the reclamation of the Northwest, which helped lay the groundwork for Democratic victories in the nineties. Do you think the Democrats ever thanked Dukakis? Bill Clinton appointed him to the board of Amtrak, and not chair of the board either.

DEATH OF COMMUNISM

On the little TV at Steve's Lunch, best Korean food in the Midwest, the Berlin Wall falls and all Popper can think about is Nadia Comăneci in her tight little leotard. Which Olympics was that? He was how old, and still, he's a nasty little letch, drooling over a prepubescent who must have toiled away in some Commie gymnast boot camp, training thirteen, fourteen hours a day in order to give pride not to herself or even to her country but to an idea—an idea that even then everybody knew was a murderous lie, and yet little Nadia had to get out there and propagandize. He should have felt sorry for the burdens placed on those small shoulders, the weight of tens of millions of people who didn't want to live and die in vain. Amazing how a few gold medals can raise a people's self-esteem, and yet even then he took no interest in the larger implications, he just couldn't take his eyes off her squat body stuffed into that leotard—not to mention those things she did on the balance beam.

Popper spears his fried egg and fishes for thin little pieces of steak in his bibimbop. November 19, 1989. On the little TV behind the counter things go on being momentous. Tom Brokaw's outthrust chin and crisp articulation = momentous. He's leaning over the wall and talking to an East German border guard.

"And how do you feel about these great changes?"

The guard shrugs. *What's it all to me? I still got a day job, bud.*

"I'm not sure about Brokaw's coat," Kat said.

"It's a loden coat. My father has one. Maybe Brokaw's trying to pay homage to German culture."

At the commercial break (Buick, Mountain Dew), Kat said, "It's not like the Communists didn't have the right idea in a lot of respects. The complete lack of consumer culture allowed them to spend more of their time worrying about more important things like sex. I mean, if you read Kundera, who is as much a philosopher as he is a novelist, he makes it seem like *all* they did was have sex, that the command economy screwed up everybody's lives but at the same time allowed the intellectuals the freedom to actually have some fun once in a while and so —"

"So I was right all along."

"'Bout what, Popperino?"

"For years, I fantasized about jumping on Nadia Comăneci. I had a poster in my closet —"

"Nadia Comăneci is like twelve. Do you have to tell me everything that pops into your head?"

"She was twelve in the seventies. So was I."

"Did your whole life happen in the seventies?"

"Didn't everybody's?"

THE FOURTH OF JULY

B est album—of all time.
This is a total no-brainer. Petty. *Hard Promises.*

I mean, I like Tom Petty also. Who doesn't like Tom Petty? But even he'd be embarrassed by your weird obsession—he'd be, like, who is this freaky Jewish redneck—

The Pogues. *Rum, Sodomy, and the Lash.* And/or *If I Should Fall from Grace with God.*

Solid choices.

Billy Bragg's *Workers Playtime.* The difficult third album.

There's hope! You're actually evolving. Right before my eyes, you're evolving. It's like you just stood up after crawling around on your hands and knees for decades.

Purple Rain.

Baby—

Anything by Johnny Cash, not excluding gospel.

Most excellent. Best song?

X, *The Fourth of July... Mexican kids are shootin' fireworks below... Hey baby, it's the Fourth of...*

Fuck me, Popper. Now, fuck me now.

1233 NORTH DAMEN

They were awarded bachelors of arts degrees of dubious worth in a packed basketball stadium with twelve thousand others. Stand up, graduates! Sit down, graduates!

Congratulations!

The guy who made *The Big Chill* gave a speech. You just experienced the very best years of your entire lives. After Michigan, the real world will pretty much suck. Life's nothing but drudgery, people. Unless, unless you keep the friends you've made here in Ann Arbor! And if ever one of your friends is getting married across the country, and you find yourself not being able to afford the flight — because, remember, you're basically unemployable — I want you to pledge right now that you will take the Greyhound to that wedding! Yay!

Popper announced it utterly insipid. Nineteen thousand and something other people wept and hugged.

They moved to their own place in Chicago, to an apartment in Wicker Park, just about the time it was beginning to be ruined by people like them. Nelson Algren is dead and lives on Long Island; long live Nelson Algren. There goes the neighborhood. Their first apartment. God, did they hate themselves. Down the street, the O'Hare/Congress/Douglass trains clacked and chuttered.

Kat would put on Curtis Mayfield and waggle around the apartment singing, *Educated fools from uneducated schools*...And she'd say, If people only listened to Curtis Mayfield—if Curtis Mayfield was President, or King, or Secretary General of the UN— then even yuppie wannabe scum like us could be forgiven for triggering higher rents.

All their kitchen chairs were unmated. They were proud of this. This is the kind of people we are. One chair Popper found in the Jewel parking lot, the red one with the shimmied seat. Another, an old iron patio loveseat, he stole from the basement of the house on Riparian. Another, the desk chair with the broken spring, Kat pulled out of a dumpster in front of a building they were tearing down on Cortez. She also liked to collect shade-less lamps. They crowded the apartment like the skeletons of thin dead men, their little bulb heads. She called them free Giacomettis.

Thanksgiving of that year. Popper went down the street to the park and played football with some neighborhood kids. It was tackle, and those local boys merrily whomped his ass. The ground was as hard as a parking lot. He came home wearing crumbly November dirt, his face bleeding. Kat had bought an enormous turkey at the Jewel. It was still lying uncooked on the table. She was lying on the floor beside the table, staring at the ceiling.

"What is basting, anyway?"

"My head's bleeding."

"Something tells me you have to cook it first, baste it second. But I really have no idea. It could just as well be the other way around."

Kat reached and opened the cabinet door beneath the sink. She pulled out a can of Ajax and held it to the ceiling like an offering.

"Who the hell was Ajax, anyway?"

"A warrior god."

"Now he's a scouring powder. Is that success?"

"Why don't you call your mother and ask her how to make the turkey?"

Kat talked to the can of Ajax. "You call your mother."

"She's in Tibet—or somewhere. I think she and Ralph went to Tibet. Don't you care about what happened to my head?"

"They really whoop it up, those two."

"After my dad, wouldn't you?"

"What was so bad about him?"

"Nothing so bad, really. But it was like he never saw us. Or he saw us too much. No, we never saw him, but that's because he made himself so hard to see, so we looked through him. Does that make any sense?"

"Not at all."

"He hit my mom once, or tried to. I can't even remember anymore. There should be more than one word for remember—"

"He hit your mom?"

"We're quiet people, middle-class people, slightly upperish-middle-class people. My father ran for office. He's a well-regarded attorney. My mother, for years, was the most popular substitute teacher on the North Shore."

"So he hit her."

"I won't be taking further questions from the press at this time."

"Well, he's alone now," Kat said.

"Mostly."

The turkey reposed on the kitchen table, pink and dead and huge. Popper silent, his face bleeding. He looked out the window at the leafless trees, stark and empty. November always his favorite, an orphan sort of month, cold, often snowless.

"Whoop," Popper said.

"Whoop," Kat said.

"Our supper is plain but we are very wonderful."

"Who said that?"

"Forgotten poet."

Kat in shorts in November lying on her back, her strong freckle-pale legs. Kat? You remember? How that fat thing sat on the kitchen table through the night, through the weekend into Monday, before it turned greenish?

ACROSS THE ALLEY

Screams from across the alley, people, people screaming, human beings. And her saying she didn't hear a thing and his trying to tell her that it isn't right, isn't natural, that sound. January of a snowless year and they were cold, always cold, and they huddled in the back room with the gurgling radiator, under the blankets and unzipped sleeping bags. Nights those voices screamed, nights she slept so hard she heard nothing. In sleep she went so far away and he was so alone, and nothing helped; it didn't matter if he read or didn't read. As soon as he turned out the light, he couldn't stop hearing them.

In the morning, Kat made coffee in a parka and shorts, an old pair of his high school gym shorts. The shorts are slowly unraveling and the tatters hang down her legs like streamers. No, not his. The faded name in the white box: *Laveneaux.*

There wasn't any point in asking if she'd been kept up, if she'd heard what he heard. The windows were crusted with snow, and the light against the panes came through as if through crystals. The kitchen had an ironing board that came out of the wall. They used it as extra counter space.

Popper said, "I'm trying to write a sad story, a good, sad story," and she said, spinning at the bop of the toast, "You know what you love most? Melancholy. Don't take this the wrong way, but sometimes I think you love the gloom more than you love the people."

"Don't take it the wrong way?"

"You want me to be the cheering section all the time?"

There is frost in the January trees and the sidewalks are the buckled ruins of ancient ant civilizations and the new cars at Bert Weinman Ford are lonely too and even the weeds are dying—

"I like it, keep going—"

And the people without houses go to the Jewel to keep warm, and on Sundays the little Mexican girls go to church in dresses with frills sewed by the fingers of long-widowed grandmothers; sometimes the girls skip, other times they walk with their hands behind their backs, with dignity, because going to church isn't something to take lightly, and it's cold, always cold, and the CTA buses lump down the streets like tired Snuffleupaguses—

Kat touching her toes with one hand, holding a piece of toast with melting lumps of butter, the parka's furry hood over her head. "Keep going, keep going. Why do you always stop?"

"That's what I do. I start things and I stop."

"Don't talk, tell—"

"It doesn't connect. Nothing ever connects."

"Just go on."

His day job: he checks IDs at the YMCA on Cybourne. He has to make sure people aren't expired. He sits by the turnstile and buzzes people in. His boss, Mr. Head, told him to make periodic checks for suicides. It can happen anytime. Lots of places to be alone in this building, Mr. Head said. And so many people come here for shelter. Sometimes the threat of having to go outside again becomes too much.

"Mr. Head?"

"That's the guy's name. Larry Head."

Kat chewed her toast. "I think you should change that. Otherwise, I really —"

So when it's slow, he leaves his post by the turnstile and wanders around. Once, they found a guy dangling from a basketball hoop in the lower gym. Even though it happened before his time, there's something about the empty gym that echoes. Yet it's not at the Y; it's at home, at night, when the voices truly wail, on the other side of the alley, beyond the rusted fence.

"I have to work on the transition from the Y back to the apartment. Feels weird. I'm trying to say he's always on a kind of death patrol, but that it's at home, in his own bed beside his completely deaf beloved —"

"Popper —"

There isn't any mystery about the screams. All he had to do was walk around the block and read the sign. It's an old-age home for the indigent, run by the state. It isn't very big. He walked right up to it and looked in the first-story window. There they were, the faces silent because it was daytime. They only start screaming after midnight, sometimes a couple of hours later. Just when you think they aren't going to scream, they scream. Not all the screams are alike. Some are sustained, operatic, almost show-

offy; others are quick stabs, loud and sharp. A few are in-
betweens. These are the worst. It's as if they don't have the strength
to carry on, to finish what they've begun. Midscream — then a
coat of blank silence.

She spins around the kitchen, half-eaten piece of toast in her
hand, her body hot beneath the big coat, the butter on her toast
melting. He tosses the story in the garbage along with the coffee
grinds and egg shells. "They scream in the night," Popper says.
"Don't you hear them? Ever?"

"I hear them, I hear them."

PEROT

POPPER *(in the darkness, reaching for her)*: ¿Quien es mas macho, myself or Ross Perot?

KAT *(laughing, edging away)*: Maybe in the morning, okay?

July 19, 1945

    I feel so rotten today—I opened a letter addressed to the ship from the wives of one of our men—His 2½ year old son was killed by a truck—and she asked the officers to talk to him to help him sort of face it out—Hell—what a life— The other day another sailor found out his wife had another kid—She put a notice in the paper that Mrs. So and So— using his name of course—just gave birth to a beautiful bouncing baby boy—Well, he's been in the South Pacific the last twelve months! The letters keep coming in, congratulating him—

J ust after dawn, bumbling to the toilet, he finds Kat alone at the kitchen table, shards of a broken plate at her feet, the refrigerator door open.

"What is it?"

"My mother always said she felt better after she broke a few plates."

"Better about what?"

"I don't know."

Kat stands and circles the little kitchen rug, careful to avoid the shards. She watches her feet in the ash light. Her toes head in the wrong direction. Dancer's feet, she calls them, though she was never a dancer. She played soccer in high school.

"F. Scott Fitzgerald was ashamed of his feet also," Popper says. "He wore shoes two sizes too big to make up for what he thought—"

"Where'd you get the idea I was ashamed of my feet?"

"You're not?"

"Ashamed of my feet?"

"Ashamed of something. What aren't I ashamed of?"

"Don't confuse us with each other."

THE BLUFF

Down the road from his father's house, the house he grew up in, his bluff, his brother's bluff. The guy who bought the Krawchecks' house after Mr. Krawcheck died put up a fence across the bluff and a no-trespassing sign. Assholes, you think you can own a view of Lake Michigan? Yes, I'm talking to you, 47 Riparian.

He took Kat there. They climbed the fence. He wanted to show her where he was from, this little spittle of land above the lake, as much home as anywhere. It was a night in April, the fog thick as cotton.

From up on the bluff, the lake in the dark. That shoving noise, that pulling away. Kat took off her shoes and tossed them over the edge of the bluff. Then she lifted her white socked feet and raised them above her head and laughed.

They listened to the lake. Off the bluff there was a wreck, or so Seymour always used to say. A mile off Highland Park, a steamship bound for Milwaukee hit a boat carrying lumber. The passengers had been attending a rally for Stephen Douglas in Chicago. Three hundred drowned, what they got for supporting the Little Giant. The debris washed up for weeks. Suitcases, a head of cabbage, innumerable unmatched shoes. Popper thought of old bones in cold water.

"There's a city of dead Milwaukeeans out there in the water."

"No doubt," Kat said.

"No really, the boat was called *The Lady Elgin*. It's still down there. Only a few people got rescued. Seymour himself swam out from the beach and saved three babies."

"There's rain in this fog," Kat said.

The fog. The fog pressing them farther into the wet. Her socks floating up there, small ghosts of her feet—

July 20, 1945

And soon this whole business will be over and we'll be back together again, hand in hand, going forward to make a beautiful life for ourselves—and maybe another couple of children, what do you say? Are you feeling prolific? I'm like a caged animal—Just waiting to get my hands on your letters and devour them—But they still don't satisfy me—I want more and more—What about a new linoleum and rug deal for the dining room?

The End of Communism II

Nadia Comăneci got a boob job."

"Say it ain't so."

"It's in *People*. Look."

"Something to be said for our system of government, I got to say."

"Yo, Popper, you got a problem with these?"

"Lemme see those."

Ziggy Marley at the Aragon Ballroom

She had a way of being alone in a crowd of dancing people, of mining out her own space in any sweaty bungle. Popper, trying to keep pace with her, only jostled people and had to keep apologizing.

"Maybe try not moving so much. Try and meet the tempo—slower, slow—it's not aerobics. Don't try and control it."

Kat in Levi's and a white T-shirt, dancing in her beat-up leather hiking boots. He'll never not think of her in Levi's, a white T-shirt, and hiking boots.

More than a basic lack of rhythm, it was a patent lack of ability to translate what he heard into any sort of actual motion. Listening and moving, and somehow the two never meeting.

"Stop thinking about it, Popper. Just move."

"Ziggy's not like his father. There's not enough political subtext."

"I can't hear a thing you're saying."

"If it was his father maybe I could get into it, because there's more political subtext."

"What?"

Them closing in on each other, shouting into each other's ears now. Where Popper likes it, where the uncertainty of music cedes to his turf: conversation, talk.

"But I guess it can't be that easy being the son of a legend. Imagine being Lisa Marie. Think about it, one day you wake up to the realization of who you happen to be. You're five or six years old and it turns out your overfat dad is—"

"Dance, Popper—try to channel your grandmother."

"It's probably different in Jamaica."

"What?"

"I said maybe fathers and sons in Jamaica—What, what am I trying to say?"

The darkness, the music heard, untranslatable. Kat, her face hot and wet, the way she gently slinked her shoulders, hardly moving but moving—to the beat, the easy vibe, the casual syncopation.

1233 North Damen

It was in the morning's *Sun-Times*. Page 3 of the metro section, the story of a sixteen-year-old girl. One guy held the gun, the other guy raped her. When the guy was done raping her, the one with the gun shot her. Later, the rapist ratted on the shooter, which is how the cops got their version of the story.

Kat said, "Shouldn't we at least—"

"What?"

"I don't know. If we aren't going to do something, shouldn't we at least say something?"

"To who? Call Richie Daley and say we're upset by the violence in this city, that he really should ask the citizens to cut it out, that Chicagoans really ought not rape and kill each other."

"Fuck Richie Daley. To at least acknowledge that it happened. Repeat it. Shouldn't we be out on the streets shouting—"

"Nobody really does that anymore."

"Or at least call up the family and say, Hey, we're—"

"Like send a card or something, or flowers?"

"If it was me, wouldn't you want somebody to at least notice. Nobody even notices."

"If it was you, people would notice."

"Doesn't that make us complicit? Doesn't that make us accomplices?"

"I don't disagree."

"Tomorrow I'll forget."

"I'll remind you."

"It's like that girl never existed. If she existed, we'd have to imagine her. And since we won't, since we refuse to even try, it's just a story, right? A horror story."

She left the paper on the ironing board and went out to the stoop to watch the traffic.

At Sea

Highland Park, 1978

Seymour never stopped lamenting the fact that he'd gone all the way to the South Pacific and the only true combat he saw up close was the age-old battle between the big fishes and the little fishes. Occasionally, he said, seabirds got in on the act. He did, though, lose a man. A young sailor felled not by enemy fire but by some kind of tropical fever.

We buried the boy, he would say, at sea. All hands bury the dead.

That was the grand talk. The not-so-grand talk was how they zipped the boy up in a canvas bag and put him on a board. A few respectful words. The slow bugle and a prayer. They slid him off the board into the ocean, and the last thing that sailor did on earth was make a splash nobody heard over the roar of the engines and the wind. Seymour still remembered that sailor's coordinates: *Latitude 12 29.26 south. Longitude 130 49.10 east. I wrote them in a letter to the mother.*

Seymour was a hard man to love, and most days he understood this and accepted it. Other times, he demanded that somebody look at him and see his sorrow. *All hands bury the dead.* Latitude 12 29.26 south, Longitude 130 49.10 east.

"Why are we spared when others, so many others, aren't?"

Seymour at his station behind his desk. Leo drawing a sketch of Seymour's head. Popper only half-listening, on the carpet turning on and off Seymour's weather radio. (*The barometric pressure is 18.45, winds out of the southeast at 32 miles per hour, small craft advisory from Calumet to Belmont...*)

"I'm asking you, boys. I'm really asking you. Why do some guys get it in the neck while others go on living? You call that God?"

"We don't know," Leo said. "How could we possibly know?"

And Seymour, his voice reaching across decades, *Hold it right there, ensign, you call this being spared?*

In Skokie

The turnout would have disappointed him. There were more empty white folding chairs than mourners. He was suspended over an open pit — a neatly cut rectangular wound — by a complicated rigging of rope and steel pulleys. This was in the big cemetery out by Old Orchard Mall. A manicured, highly regulated place. No flowers or any other adornment permitted, as per Jewish law. Thou shalt not sugarcoat the end of things. It means you spend the rest of the world in a hole in Skokie.

It was early June. They tried to stay focused and not enjoy the sun on their faces. There was a naval honor guard, and the sailors also wore their best solemn looks. Popper had never seen Kat so snazzed up.

"Liking the tights," he said.

"Shhhhh."

A woman nobody recognized, wearing an enormous yellow hat, began to moan, a low moan from the bottom of her throat, like a dying dog.

"What's with the sombrero?" Leo whispered.

Kat tried not to laugh.

"You can laugh," Popper said. "We're a modern ironical family."

Popper thought of him in there, in that steel casket, in his peaked American Legion hat, in his suit and well-knotted tie, ready to deny a loan.

The woman in the yellow hat moaned louder. And yet he was theirs. Ours is ours. Who are you to come here with fresh tears, lady?

Later, back at the house, Bernice said it must have been Irma Bluestein, an old friend of theirs from Lunt Avenue. "We haven't spoken to her in years. She must scour the obituaries. Or perhaps that's not who it was. It doesn't matter. Why would it matter?"

The service didn't last long. The rabbi was concise and proper and celebrated Seymour Popper for the things he had been, husband, father, grandfather, Navy captain, insurance company executive, suburban banker. As he went down the list, Popper thought about how much work all our failure takes, and he gripped his knees in terror as they started to lower the pulleys. *Therefore, by the All-Merciful One, offer shelter to Seymour beneath this humble earth.* And the rifles saluted him. God, would he have loved the guns, every jolt of every report, the way the reverberations of the shots hung in the air after. He would have chatted up the men: *Hey, sailors, what ship? I myself started in the Coast Guard, but as you all know, the Coast Guard's for puffs. I went to war in autumn of '44, better appear in the last act of the show than never.* The men cleared away the ropes and pulleys. One by one, they took their turns with the spade and rained dirt and gravel down upon the casket. That outrageous final thumping. Everybody took turns holding Bernice, who then walked slowly away from the grave. As Philip was helping her back in the limousine, she stooped, plucked a handful of grass, and stuffed it in her purse.

HOLLIS

The funeral over, everyone began heading back to Bernice's for cold cuts, Kat and Popper were still searching the unmowed grass on the other side of the little road.

"He's got to be around here somewhere," Popper said.

"Who was he? A black-sheep uncle or something? Why's he over here?"

"He worked for us. Our houseman. He had a heart attack in the basement. My mom always said he died of loneliness."

"Your houseman?"

"He put up the storm windows, cooked, baby-sat, drank whiskey with my mom. That sort of thing. We loved him. Or we said we loved him. His name was Hollis Osgood. When he died, his family didn't want to take him home to Alabama. So we buried him with us."

"Why's he over here?"

"Because he's not Jewish. If you're not Jewish, they put you on the other side of the road. In cemeteries that aren't Jewish, they put the Jews on the other side of the road or outside the fence or wherever. Or they don't let them in there at all. It all evens out."

"There's nobody else buried over here."

"Not that many housemen. Hollis was unique."

"But now you lost him," Kat said.

"We didn't lose him."

"Then where is he?"

Popper didn't answer, on his hands and knees now, pulling the grass by the roots, searching the moist dirt with his fingers.

Our hold on people, even our own people—

Heat Wave

July 1995. On the news, the old people were dying like flies in sweltering apartments. No, not like flies — flies died with more dignity. The old people slumped over in the thick, fetid air and nobody collected their bodies for days.

Popper sat on the stoop in front of 1233 North Damen trying to breathe, a wad of twisted Kleenex up his nose. It had been too hot for sexual congress for weeks, or for that matter, even sexual dictatorship, if you know what I mean. Popper further philosophizes: If sneezing is a form of orgasm, then you could say that all total celibacy really amounts to is not sneezing. I mean, I love sneezing. Who doesn't love sneezing?

Kat just back from a run. All through those panting days — the heat index up to 120 degrees — Kat ran the melting streets.

Her face red, her neck, her hair sweat-stuck to her ears. Ten days ago, at three in the morning, they went to the Golden Nugget for the air conditioning. Out of mercy, Kat gave him a hand job using the oil from the salad-dressing rack on the table. Since then, nada.

"What happened to your nose?"

"I'm trying to not sneeze."

"I'll make salad," Kat said, and went inside. The door whacked. She'd recently been accepted into the graduate program in philosophy at the University of Chicago. Now everything she did was terrible and purposeful. Now she ran, now she made graduate school salad.

That night, their sweat pooling in the hollow of their futon, Popper said, I could lie beside you like a Sunday roast.

"Who said that?"

"I forget. A. J. Liebling maybe. No, he probably just said, 'I want to lie by a roast.'"

She raised her head and kissed him, daintily, un-Katlike, as a small reward. For stealing a line? For A. J. Liebling?

Now she brought a small tower of books to bed with her every night. She fell asleep holding Hannah Arendt.

The three fans only flung the heat around and made it hotter.

He stood up and yanked the light cord, that cord that dangled above their lives as they slept, like some ceiling god was fishing for them.

"Hey, I'm reading."

"You were snoring and that bulb's like the Stasi."

"I've never snored once in my entire life."

He stood up again and yanked the light on again.

Kat went back to sleep with her book in her hands, snored.

He nuggled closer to her. "Did you know that the Nazis forbade Jews asparagus? I mean what kind of bureaucrat thinks that shit up?"

"Popper—"

"Well, we've rounded them up, machine-gunned, gassed, burned alive their babies—now let's forbid them an esoteric vegetable."

Kat opened her eyes a crack, read a paragraph. Then she said, "Why is it always back to the Nazis?—Jesus, that's it, so obvious—Nazis give you a hard-on."

"It must be the sadness."

"Arendt says there isn't anything particularly unique about the Nazis, only that they were better accountants than, say, Kubla Khan or Oliver Cromwell."

"The sadness, the grief, it must, you know, increase the old firepower—Arendt's completely full of shit. And Kubla Khan was in it for territorial expansion. I forget who Cromwell was. A mean Englishman? I remember Benny Hill doing some bit—"

"Go slow, Popper. Woo me a little."

Her naked already. Him naked but for his Sox hat. If they could have torn off their skins they would have.

"Take off your hat, Popper."

"Never."

Like two wet seals thumping. They kept losing their grips on each other's greasiness. Kat almost fell off the bed. Two and a half minutes tops.

He edged downward. "Let me correct the imbalance."

"No. Not now. Later, okay?"

She got up and took another shower. He stared at the bulb above the bed and listened to the trickling of the water. They had very low water pressure that summer. The whole city did, according to *Eyewitness News*. He stared at the bulb and thought of the water slowly falling, draining down her body into the abyss of the drain.

1233 NORTH DAMEN

It's the sex. Lack thereof.

Why don't you just go back to sleep? I'm just thinking.

On the floor?

I like it.

Want a pillow?

No, thanks.

I specialize in anticlimax, which, when you think about it, has its own subtle excitement.

I'm just thinking. Not about that.

You want to get some toys or something? Spice things up. There's a place on Western Ave I could go and pick up some stuff. How about porn? I grew up with porn. My father had a ton of it. I think of it as a character-forming aspect of my childhood.

Let me think, Popper. I'll come back.

It's the sex.

No, it's more than that. Or less. Fuck, I don't even know. Sometimes I've got no want. I don't even want to want. Do you know what I mean?

July 28, 1945

So little to say — Nothing's changing — At night all sorts of past experiences keep popping up in my mind — of you and I arguing about this or that while I drive — This is such an artificial life in a way, and yet it is so intense — one loses all sense of place and time — I wonder if where we are at any given time is even important — It's just where we come from that means anything at all — This is no life for a family man — I'm no different from the rest of the men — When we censor the crew's mail, I can see how much they miss their wives and kids, too — What a fine bunch of stay-at-homes this war is going to make of all of us —

DINER GRILL, IRVING PARK

We have no destinations.

—Ben Hecht, *A Thousand and One Afternoons in Chicago*

anting to be alone but not free of voices, he drives his mother's tired Chevelle to the Diner Grill, where the taxi drivers go for late-night coffee and cheeseburgers. Three in the morning, he sits on a stool facing the wide, empty street, a double-parked cab idles with the windows open, the dispatcher calling out an address: *37, I got a pickup at 1673 Aldine, copy. 37. 37, I got a fare standing by. 37, where in the fuck are you? You got to stop disappearing on me, 37.* And at the end of the counter slumps an ancient man, not a driver, maybe he was one in the past and now—not being able to sleep either—he comes to be around the old talk. Always a plate of fries in front of him. *Just fries, no burger, Ken, thanks.*

A new driver pulls up. He comes in and sits next to Popper.

Couple of fried eggs, Ken.

Hash browns?

Sure thing, Ken.

Outside it's getting colder but inside the windows sweat from the hot breath of the men who don't tell the stories Popper is looking for—about the holdups, the fare-skippers, the drug-addled. One driver talks about a homemade remedy for hemorrhoids and Hash Browns says, That's all a crock. And the creams don't work, either. The only surefire way to lose them is to shell out the money and get the operation. Any other way just buries the pain temporarily.

Popper gets back in the car and drives block after block looking for lighted windows. This is September 23, 1995. It's 3:45 in the morning, your light is on. The corner of Ashland and Milwaukee. Fourth-floor apartment above Vasilatos and Sons Real Estate. Who are you? What are you doing? Right now, tell me, what are you thinking about?

1233 NORTH DAMEN

Sunday and Popper lying on their bed with his shoes on, a sacred indulgence. The weight of one's shoes relaxes the feet, providing a kind of wonderfully decadent encasement, a double set of wombs for each foot, if you will, or two little comfortable tombs, to put it another way. Interesting, womb and tomb. All you have to do is switch a letter.

Kat was digging around for something in the closet. All he could see was her ankles and the backs of her bare feet, dust-coated from pacing around the apartment all afternoon.

"Maybe I'll go to law school," Popper said to her feet. "I'll defeat the class system from the inside. They'll never know what hit them."

"Who?"

"The class system."

Kat stood and stepped out of the closet. She held a gray dress he'd never seen her wear. "You think this is too frumpy?"

"Put it on."

And she did. He watched her pull off her sweats. Blue underwear, no bra. Remember this: her blue underwear, no bra. Breasts inflated like wind socks, like for a small regional airport. She's my Meigs Field, my Palwaukee...

354

Being nearly naked somehow made her taller. She was like his father this way, short but this didn't mean she didn't have a way of looming. She raised her arms and pulled the dress over her head. It had little frills on the sleeves.

"I want to go to the front lines. I'm talking about real change. Without lawyers there'd be no minimum wage, child labor would be rampant. We'd still be driving Pintos. And don't forget Gandhi was an attorney. So is Fidel Castro."

"Popper?"

"Or maybe I'll just take up Tae Kwan Do—It's not frumpy."

"But it's a little biggish?"

"I had my yellow stripe in high school. I wonder if it's still valid."

"Popper?"

"Yeah?"

"I'm pregnant."

"All right, I won't go to law school."

"Popper," Kat said. A slightly different emphasis on the *er,* as if the name had slightly more weight in the world. His name?

"Behold immaculate conception."

"Yes."

"Yes? Actually yes?"

"I mean no, not that. But yes. Yes."

"Damn, I feel like Daniel Ortega. He's probably a lawyer—"

"I think I'd like to go ahead with it." She stopped but didn't step toward him. Only her eyes got closer. She stood there in that gray dress with little frills on the biceps.

"Serious?"

"Serious."

Popper got off the bed and went to the window. A couple mosey-ing down the alley paused to grope each other before walking on. He opened the window, he closed the window, he opened the window, he closed the window. He wanted to shout out to them. Hey, you beautiful, carefree hoodlums. Something has happened. Up here. Look up here. An occurrence. It's about time. Plot! Up in this window. You're not even looking. Hey, up here, have a look up—

"You think you'd like to go ahead with it?"

"This doesn't make me any less pro-choice, does it?"

"Huh?"

"And I admit, the fatness part bothers me. I'm as vain as anybody."

"Go ahead with it?"

"I'm asking you."

"What do I think?"

"A kid, Popper, a bambino."

"Jesus. The heat wave."

"Right."

"Want to fool around? Suddenly I feel like—"

"I do, actually."

1233 North Damen

And another thing, Popper, does the world really need another privileged overeducated white kid? Haven't we done enough to destroy the world?

You're having second thoughts.

I didn't say that. I'm just feeling guilty. I need you to help me justify.

At least ours will be a poor privileged overeducated white kid.

That's true. Wait, is that good? The kid's expectations will be so out of whack with reality, with what we can provide, he'll become more enamored with money than if we had it, and then—

Shit, we're so fucking white.

But we're also minorities. Don't forget that—

I'm only half a minority.

That makes you a minority's minority.

Give it a rest. And I'm fine with being half-Jewish, more than fine. My father used to say he had enough trouble being a human being from Wisconsin. He said if people worried less about their own nationalistic identities, we'd have one less excuse for killing each other.

The kid will be three-quarters Jewish, not bad, not bad at all, said the reform rabbi!

Popper, I'm so tired. Can't I be less tired?

I rented *Ordinary People*.

Again?

Ordinary People is —

I know, I know, the greatest war movie of all time. *Ordinary People* makes *Apocalypse Now* look like *Charlie and the Chocolate Factory* —

Right, not that *Charlie and the Chocolate Factory* is for slouches, not at all —

I know, Popper, I know.

PHILIP, MICHIGAN AVENUE

H e pauses in front of the Wrigley Building and looks north. Six o'clock in early October and the light is white gray. And the people flee. And the cabs scuttle for position like crabs. Above it all, the Hancock Building. Philip thinks of birds. Always, when he looks at the Hancock he thinks of birds. When the building was finally finished in the late sixties, triumphantly, they flipped on the airplane lights. We all cheered but the birds didn't. The lights must have baffled them and that first night bird after bird slammed into the windows. Small thumps nobody heard. In the morning, carnage. Philip remembers the picture in the paper, the birds lined up like earthquake victims on the sidewalk, tags around their necks.

August 2, 1945

   *Start brushing the moths out of my clothes—all the talk
is we may well be heading home soon—I want to be ready
to hop into civvies as soon as I get back—You know my tails
are still at Dapper Cleaners in storage—I still have the
receipt for them—Anybody going formal? Ah, sweetheart,
we're so close and we can start right up again—Oh, my
darling—Whatever needs fixing with the house—let it go—
I'll fix it—What about some new drapes for the living room?*

1233 North Damen

They talked about getting curtains. Neither of them could figure out how to measure the windows. Kat slept a lot during the afternoons, when she wasn't working at the bookstore or in class. He'd join her. He always had the time. Three nights a week he was still doing overnights at the Y, but even so, he always had the afternoons.

"You know what my mother told me once? She said she and my Dad stayed together so long because of the children and I actually said, I swear, What children?"

"That's sad. Everything about that is sad."

A shallow daylight sleep, on top of the covers most of the time. The long quiets of those afternoons, not even much traffic on Damen.

August 4, 1945

    When you do write you never seem to mention much about my letters — are you getting them at all? —

Montrose Beach

O dd that an abstract notion like fatherhood could make him feel more alone than ever. No wind this morning and the lake is lumpish. The bloated waves curl slowly toward the shore. Only at the last moment do they collapse. This bedraggled city beach, broken glass, a few tires, a single slatless bench, faded letters, *Prk Dist. of Chic.* Scattered styrofoam like unmeltable snow. Even the water crib, five miles off the beach, has faded into just another tired old building. It used to give him such joy as a kid— that magic floating house in the middle of Lake Michigan. Miriam once said only in Chicago would the powers that be build a cathedral just for the fish.

Water Crib, Wilson Avenue

12

THE COMFORT INN

THEATETUS: The very next question which I am going to ask
you is an extraordinary one, although expressed in per-
fectly ordinary language.
SOCRATES: There is no need to warn me: I am all ears.
THEATETUS: What did I say between your last two interrup-
tions, Socrates?

—Karl Popper, "Self-Reference and Meaning
in Ordinary Language"

Boyhood Home

December of 1995, and Kat read that Ronald Reagan's boyhood home in Dixon had been restored to its original splendor and was now open for pilgrimages.

"We're not the faithful," Popper said.

"I'm just thinking maybe his goofy-ass house will explain—"

"Explain what?"

"Who this country is."

"We're all Clinton now. Bill Clinton's this baby's daddy."

"Let's hope the kid doesn't end up on welfare."

"He had to sign that bill."

"He had to sell the poor down the river?"

"It's called politics, Kat."

"It's beyond revolting."

"Anyway, poor Dutch has Alzheimer's."

"Isn't it too poetic? He's the one who gets to slip away so easy into forgetting while the Guatemalans eat—what do Guatemalans eat?"

"Papaya?"

They drove up on Saturday. They stopped in Mooseheart, where Popper bought a key ring at the Citgo: *Mooseheart, Illinois: City of Children.*

Back in the car he said, "Maybe in time all parents become Republicans. This means us. You know my father, the great Democrat, voted for Reagan the second time around. But part of that was because—"

"Because your mom slept with Walter Mondale."

"I told you that? That's a closely held and sacred family secret."

At the boyhood home, a little blue-haired tour guide doubling as the gift-shop lady cried in a piercing voice, "Welcome! Welcome! And when does your little precious arrive?"

She showed them sacred artifacts in glass cases. A leather football helmet. His varsity letters. A replica of the hutch where Ronnie raised his rabbits. Photographs of his childhood dogs: Stoney, Taddy, and a short-lived shepherd (a runaway) named Doug. A story: "Once Ronnie was fined fourteen dollars and fifty cents for lighting off fireworks. And he thought he'd get off easy because his daddy played pinochle with the chief of police. Fat chance of that! It took Ronnie half a summer to pay that off. Now this is the President's room. He shared it with his beloved brother Neal, also called Moons."

"Is this where he first started hearing Commies under the bed?" Kat asked.

"Listen, missy," the woman growled, at a much much lower register, "you don't have to be grateful to him, but you don't have to be an ignoramus, either."

Her hair wasn't blue, either. Where did Popper get the idea it was blue?

Hardly pausing for breath, the woman went back up to her gift-shop voice. "And this watch here is not a replica. This is Ronnie's first Timex. (He remained loyal to the brand throughout his entire life.) He bought it with his own money in 1929, which, as you know, was an inauspicious year to be buying anything, and yet Ronnie was ever the optimist, never once did he believe that tomorrow wouldn't bring more blessings than…"

Before they left, they bought a coffee cup, two T-shirts, eight postcards, a Reagan bobble-head, and promised to return with the baby.

They ate roast beef sandwiches at Arby's and got a room at the Comfort Inn. The gray stucco walls were covered with glazed pebbles. The television remote control was screwed into the night table. In the dark, they held each other. It was 5 degrees outside. In the room, they couldn't turn down the heat.

"I feel like a wildebeest," Kat said.

"You're fine."

"A Weeble Wobble inflated up with a bike pump. I mean, have you looked at my cheeks lately?"

A half hour later, she reached and turned the light on. She got up and sat on the other bed, held her stomach in her hands. Popper squinted, blue spots in his eyes.

"Bumpy's keeping me up again."

"What do you think of the name Ottla? She was Kafka's favorite sister."

"It's like she doesn't want me to sleep."

"She died in a camp."

"Who?"

"Ottla. Get high?"

"You want her to have six toes?"

"Read? I think she likes it. More *Herzog*?"

"Enough with Saul Bellow. He's a blowhard, all his characters are blowhards, and they all sound like him."

"I'll disregard the blasphemy because of your condition. Chekhov?"

"Fine."

He got the book out of his bag and started a story. It was about a famous professor who, needing to escape the treachery and rigor of St. Petersburg, goes to the country estate of an old friend. The country estate of an old friend *whose wife he happens to love.*

As Popper finished the first paragraph, he looked up. Kat was lying on her back, arms folded across Bumpy, her bare feet sticking out across the abyss between the beds. He stretched his own bare feet to meet hers, but she recoiled.

"The water stain looks like Idaho," she said. "See the panhandle?"

"Where?"

"In the corner. Aren't you going to go on?"

The old friend drags the professor around the estate to show him what's new in the greenhouses. The professor fidgets. All he wants is a minute alone with Mayra. The problem is that every time he is able to sneak a private word, Mayra wonders out loud, "Don't you find me terribly dull? Wouldn't you rather be with your friend?"

Now, Miss Mayra, there's something I absolutely must—

"Hey, Popper."

"Yeah?"

"Your feet. I'm asphyxiating. Wash them, will you?"

"Now?"

"After."

The drama continued to not unfold. The professor listens to his old friend describe the new species he's collected. The old friend has long clung to the belief that the professor is the single person in the whole of Russia who can appreciate his passion for rare flora and fauna.

Sudden good fortune! The old friend is called away to the village. Something having to do with a drunken peasant wreaking havoc with someone else's mule. *Oh, my dear professor, I am so sorry, this will only take a bit. And the agitators want land reform! Ha!* The door closes. The professor and Mayra alone at last. Again she protests, "Don't you find me so terribly boring?"

The professor lays it on the table.

Mayra swoons and nearly faints in the arms of the dazed professor, for whom the feel of her flesh, of her pink and naked arms, is enough to—

"All right, wash."

"What about the consummation?"

"There isn't going to be any."

"How do you know?"

"Because Mayra's going to be loyal to her husband, even though he's a dolt, and the professor's going to be loyal to his old friend, even though he wants to murder him. Can't you see what's coming? They're all weak. Every character in the story is weak willed except for maybe the housemaid and the gardener. Maids and gardeners are always strong in Russian literature. Maybe you've got a fungus. My father used to have that. He kept some kind of powder in his shoe."

Popper went to the bathroom and closed the door. He examined his face in the mirror, in the murked yellow light. He unwrapped a little white bar of soap and stuck his foot in the sink, scrubbed. He took it out and dried it and stuck the other foot in the sink, when a couple next door began going at it in the shower. The sink shook. They were like a ramming snowplow. She— *Mayra?*—began roaring. Full-mouthed roars with an erotic gurgle in her mouth. Yes! My God. Yes. Jesus Christ. Yes. Mary, Mother of God. Yes. Yes!

Popper considered quickly jerking off. Then, deciding this was in bad taste, he finished his other foot. He noticed that the two water glasses wore little white hats with perforated edges. A nice touch. He filled one up with water and put the hat back, brought the glass out to Kat.

"Water?"

"Thanks."

"You like the little hat?"

"I do."

"How's it going?"

"She forgot Joseph."

"Ralph says the only problem with atheism is that you have no one to yell to when you're in the throes. Want me to go on with the story?"

"Okay."

The professor and Mayra's lips are about to meet. The front door flings open. *Dmitri, old friend, back so soon from the village?*

And Popper stood on the bed and read the last couple of pages, outshouting the couple next door. Kat squeezed a pillow over her ears and laughed.

The professor departs in a noisy horse-and-buggy flourish, Dmitri and Mayra shouting, *Don't forget your country friends! Don't forget your country friends!*

And when it was over, the professor safely on the road back to Petersburg, their neighbors, as if on cue, moved out of the shower to the bed for a more traditional wall-slapping motel romp. But this time Mayra's shouting had died down and been replaced by a keening that sounded like a dog who's been waiting for you to come home all day, so joyful her noises became agony.

"Before she was faking."

"Yeah."

"Not anymore."

"No."

Kat stood up and went to the window and looked out at the parking lot through the veins of ice. She put her hand flat against the glass.

"What are you thinking?"

"Why do you ask me that?"

"Because I want to know."

"You never want to know."

"Tell me."

She kept her hand against the glass, but turned to face him. He still wished he could describe it, her face. How her eyes always seemed slightly hidden until she laughed.

"This place."

"Why are you whispering?"

"I was thinking about this place."

"The Comfort Inn?"

"I'm thinking how I might drive by this place someday and point to it and tell somebody—nobody in particular—'Before I knew you, I stayed there once. See it? That place that looks like they built it in thirteen seconds? It's a part of my life.' And that person will nod but not really be interested, but say, 'Really? You stayed there, huh?' Then that person will ask me if I'm hungry, because at that point that person will be hungry and not in the mood for any stories."

August 13, 1945

*We're under strict orders not to mention recent events —
Suffice it to say that all the officers met in the captain's
stateroom and split a quart of whiskey into nine drinks — the
captain proposed a toast—"to eternal peace!" — We were
amazed to learn over the radio that so many people in the
States wanted war to continue over what appears to be a
mere quibble over words—whether or not the emperor keeps
his title or whatnot—What's the matter with those people?
We out here know what a drubbing the Japs have taken —
Not without loss to us—But if this should prove to be a Jap
trick, which hardly seems within the realm of reason, nothing will stop us from wiping them off the face of the earth —*

The Comfort Inn

I t's not my hormones."

"What are you saying, then?"

That motel room, the wet heat, Kat's hand melting the window.

"Don't ask me what I'm thinking if you don't want to know."

"I don't get it."

"This isn't anything new."

"It's that fucking Hansel in your program."

"Hans. It's not Hans. I said it's nobody in particular. I wasn't sure, Popper. From before the baby—from before any idea of any baby—and you know it. Don't pretend this is out of nowhere with your selective—"

"You weren't sure?"

He looked at the terrible, perfect, unstained carpet. Popper had the feeling—not for the first time—that his life was largely made up of overheard dialogue from the other side of somebody else's wall. It made him think of listening to his parents in the kitchen. Not what they said to each other, never what they said, but the indifference with which they said it, and the indifference of the kitchen.

"All right, I slept with Lindy Schwartz."

"What?"

"I said I slept with Lindy Schwartz."

"You did? The bitch. When?"

"Senior year. When you were in Cincinnati for your aunt's funeral. And your friend in your program, the one from Paraguay with the little glasses—every time I see her, I want to climb across the table."

"Sofia Galeano?"

"That's right. And also—"

"Popper, stop confessing."

"Fuck you."

"I'm trying to be kind. Don't try and stop me from being decent. There must be a way to do this—"

"Hansel and Gretel. And what? He gets my little piggy, too?"

"I'm not talking about anybody else. Don't you see it would be easier to explain if there was? Chekhov doesn't need any easy devices."

"Chekhov?"

She took her hand off the glass and looked at her palm, then pressed it into her stomach.

"Nobody's getting your piggy."

"Why now, of all times—"

"Wouldn't now be better?"

"I suffocate you."

"That's closer."

1233 NORTH DAMEN

At first he thought it was the old people across the fence, but this screaming wasn't coming from outside the apartment.

The guy at the hardware store said a glue trap is supposed to kill them more humanely, but if it were me, the guy said, and I wanted to get rid of something, I'd buy a normal trap and break its neck clean and easy.

"Give me the glue trap," Popper said.

But it does not kill. It merely glues. The mouse eeks in terror. All night long, stuck to a pad. Popper listens, he watches the walls. You never see a room more clearly than after someone leaves it and a mouse is begging for its life in the kitchen. The pale green walls, the scattered pockmarks, the pictures she took, the pictures she left. She left his license plate collection. She left her framed Billy Bragg poster. Not just love that's unrequited, it's everything. And then you get glued.

All night long, the little screams. At dawn, it's quiet. He saw what passes for the sunrise in Chicago more often in those months than any other time in his life. That unhesitant cement dawn, like pulling a sheet off a corpse. Popper goes to the kitchen and kneels beside the pad, leans in, tries to hear its breath. Can you hear a mouse breathe? The terror's gone. But the tiny stomach still rises.

376

One of us has got to kill it off, Popper, Nobody says. *You want me to do it?*

You think I can't? Nobody answers.

He goes outside to get a brick from under the steps. 1233 Damen, alone. Last days of February 1996.

ELLA

That part of him (a fraction) that wasn't watching himself watch the bloody scene proceed felt the whole ordeal was less the inspiring miracle it had been touted to be and more like some science experiment gone horribly wrong. Kat thoroughly embraced the chaos. She moaned with "wild abandon" like they'd taught her to in the class. Having a baby isn't the time to be inhibited! Having a baby is a time to roar! And before the drugs kicked in, she'd reached for him when the pain got to be too much. *I curse to hell every male of every species on the entire fucking planet, hold my arms—*

You want a cookie?

Hold my arms, Popper.

Ella Ottla Rubin-Popper. Born Northwestern Memorial Hospital, March 12, 1996, at 4:16 p.m. Height: tall, twenty inches. How'd that happen, parents being near-midgets? Weight: about as heavy as a small bag of groceries. Face: scrunched, folded, looks a lot like Great-grandmother Wasserkrueg, actually.

———

When he ran out to the nurse's station and called Miriam, he had to put the phone down, slobbering so much he couldn't speak.

"Oh, honey," Miriam said. "Can you believe it? In spite of the obvious complications, you're someone's father now. The only father she has in this entire world is you."

August 15, 1945

It's over!!!!!!!!!! Just five minutes ago the word came through — This afternoon we're going to knock off early and have holiday routine, with an extra beer ration — I can only imagine how it must be at home — All our prayers have been answered — Are you happy, darling?

5643 SOUTH BLACKSTONE, APT C

He has been told that daughters are supposed to take after their fathers. This apparent evolutionary precaution was inaugurated back in Paleolithic times to ensure that Barney Rubble wouldn't throw Bamm-Bamm against the wall of the cave. Popper looks, for hours he looks, but he can't find his own face in Ella's. Her mother's face, her coffee eyes, the same small wings of nose and slight downcurve of the pointy tip, the little nodge above her chin — all her mother's — and the way she kept her mouth closed, always, until she laughed.

She had, though, his cold hands. The doctor said poor circulation isn't necessarily hereditary and that with proper diet and normal development —

Popper will take what he can get.

"This is my kid."

"Who said she wasn't?"

"Wait, Bamm-Bamm *was* adopted. I just remembered the episode. Fred lent Barney his entire life savings so Barney and Betty would look like qualified parents."

"What about Pebbles?"

"No, Pebbles wasn't adopted."

Her stillness, her concentration. That didn't come from either of them. Where did she get it, then? In the beginning Kat got upset because she didn't cry enough. She was sure something was wrong. It soon became obvious that Ella was, very early, too busy paying attention to do much wailing. Miriam said that girls notice the rest of the world before boys do, and some men, well, you already know about some men, some men never do notice—

They gave rise to a watcher. Ella watched her parents with a detached but intense curiosity. It wasn't what they did that was so fascinating; it was only that, for the moment, they were the only show in town.

The weight of her, what he missed most in the other hours was the weight of her in his hands. Kat, her hair wet from the shower, takes Ella back into her arms. When Popper came over, she took some time for herself.

And when it was time to go, Ella watched her father out of the room, out the door. The Hyde Park night, the drive back home, north on the Dan Ryan.

ELLA

Kat telling him on the phone about waking up with Ella, and he heard nothing after that, only waking up with Ella, and still holding the phone, he went to the kitchen and pressed a fork into the veins of his wrist. *She sleeps like a holdup victim with her hands over her head. It's like she's practicing to get mugged... Popper?*

HYDE PARK MORNING

Other nights he stayed over. He'd take Ella back to the couch with him and coax her to sleep until she woke up hungry again. He shoved the coffee table next to the couch so if he fell asleep and lost his grip the kid wouldn't drop on the floor.

Here the light is different from the North Side. Something vinegar, almost sepia, about the light. Popper stands at the window and watches as the street begins to wake. The canopy of elms, their branches reaching, the row of cars, lumped one after the other, the cracked sidewalks running up and down both sides of the street like smaller, parallel streams. A man in a bowler and a camel-hair coat walks his dog while reading a novel. In front of the church across the street, there's a for-sale sign. *Call Judy Pabluca at Century 21 today!* It's a massive, feudal thing with giant iron doors, palace doors. Bang on those doors for an eternity and get no answer. Kat comes out of her room. She's dressed. Now when she comes out of her room in the morning, she's dressed.

"She asleep?"

"Finally. I think she hates that crib."

"Why don't you go back to sleep?"

"I tried. I can't. I feel berserk. Now I just need coffee."

"The church is for sale."

"I saw that. I wonder if the Pope knows."

"It's Christian Scientist."

"Mary Baker Eddy know?"

"I'm thinking about buying it."

"Need coffee."

"You're dressed. Six-thirty in the morning and you're dressed like I'm a guest."

"Popper, don't."

Miriam and Philip

The Wednesday before Thanksgiving, that mad scramble, and Popper has driven out to Highland Park early in preparation for tomorrow's holiday shuffle. First shift: brunch, with Miriam and Ralph and Ralph's terrible kids. (The twins, Brad and Cindy. *We aren't identical, but we certainly think alike!* Both have jobs downtown in finance. They both work out a lot and talk about it.) Second shift: Philip and Bernice, a lonelier, quieter, early dinner.

Leo's coming in from Washington in the morning.

Miriam calls and asks, since he's in town, if he wouldn't mind picking her up at the train. She's recently opened her own art gallery in Bucktown.

"If I'd known you were downtown, we could have driven together."

"You know how much I love the train. No offense, honey."

"Which train are you on?"

"The 5:19."

They no longer call the train the Chicago and Northwestern. Now it is called the Metra Rail. Metra must stand for something. In the crowd, getting off the 5:19, his mother appears, and then behind her, bobbing, his father. Popper watches his father tap his mother on the shoulder. Miriam turns. He can't see her face, but there is something about the way she throws her head back, slightly. Not the recognition of seeing an old friend after all these years. Not quite that. Yet there's something in her posture that pauses, it seems to Popper, though he still can't see her face, something that pauses and breathes, *Oh, it's you*. Another moment before either speaks. Popper watches the two of them talk a little. Together they walk toward the car. His mother peeks in the open passenger window.

"Honey, you don't mind giving your father a ride?"

"Huh?"

"His car's in the shop."

Philip yanks the door open and clambers into the backseat. He leans over and grazes Popper's cheek with his lips. His mother gets in and asks Philip if he has enough room.

"It's your new husband that has the long legs."

(Miriam jolly laughter.)

Popper hasn't been alone with them together since the Iran hostage crisis.

"Beautiful day," Philip says.

"It is," Miriam says. "It really is."

"My parents," Popper says, and this startles them. Philip and Miriam giggle. Who, us? We're not parents; we're just two people who happened to get off the 5:19 at the same time.

"My parents," Popper repeats, but he can't think of anything more to add. He drives toward the house on Riparian Lane. It isn't that he expected some sort of fireworks. It's only that one would think proximity would change the equation. Being apart for years is an abstraction. When you are so close that you can feel someone on your skin even if you don't touch — shouldn't that make for a reaction?

"Where's Ella?" Philip says.

"She's with Kat," Popper says. "Her parents are in town from Ashland. I have her most of Friday."

"You know, you really must see a judge, get something on paper like your mother and I. Establish some clear rights. Not this loosey-goosey—"

"The last thing I want to emulate is—"

"What if she moves out of state? What's to stop her from taking the kid and moving out of state?"

"He's still hoping they get back together, Phil—"

"No, I'm not. Who told you that? Leo?"

"Let's talk about something else," Miriam says.

"Happy Wustrin died," Philip says.

"I know, I *know*. Can you believe it? We've begun to die."

"Was she still with Ira?"

"God no, Phil. Where have you been? She left Ira eons ago."

The two of them chatting. In the rearview his father's eyes sag. The droop of all the years without her.

September 9, 1945

What a thrill I had the other day when we finally received our mail—Fourteen letters, no less—Was that delicious?—I spent all one afternoon just going over them—You simply cannot imagine what mail can mean—My only regret was that all fourteen were not from you—

The Law of Intent

At John Marshall, Popper's mind mostly roamed backward. But he liked to hear all about other people's problems for a change. He found that the study of law, finally, boiled down to this, case after case after case of other people's problems. And the pure volume of pages of these problems battered his consciousness into a comatose submission that wasn't at all unpleasant. It gave his brain somewhere to go.

He especially loved trusts and estates. Who didn't leave what to whom. The most personal agonies played out in the most turgid prose, prose he also was starting to emulate in the conversations he was beginning to have with himself.

You'd think to the contrary but criminal law, by far, was the most tedious. Everything tends to go completely downhill after the excitement of a crime itself. Procedural questions were especially numbing, though he appreciated the spirit behind the general rule (riddled with exceptions) that a thousand of one's past crimes couldn't be used, per se, to prove one's guilt in an instant case.

One issue, however, concerning the question of criminal intent (*mens rea*), couldn't help but intrigue. How do we determine intent of the perpetrator in so-called crime-of-passion cases? In other words, those murder cases where there was no pre-planning, when intent wasn't formed until the very heat of the moment. You come home from work early. Surprise. Your wife's in bed with your best friend. So you strangle your wife. (Your friend escapes out the window in his underwear.) That sort of case. Now the crux is this: At what point between the seeing (surprise) and the strangling (I'll kill you with my bare hands) did the requisite *mens rea* to prove murder in the first degree form? Or did it? Was the murder simply a reflex devoid of any intention at all? In such a case, we're looking at a manslaughter conviction at most. Now, what about those people who are less decisive? The irony is that hesitators fare worse in cases like these. The guy who wants to talk things over with his wife (you know, process it) before he wrings her neck. Popper counts himself in this camp. Whatever the decision—murder, what to have for lunch, which book to read—he'll take an hour to make up his mind. And the more time it takes a person to decide, the more evidence there is of intent. Hence, don't be a thoughtful murderer.

"Did I wake you up?"

"I don't know."

"What are you doing?"

"Thinking about manslaughter. Or dreaming about it. I don't know."

"Ella's imaginary friend died."

"Chauncey?"

"Yeah."

"She said he died?"

"She said he got hit by a bus tonight. At Stony Island and 57th. Squashed."

"Any indication the driver saw Chauncey and didn't stop intentionally? We might have an action against the CTA."

"What?"

"Tell her I'm sorry. Is she sad?"

"She's being pretty stoic about it. Shouldn't she be sadder? How are we supposed to know? What time will you be here tomorrow?"

"I've got class till eleven. What time is yours?"

"Three. Can you take her from 11:30 to 2:30?"

"Okay."

"Okay. So, see you—"

13

WE INVENTED THE SPIRAL NOTEBOOK

Is the past a story we are persuaded to believe in,
in the teeth of the life we endure in the present?

—Wright Morris, *Plains Song*

The Judges

Chicago, 1998

The old judges may no longer swim naked in the Standard Club pool.

Women. Time was they weren't even allowed in the club. And now? But the judges, the ones who are left—Abe Marovitz turned ninety-two this year and still does his laps—don't complain. They of all people know what to expect. Who knows better than they the tide of this reprehensible epoch? Respect, there simply isn't any respect anymore. Enthroned, impassive in their Civic Center courtrooms, they watch the world litigate its way to madness. Louis Brandeis is dead and gone and unremembered. And Picasso on the outside does nothing for the culture inside. It doesn't matter who you are anymore, and lady lawyers strut into court in pants. Yet even now, as they swim their laps in bathing trunks, they wonder if it was ever true—if the world, their world, was really any better. Lunches in the Walnut Room at the Bismarck Hotel. Long dinners with their beautiful wives at Gene & Georgetti's or Mike Fish's. Black-tie nights at the opera, Puccini on the Plains. Now they're sure of nothing. Were their wives ever beautiful? Were they ever as grand in life as they were in the stories they told themselves? Or was it all as much an illusion as the sight of a two-piece bathing suit emerging from the chlorine-drenched mist—

by God, a bikini—on this the deck of their sacred Standard Club pool. *You're in contempt, madam! Bailiff, please remove her!* Even the water—that first engulfing isn't the same. You need to feel it like a return to the womb. A Speedo doesn't cut it—the ancient dick needs to wiggle free. It will never be the same.

38 SYLVESTER PLACE

Highland Park, 1977

I n the attic of the house on Sylvester Place was a baby carriage, an old-style one with big white-wall tires and spoked wheels and a coffin-like black rubber hood. It was Philip's and then Esther's, and long since retired. But Leo found a use for it. He ordained it the final resting place of the ghost baby.

It was hard not to think of death in the attic with all that dead stuff. A hamper full of old nightgowns. A pile of worn-out ballet slippers that still, when Popper put his nose in, smelled sweetly of sweat. He found it fitting somehow that sweat outlasts the work it took to make it.

Because didn't they have something dead also? Miriam had told them they'd had another brother once. That he hadn't lived long. He hadn't lived at all, actually, but that doesn't mean he hadn't existed.

Popper would put on one of Bernice's flowered shower caps and play the hauntboy. He'd lie in the carriage with that shower hat on his head and his feet hanging over the side and Leo would push him around the attic and softly whisper to him all the things he'd missed by not being alive, like, for instance, Watergate.

"What else happened?"

"We went to the moon. At first it was a big deal. After that nobody much cared unless the rocket blew up."

"What else?"

"Ford pardoned Nixon."

"Come on —"

"Mom left Dad in the dust."

"That hasn't happened yet."

"You don't know that."

"I don't get it."

"You don't know anything. You've been in the ground all these years."

"What was my name?"

"You would have been Leo."

"And you?"

"Alexander, I would have been Alexander. Mom told me once they picked out two names beforehand —"

"And me?"

"Which you?"

"You know what I'm asking."

"I'm not sure you really get the full importance of the Ford pardon. You see, on the one hand, Ford had the country to think about, and on the other, his own skin, and for once a politician —"

Popper went by 38 Sylvester Place the other day. That house always felt bigger when you were in it than when you were standing outside. The new owners painted the shutters the wrong color. They're supposed to be rusty. Now they're blue. Blue shutters on the house at 38 Sylvester Place? When Leo drove him around in that carriage, all the old attic dust would kick up, and it would combine with the light streaming in through the windows. He'd reach out, try and wrap his hand around that dust.

BERNICE

Now you ask questions? Why bother with any of it anymore? It's a mistake, Alexander, to love the dead too much. The dead are easy. They can't kick you back.

You aren't dead.

It was my father who started me dancing. In Warsaw, he'd once gone to the ballet. It was Petipa's *The Pharaoh's Daughter.* The man could never get those dancing mummies out of his head. As soon as I could stand, my father had me up on my toes. My mother thought it a waste of time. You see, my mother wasn't interested in anything that wouldn't pay. As a young girl, just out of teacher's college, she'd gone to work for P. K. Wrigley as his personal secretary. Everybody in her family was impressed. My mother wasn't impressed. She said Mr. Wrigley's teeth stank. The man manufactures every stick of chewing gum in the universe and get a load of that—the man's teeth stink. P. K. Wrigley didn't hire my mother because she was beautiful. He had other girls to look good. He hired her because she was good with figures. She was still working for Wrigley when she met my father. He was ten years older, born in Warsaw. They met on the street. The family said she was marrying beneath her. A man you met on the street? A foreigner? My mother said, Beneath what? Besides, aren't I thirty? Not only was my father not even an American, he also stuttered when he spoke English. Yiddish he didn't stutter. Now in those days of course when you married you didn't work. And so the family said, *You're tossing over P. K. Wrigley for a filthy Polack?* This from a family of Jews from Poland. What could she do? She loved the man. My father owned a bookbindery with his brothers. He bound bibles, law books, all sorts of books. He used to say, "Anything between two covers, I can bring it t-t-t-together." A year after they were married, my parents bought a triple-decker in Rogers Park, 7232 Fargo Avenue. They rented out the other two apartments. My mother said, "This is how the rich must do it. Sit in a chair, do nothing, collect money." We lived on the middle floor. She wanted to be able to keep an ear on both tenants. When the market went under, my parents couldn't keep up with the payments. We lost Fargo Avenue. My father's bindery went under, too. After that they opened the store on Pratt Boulevard and my father began, slowly, to die. Even so, Alexander, a happy marriage. Who ever heard of such a thing? And no one can say that my mother wasn't bright. I didn't get any of her brightness. Wish I did. I was an only child, all she had, a disappointment. She'd grab ahold of my chin and say— *Bernice, of all the ridiculous. Take a wink of me. A wink of your father. Us still peasants and you swan around the Gish sisters? You'll end up without a roof.* She was wrong about the roof. You know, I always say I gave up dancing because I married Seymour. But how to say this other than just to say it? I didn't have the talent to make it in New York and so I came home and married Seymour. Then the children, then the war, and how could anybody dance seriously during the war? Maybe this is even true. After I became afraid of dancing it didn't matter what I did.

But you taught it, Granbean, for years and years, you taught—

That's not dancing.

September 12, 1945

I must admit it was a thrill to sail up Tokyo Bay and see our fleet—what a tremendous sight—battleships, cruisers, carriers, destroyers, Liberties, tankers, LSTs and MSMs—as far as the eye can see. Ships, ships, ships—What a magnificent demonstration of American power! Oh, darling, what can't this country accomplish?

Van Buren and LaSalle

T he steady rain softly pelting his head, Popper was standing
on the corner. Even though the light had changed, he was
still waiting for it—or waiting for something. Like when you
wake up and try to will yourself back into a dream, you wait for a
story that won't return? He watched the world through the rain.
He'd gone someplace else, someplace far, when someone clamped
his elbow and squeezed it—hard.

"Nellie! Where's your bonnet?"

"Leah Harvey?"

The two of them stood in the rain and talked for a few
moments before parting. Popper pretended not to look her over
as he looked her over. He coughed into his hand and peeked. A
squat woman in a pinstripe suit, no makeup on her healthy red
cheeks. Squat but not unstately, Marthalike in her poise, in her
direct stare. She stood her ground on the sidewalk. People didn't
jostle Leah Rosencrantz, they arced around her. She looked Popper over and didn't pretend not to. Found him barely passable. He
felt a dig of lust pierce his gut.

The years have ground the Rosencrantzes down to a more
Popperish size. Like their father before them, they are lawyers in
this city. Leah does estate planning, which was what Hal did after

403

Abrahamson and Smoot collapsed in the mid-nineties. Eli's a junior partner at Rothstein, Korshak, and Preskill. Neither Leah nor Eli has become as successful as their father in his heyday. At what point do we become our limitations?

Alexander Popper? He works for the Cook County Public Defender, where he handles mostly misdemeanor cases, petty vandalism, petty theft, trespassing, an occasional assault and battery, a little drunk and disorderly, some moral turpitude. Nothing he couldn't imagine himself committing on a bad day. He's always felt most at home around the guilty. But even guilt's no requirement. All that counts is to be accused.

All these years and they've never run into each other on the street.

"I've got a daughter now," he said.

"I know. Your mother told my mother. Mazel tov."

"They talk?"

"Why not? See you, Nellie. I've got a hearing."

Popper waved. Leah waved. They both crossed the street at the same time. There was that weirdness that happens after you've said goodbye to someone but you are both still walking in the same direction.

"Well."

"Well."

"Okay, then."

"Right. So long."

Popper stopped in the middle of the intersection and scratched the underside of his knee. He watched her stomp down LaSalle with the rest of the crowd. All the umbrellas like bobbing mushrooms. In the rain, in Chicago, everybody looks alike. Popper, baffled by the ruthless piling of the years, gazes up at the Board of Trade, looming at the end of the block like a giant stopper.

They don't call this the Loop for nothing. *Loop, deloop, deloop.* Here I am myself again. Nobody as exiled as people who never leave home. He's got a pre-trial conference for a shoplifting case in an hour. The defendant stole eight perfume bottles from Field's. ("Why eight?" Popper had asked. "They were on sale," she said.)

Hey, Leah, you want to grab a beer sometime?

GUN SAFETY PRECAUTIONS

1. Never point a rifle or pistol at anyone you do not intend to shoot.
— *Bluejackets Manual*, page 102

105 Riparian Lane

I'll sue you for libel."

"Wouldn't it be slander? I haven't written anything. It's only a verbal accusation, and it's not even an accusation. I'm only asking you."

They're on the back patio. Philip is on his knees, weeding along the low wall where some years he grows long-stem roses. Beside his knees is a tall glass of iced tea with a floating lemon wedge. He tugs up another weed, long, dirty-rooted, and tosses it to Popper.

"Throw it in the basket, will you?"

"Come on, it was a long time ago. No harm, no foul. Statute of limitations. Did you rob the White Cedar apartment?"

His father used to say phooey when he got angry. Leo and Popper have lampooned this for years. It always came out fast, in a rush of spit, more like *Fwi! Fwi! Fwi!* But Philip's calm now. He only says, "Enough with the goddamn law. I'm tired of it. I'm going to give it up in three years. Now I just want to garden."

"You only took Mom's engagement ring and a ring of your grandmother's that Grandbean gave Mom when you guys got married."

Philip took a sip of tea.

"More lies, lies upon lies."

Popper thinks of the way his father used to comb his hair for him when he refused to do it himself, mashing the teeth of the comb across Popper's scalp. He's never used a comb since. And he thinks, though later he will not even admit to himself that he thought it, Who knew? Like me, true, no argument on that from me. But my father? A nobody? The garage door would begin its slow upward grind, and everybody in the house would run for cover, like it was Ahab home from the sea. Who were we running from?

"What about the couch?"

His father's face doesn't move, but his hands dig deeper into the soil.

"What couch?"

"Upstairs in the TV room. The green couch. When you threw Mom—"

"Is this an ambush? You come here after how many months of not setting foot? Is it a year now? You live a half hour away. I see my own granddaughter, what, every six months? And this is what you come to talk about?"

"Ella doesn't like the suburbs. She cries the entire ride out here."

"I did not rob your mother's apartment, and I certainly never threw her on any couch."

Nothing has changed, nothing has ever changed. The fountain still burbles, the turtle still drools. The turtle will never stop drooling. And the boy holding him? Popper wonders if there really is a dick under there or if the sculptor put a leaf to cover up only what people would expect needed covering up.

"Do you still hate Hal Rosencrantz?"

"Hal? He's dead, leave him be. Leave us all be."

"I mean, you two were pretty close friends, so it must have—"

"Alex, in those years everybody was sleeping with everybody. And don't kid yourself, everybody is always sleeping with everybody. Your mother and I, that wasn't our problem. Forget Hal Rosencrantz. Miriam and I had zero in common. Any idiot could have seen that a mile away. What's the big story?"

His father's hair is thinner now and wispy. The wind makes it flap upward, as if it's hinged.

"I'm only trying to build a record."

Philip stands and leans toward him and nearly gently kisses Popper's neck.

"You're building ruins."

To: Ella
FROM: Your Father
RE: Questions of Cowardice

When I'm not with you I spend a lot of my day thinking about things that happened before you even existed. I much prefer this to actually working.* A few years ago I got mugged. I was riding on the path through Lincoln Park by the lake and a guy—he wasn't much more than a kid—jumped out from behind one of those cement planters and knocked me off my bike. This was the second time in my life that happened to me. The other time I was little and on my way to your Uncle Manny's. I was as scared a few years ago as I was when I was six. So this kid knocks me off and takes my bike and rides away down the path. The sort of thing I deal with every day at work. Assault and battery. Class 2 robbery (unarmed). I pretended to chase him. Later, I told people he had a knife to make the story better. He didn't. He was able to take my bike because he scared the hell out of me. I'm not sure if this makes me a

---

*Munchkin, this is what we call in legal jargon "putting a note in the case file," in other words, something to be filed away and never read by human eyes (unless it's subpoenaed or found while scavenging a dead man's papers).

coward. Maybe it does. But also, it's true, I've never much believed in chasing people. Nobody is more determined than a person running away. This is about the only thing I know for certain. Your mother wanted something else. She wasn't sure what, but she wanted something else. Nothing in your nature suggests that you will ever blame her. Nor do I think you'll ever blame me for not trying harder to change her mind. But we do tend to judge our fathers. For what exactly, we don't always even know.

In the New House

In the kitchen of the new house on Ridge Road, west of the highway. Years since they sold the 38 Sylvester Place house and still they call it the new house. Nobody ever remembers the address. Only that it's a block off Lake Cook Road, near Northbrook Court. Maroon brick house, white roof.

The two of them, two cups of cold Folgers, the afternoon light slowly retreating, a deer idly munching the brown grass in the little backyard.

"It's time I told you," Bernice said. "We invented the spiral notebook."

"Say again?"

"My father. At our kitchen table in 1919. I was standing by his elbow when it finally worked. He'd been at it for years and years. The man was a real perfectionist. One day he did it. He invented the spiral notebook. But a cousin, a lawyer by the name of Gus Hirsch, tricked him out of the patent. Never trust a lawyer, even if you're related, especially if you're related."

"Granbean, walk three feet in this family and you step on a lawyer."

Bernice swatted the air. "I'm talking about my own father. I'm talking about Slanskys, not Poppers. Imagine the money! Every time anybody in the universe buys a spiral notebook, we're supposed to make at least three and a half cents on the dollar. I choreographed a little dance in my father's honor. *The Notebook Dance.* I wish I remembered it."

It could even be true. Popper's great-grandfather Louie was a bookbinder, this much is certain. Popper has in his possession an Illinois Blue Book from 1922. Slansky Brothers, Printers, 148 Monroe St., Chicago. There's only one surviving photograph of the man. In it he is standing alone, a big-eared, scrunch-faced man with small hands that he is holding out in front of him like these empty hands are all he has to offer. Think of the man sitting at the kitchen table tinkering (years of him sitting at that kitchen table tinkering) with wire and paper. Tinkering and tinkering until one day, *voilà*—How do you say *voilà* in Yiddish?—you can turn the page and turn the page! *Hey, Louie, call a lawyer. You ought to get a thing like this patented. What about Gus? Isn't Gus Hirsch a lawyer?* The rest being history, their history, the only thing that can't be ripped off by an unscrupulous cousin.

"But complain?" Bernice says. "Complain? My father? He loved this country even if it didn't make him rich. He was a simple man. He thought there was more to life than the money he'd never have. He'd come home from the bindery, collapse in his chair. I've never seen tiredness like my father's tiredness. My mother— she'd complain, she was the one who complained. Yes, she wanted something better, always something better, but there wasn't a day she didn't bring him a bowl of warm water to soak his hands in when he came from work. He'd walk around the house with bandaged hands, pretending to be a boxer, my little father."

The light in the kitchen fades. Neither of them bothers to flip the switch. They are no longer in the not-so-new house on Ridge Road, this house they never look at, never remember, but instead are back on Sylvester Place. Seymour coughs in his study. He's reading. In the den with the big picture window the TV talks to no one. The living room remains an unsealed tomb. His grandmother, her hair—still beauty-shop perfect. Her face, her wartime starlet eyes.

"Enough about me. What about you? Anybody new on the horizon?"

"Nobody much."

"How's Ella?"

"She wants a dog, a big one, a St. Bernard."

"Get her a stuffed one. Bring her next time. I promised her I'd teach her to pirouette."

"I will. How come you've never liked dogs? Something happen when you were small or something? Did you get bit during the Depression or something?"

"Talk about you. You're suffering?"

"No, I'm not suffering. Who said I was suffering?"

"Right, because there's suffering and there's suffering, and you know the difference. You've told me. They suffer in India. A little, you're suffering a little? From your divorce?"

"We never got married."

"Good for you. Who needs it?"

"Anyway, it's been almost three years now. I'm fine. How can we get some of this spiral notebook loot?"

"You call three years 'years'?"

"What do you call them?"

"Pinpricks, Alexander."

"It's true, days feel swallowed sometimes. I mean Ella, seeing Ella, but—"

He stops, shrugs. They both look away from each other and

try to find some place in this near-empty kitchen to moor their eyes. Popper looks out the curtained window; Bernice at the digital clock. 6:37.

"You've always been sad. Even as a boy you were sad."

"I'm fine."

"You're letting your hair grow a little. That's good. You've lost some weight."

"I have?"

"Roll up your sleeves. Let me see the backs of your arms."

"All right."

"Dry, always so — Seymour always said that even men —"

"I know, I know."

October 5, 1945

 And now for the big news—You can step up and call me Captain—captain of an overwith war—I took over command yesterday when the skipper finally got relieved to go home— He was such a nervous wreck, another day on this boat and we would have had to carry him off—For the last few months he couldn't eat anything without having violent gas pains— So yesterday we had to close out all the books and records and change command, which is just like closing a million-dollar deal—But it's you, Beanie, who deserves the promo-tion to Chief House Frau—You've proved yourself a whole lot better than the common clay through this entire ordeal—

Brooks Brothers Afternoon

Philip roams Brooks Brothers like a leopard in his own jungle. This particular hue of blue all his. Today, though, he's not on the prowl. He's come in for—

What has he come in for?

A suit salesman gradually approaches. He's got a pronounced limp that makes him sway from side to side as he moves soundlessly across the thick carpet. Longish face. Eyes set forward in his head, not quite buggy, but almost. Large fleshy nose. Not a handsome man, Philip thinks. Yet not without dignity in his homeliness. Old, though, very old, even too old to be selling suits. Wonder where Charlie is.

"What can I do for you, Counselor?"

"How did you know I was an attorney?"

"You have that look about you. A man in charge. Important affairs. A briefcase full of secrets. What's on your mind today, sir?"

Philip's not sure what to say. *I've only come here for refuge.* How would this sound? He stares at the unfamiliar salesman. The salesman looks for a moment at Philip's cordovans, then back at Philip's face, as if he's begun to understand. His eyes moisten slightly. *There is comfort in our blueality. I know it. You know it. Nothing to be ashamed of. Here the harshness of the world is lessened.*

"Where'd you get the limp?" Philip says.

"Born with it," the salesman says.

"Oh," Philip says. He'd like to lean up against the false mahogany and whistle. Just passing the time. "So you weren't in the war?"

"No."

"My father was in the South Pacific. Saw action at Okinawa. Terrible scene. Lucky he didn't get his head shot off."

The salesman nods respectfully. The store is mostly empty. A couple of younger salesmen murmur to each other in the back. No sign of Charlie.

"So," Philip says, setting his briefcase on the carpet. "How's the spring line?" Again as one Brooks man to another. He only wants to talk a little shop with someone on the inside.

"Seersucker's back," the salesman says.

"Again?"

"In yellow and pale blue."

"Hmmmmm," Philip says. "Hmmmm. Anything else?"

"They're bringing back the three-button."

"The three-button? When did they get rid of it?"

"Last year. It was foolish. Last year everything was two-button with double vents."

Double vents. Awful. A kinsman.

"You haven't been here long," Philip says.

"No. I've been out in the suburbs. Transferred here last month."

"Transferred? Like in the Army."

"In a way," the salesman says. "We are, after all, on the front line of fashion."

The salesman and Philip laugh together. When they stop, Philip says quietly, "It's lonely, moving around like that?"

He's feeling a little wobbly. Drunkish at 4:00 in the afternoon on a Monday? Lonely? What's he talking about?

The salesman nods and half smiles. He doesn't show his teeth unless he has to. Again, it's as if he understands what Philip's getting at in spite of the fact that Philip isn't sure himself what he's trying to say.

"You get attached to a place," the salesman says.

"I've been in the same office on the sixteenth floor of the Monadnock for as long as I remember," Philip says.

The salesman breaks in, he can't help himself. "I've worked everywhere. Southside, Northside. Northwest suburbs. I was at the Brooks in Woodfield Mall for seven years."

"In Schaumburg? Good God, man."

"At Lake Forest for another five or so. That took endurance, too."

"Snoots," Philip says. "When you're born up there, the doctor shoves a polo stick up your ass."

"So you know!" The salesman practically yelps.

"Jews know all about Lake Forest."

The salesman rolls back on his feet and laughs harder now, and again, he and Philip—kinsmen—laugh together until neither of them is laughing anymore but they're still laughing.

"Not a religious man myself," Philip says.

"Neither me," the salesman says. "Still, you drag it along."

"That's right," Philip says, and reaches for a display of belts hanging nearby. They look like a set of decapitated tongues. He reaches for one and fondles it. "Alligator?"

"Cowhide," the salesman says.

True, Brooks has never been known for its leather. Even so, Philip thinks, you can never have enough quality belts.

"Say," Philip says, "what happened to dear old Charlie?"

"Charlie Hubbard?" the salesman says. "Oh, they sent Charlie out to pasture."

Philip grips the belt. Charlie, who sold him his suits for decades. Stories about growing up on a dairy farm in Wisconsin. Always sucking a cough drop that made him slur his words when he talked. One about a boot getting lost in the muck. Having to hop back to the house on one foot. And in the spring of that year, a shoot of corn growing up out of that boot!

He thinks of Charlie in a seersucker suit on all fours in a field munching grass. When this city's through with you, it spits you home to Oshkosh. It'll happen to us all. We've all got our Oshkoshes.

"Oshkosh," Philip burbles. Still wobbly.

"I'm sorry, sir. I didn't catch that."

"Oshkosh," Philip says. "Oshkosh, Wisconsin."

Again the salesman nods. Again, he seems to get it. He gets Oshkosh. When the world is through with you, it spits you home to— *Who is this person?* Philip thinks. Philip wonders. He tries to look in the salesman's eyes, but doesn't get very far. It's as if the man's eyes are varnished over. He's hiding somewhere in there and Philip can't find him. *Uncle Mose? But you've been dead a thousand years.* This is all very off. We stumble from late fall to early winter. Where did that come from? Did I read it somewhere? Dizzier now, discombobulated. Brooks Brothers afternoon. Outside, the steam rises from the vents in the sidewalk, the underground boilers, a burbling cauldron beneath these streets. In here a sinkingness, a muffled feeling, not at all unpleasant. The salesman might be saying something else, but his voice is so far away now.

Night, Golf

He comes to him in the night and orders Popper to play golf. Recognizing the turrets of a castle rising in the distance, Popper says, "Hey, isn't this Migweth Country Club? Why don't you play at your own club? I thought they don't allow Jews here."

"Dead ones are all right," Seymour says. "And I'm entitled to bring a guest."

"I loathe golf and everything it stands for. Do you know how many homeless people could live on a golf course?"

"Don't give me the business."

They play. Seymour tees off. Beautiful, arcing, heavenward, 250 yards at least.

"Nice," Popper says.

Seymour smiles. "I've been playing five, six days a week lately." He smiles some more. His teeth are very white.

Popper tees off. Twenty-seven yards with a kerplunking divot the size of a small farm.

"Shoulders down. Widen your stance three degrees."

Our dead, the distances they travel to reach us. Popper's comes in a golf cart wearing plaid, spikes on his shoes.

They drive, slowly, toward Popper's ball. It's not very far. Popper gets out again. His feet, his bare sleeping feet, sink in the soft loamish ground. It feels lovely, actually. No wonder this place is so exclusive. He hits the ball again. Maybe thirty-five yards this time. Still, Seymour doesn't comment, nor does he question why Popper used a 9 iron when his ball is still practically on the tee. No, as they move down the fairway under the tall trees, Seymour chats. Here's the thing, though. Seymour's mouth moves at the wrong times. It doesn't correspond with his actual words. It's as though he's been badly dubbed.

Popper's ball whacks a tree and flings backward for his longest shot yet, yardwise, and lands in a sand trap. Seymour is a big plaid paragon of support and patience.

"Bravo! There's the killer instinct!" Popper gets back in the cart. His grandfather grips him by the shoulder. "So what's the latest?"

"I'm a lawyer."

"Passed the bar and everything?"

"Took it twice, but on the second—"

"Marvelous!"

"Marvelous?"

"What else you got cooking?"

"I don't want to talk about it."

"Ah hell, Alexander, don't you know you've got it all? You know it's a hoot. I see Brezhnev at the driving range—he doesn't play, he only scowls at the bourgeoisie—and I say, 'Hey, Lenny, loosen your balls a little, huh? It's all over now. There's a McDonald's across the street from the Kremlin.' Talk to me, kid. You think getting here was easy?"

"Do you remember Kat?"

"Funny girl? Had a tongue, that one. I always liked her. Bleedyheart, but all you dopes are bleedyhearts."

"She left me for someone she hadn't met yet. Then she had the baby, ours. Your great-granddaughter—"

"And all this time I thought you were a poof!"

Popper gets out of the cart and heads to his ball in the sand.

"A what?"

"A poof! A fagela!"

"Oh. No, that's Leo. Why are you shouting?"

"Leo's a poof?"

"I think he'd object to poof. He's lived with Ahmed for six years. They're both lawyers in Washington. Leo works on the Hill."

"Ahmed?"

"They met at Tufts."

"Well, I knew some in the service. Never had a thing against them as long as they were discreet about it. Some of the very best men in the navy were poofs. And your papasha?"

"My what?"

"Phil, my boy, thrill of my loins, the old son of a gun!"

Seymour's eyes are still calm, mild. It's only that mouth — it's like one of those freaky fist puppets from the seventies that would talk in slow motion.

"You and he spent entire decades at each other's throats."

"Fathers and sons. But there's warp and woof all over, isn't there? Even, it's true, in the leading corporations. Go to a board meeting someday. And yet how it appears to outsiders isn't always how it is with people in their heart of hearts, if you know what I mean. Between Phil and me there was a lotta—"

"Heart of hearts is a phrase of my mother's."

"You think I never knew Miriam?"

"You're rewriting history."

"Shucks. Who do you think wrote it in the first place? You replace my lies with yours and call it what happened? Who cares. Tell the little tiger I miss him, roar! Roar!"

Above, the honk of geese. Little green shits plop from the sky. Seymour in the golf cart, his feet up on the little hood, his yellow socks. Popper in the sand trap. He swings at his ball and misses.

"I thought you knew."

"Knew what?"

"Last year, Dad had a heart attack at Brooks Brothers."

"Don't laugh at your own father."

"I'm not laughing."

His mouth will not move. "Stop it. Honor thy!"

"I'm not laughing."

"It's cruel."

Seymour gets out of the cart and joins Popper in the sand. His bald, sunburned head. His face begins to cave in. Eyes and nose fall inward, mouth and jaw disintegrate. He lies down and begins to pull sand over himself until all that's left of him are his hands and forearms and the mush of what's left of his head.

"I thought you knew. He's buried right—"

"When did you become cruel?"

A Pleasure Dome

Highland Park, 1972

Coleridge by flashlight. Philip doesn't try to sell the poem. He just tells it, and though there are parts he has long since memorized, *In Xanadu did Kubla Khan,* Philip repeats the words as if he doesn't know them at all, as if this is the first time he's heard about any of this, as if he's reading about the Kubla Khan's fantasies out of today's news, and Popper lingers on the bluff of sleep, his father's voice faint, as if from miles away.

Kubla Khan telling his slaves, *Listen, I want you to build me a good-time dome down in Xanadu. I want sunshine and I want ice. This place is going to be so fantastic even the rocks are gonna dance, follow me? And hey and I want this thing built fast, I'm getting word from people in the know that there's war coming, I want to have some excellent times before all hell breaks loose in the kingdom.*

Later, Popper will learn that it was all some freaky English dope dream and Xanadu was no more real than the town of Bedrock, but that will never take away his father knowing the story but reading as if he didn't know a thing about it, like he'd never heard of any Khan or any pleasure dome deep in a hole in the earth — which is the only way to reread anything.

His mother's voice: *Is he asleep, Phil?* Quick touch of her lips on his eyelids. He can't raise his head off the pillow. Soundlessly, he shouts, *I'm not asleep!*

425

To: Ella
From: Your Father
Re: Conception

Your mother and I have told you that you were conceived during a heat wave. The verb conceived makes it
sound as though we knew what we were doing, but the fact
is, we had no idea. The heat wave killed hundreds of old
people. This was in the summer of 1995. It shouldn't have
happened. Not in our city, not anywhere. But what I want
to tell you is that your mom and I used to say, quietly, only
to each other, that of all those people who died, one of
them came back as you. God knows where we got this
idea. Maybe it's Buddhist or something. You know how
much eclectic reading your mother does. She must have
read it somewhere. I leave it to you to decide if it was ridiculous or whether we were on to something. My only point
is that we used to talk, your mom and I, and this was just
one small thing out of the thousands of other things we
said. I tell you this only so you know that you were born
out of that talking. One other thing. I remember looking at
you when you were still only a blur of tissue on a computer
screen. The lab technician pointed out the pumping of
your aorta. It looked like a yapping mouth in a tiny skull.
I'll never get over this.

December 3, 1945

Other than what to do with all these Jap prisoners stinking up my deck, the next most important topic around here is the making of a home—and getting a job—All the officers but one are recently married—They've never had a home, of course, and you should hear them talking about buying furniture and pots and pans—It's really a scream—

The Leaning Tower

The architect who designed it used a postcard of the real one, and he didn't do that bad a job. It leans. Except this leaning tower is only three and a half stories high and next door to a used-car lot in Niles. On their way home from cards at Twin Orchard Country Club, Bernice Popper and Gert Zetland always stop at a coffee shop across the street. Just a stupid funny thing. A whim of Gert's. Always made her think of her honeymoon in Italy, although they never made it to Pisa. Milt's stomach acted up in Rome. All that rich food.

They are sitting at their table by the window and Bernice is listening to Gert yatter on about her nephew Jerry, the maverick tort lawyer. They've both ordered egg salad sandwiches. Cars whiz by on Touhy Avenue. Occasionally someone slows down, someone who hasn't seen the tower before, and there's all kinds of honking.

What do you want to look at that fake thing for? Move it, move it. What are you, a tourist? In Niles?

"Did you hear Sid Kaufman died?" Bernice says.

"How could I not have heard?" Gert says. "It's like the Pope has passed. I'm waiting for the white smoke to rise from the Standard Oil Building. I mean, the man was a professional gossiper, for

God's sake. Now listen, Beanie, you're not going to believe this one…"

Gert's voice, after all these years, has become an almost pleasant background gurgle. Occasionally Bernice sighs over one of Jerry's triumphs. Hears none of it. She watches the busboy clear away the cups and crusty soup bowls, a young man with tapered black hair and invisible buttocks. She wonders what he sits on. If it hurts in the bones he doesn't even seem to have. Maybe he never sits. Maybe he never sleeps. Clears tables. Clears tables. There is no end to the clearing of our tables. Mexican, he probably crawled across the border in his underwear.

Gert reaches and pinches Bernice's forearm. "And so they offered eighty thousand to settle and Jerry says to them, 'Blow it out your nozzle.' Oh, I know he said something far more off-color, but that's what he told his delicate-eared aunt, always trying to protect me from anything untoward. He thinks I was born in the seventeenth century. Even people born in the seventeenth century weren't born in the seventeenth century. Blow your eighty thousand out your nozzle! Can you imagine?"

"Nozzle?"

"Nose, Bernice, nose. Blow it out your nose. What's wrong with you?"

Bernice waves her off. She sighs appreciatively over Jerry. Gert's hair frostier than usual today. It looks like if you touched it, you'd get snow on your fingers. She thinks of mountains. God knows where they were, somewhere north of here where there's mountains, Michigan maybe, and Seymour said, *Look, Bernice, look what the wind did. Like somebody came up here with a paintbrush.* He was right, Seymour, for once. The snow didn't even look cold. It looked like sugar. And she remembers being vaguely afraid of those trees, remembers thinking that the snow was cruel to be so deceptive. How long ago? Seymour insisting we go walking in the snow in the mountains, of all the cockamamie things, and us getting in the car and driving for hours. Were the children with us? I can't even remember.

"Why don't they tear that thing down already?" Bernice says.

Gert pauses her Jerry narrative and looks curiously at Bernice. "What thing?"

"That."

Oh, the tower. Gert laughs. Well, the tower. Who gives a damn about the tower? But Gert leans forward and looks into Bernice's glossy eyes and nearly gasps. She's withering. Poor darling. First Esther. Then Seymour. Then Philip. It's too much.

"And you know, I saw the real one," Bernice says. "And you know what?"

"What?"

"It's taller, but every inch as dull."

"Dear—"

Bernice ignores her, honks into her napkin, and says, "In fact, I hated Italy."

"You did?"

"They say the French are bad. Seymour said it was impossible, that nobody in their right mind had ever hated Italy, that nobody on the face of the earth had ever once hated a single thing about Italy—"

"Dear—"

"Yes?"

"Are you ogling the busboy?"

"What if I am? I'm an old bitty."

What do you say to that? Nothing, Gert thinks. You don't say anything to that. You let it go. These days you let a lot of things go.

"You know, during the war I had a man."

"Oh, Beanie, during the war everybody had a man. Milt was 4F and even I had a man."

Bernice looks down at her sandwich. "It was Sid."

"You and Sid Kaufman?"

"He didn't only go for actresses. Dancers also. Even washed-up ones. And I thought he was dashing until I knew him better. What a blowhard!"

"How long did it take for you to realize Sid Kaufman was a blowhard?"

"I almost left Seymour. Isn't that funny to think of now? I almost packed up the children and left and ran away with Sid. Hours and hours we'd talk about it. But he wasn't here to leave. How could I leave him if he wasn't here to leave?"

Gert watches Bernice, who is once again staring at the busboy, except she wasn't seeing him anymore. She was staring past him at someone or something or someplace long gone. She seemed asleep, everything about her seemed asleep except for her eyes.

"Bernice, aren't you going to finish your sandwich?"

THE OTTER

Chicago, 2001

Lincoln Park Zoo, October leaden-eyed sky, nobody around, father and daughter sit huddled, shoes touching, watching the otter. Occasionally the otter rises from the water, croaks, gnaws its teeth a little, squirms up over the lip of the pool, swaddles forward along the rocks, croaks some more, gets back in the water, swims, loops, climbs out again. Bury me, Popper thinks, at Lincoln Park Zoo, in the autumn, amid these scrawny trees and old copper-topped pavilions, all the sad animals. He wonders if he donated money he'll never have, if they'd let him rest from his labors here. Just a little patch of grass in some out-of-the-way corner by the flamingos.

Ella watches the otter with an attention he can't match. She slumps against him, how easily she slumps against him.

"I can't get enough of these fake volcanic rocks. Can you?"

"Mmmmm."

"Did you know that the land we are sitting on was formed by the recession of Wisconsin Glacial Episode? I'm not sure this involved any volcanic activity, but science, as you know, has never been my strong point. I've decided to try to learn something new every day, because I feel like I'm losing my memory, that moments are slipping through my fingers and that by collecting cold hard facts — Ella?"

"Mmmmm."

When Ella learned to talk, Popper tried to unlearn, but it hadn't taken.

"In Xanadu, what did Marco Polo do?"

"He went to the zoo," Ella says.

"Want to go to the lion house?"

"Stay here."

"Polar bear? Fat feet against the glass?"

"Nope."

"Want a Moderama?"

"Nope either."

"You don't want to see Kumba?"

"Later."

"The farm in the zoo? The goats, the sheep?"

"Closed."

"How do you know?"

"Here last week."

"With Mom? Why didn't you tell me?"

"Because the zoo is your thing."

She rarely calls him Dad. Sometimes she says it with her eyes, rarely out loud. Sometimes she adds it invisibly to the end of sentences.

"Aren't you cold?"

"I'm never cold."

I've sired a Chicagoan. If I am weak and my daughter is strong, does this not make me the father of strength?

The otter swims, sleek and eelishly through the water, that graceful surge, not ever having to think about it, surging forward and upward, rising above the surface without effort.

"You know, there's this concept in law called adverse possession. It's one of my favorites. It means if you stay in a place you don't own long enough, that place can become yours simply because you stuck around. So if we keep sitting on this bench for the statutorily required two years, this otter pond could be all ours."

"They'd kick us out. Security."

"Not if we remained very still. They'd think we were a couple of statues, Chicago's full of—"

Ella unslumps against him and blows into her hands.

"Where are your mittens?"

"Dunno."

She was constantly shedding clothes, dropping hats—So long, hat.

"Mittens cost money."

"I know."

"Ella?"

"Uh-huh."

"Do something for me?"

"What?"

"Leave here. At some point, when you're old enough. Your Mom and I will always be here and you can always come back to this city but I want you—"

"You just said—"

"I changed my mind. Go forth, kid."

"Wait."

"Wait for what?"

"Mmmmm."

"It's raining harder, Ella."

"Otter's not done swimming."

December 21, 1945

I just saw Meet Me in St. Louis—*That little girl was so cute, she reminded me so much of Esther I almost cried— What do you say, another one? Two? Well, baby, the rumor is now "Meet Me in San Francisco." And you're going to be there when we pull in—at the government's expense, too— My tongue is positively hanging out to see what you've done with the house—It was so cute of you to send those wallpaper samples—I've been walking around with them all day— the guys like the one with the tulips—Sweetheart, hold tight—We are going to have so much happiness in the future it's going to feel like exquisite torture—We'll never want to go to sleep—*

Capt. S. Popper
LST 504
F.P.O. San Francisco

January 16, 1946

Darling,

Today I surely expected a cable saying to meet you, but so far no such luck. Everyone is home now but you, that is all the people we know that went in the service, but of course that was not too many people.

Nothing new here. There's a meat cutters' strike on. We went to a concert at Orchestra Hall yesterday. Philip came downtown all by himself. Esther had her dancing lesson in the afternoon. Later, we all met Sid and Babette at the Blackhawk for dinner.

All the kids talk about is your homecoming, how they'll act, what they'll say, all the stories. You know, you left two babies almost two years ago—you're coming home to two almost-grown people. All I can say, darling, is that please forget any notion you might have about more family, frankly I am finished. I hope we will see eye to eye on this and most other things. Well, darling, here's hoping to hear from you quickly, I am waiting patiently for news.

Bernice

MIRIAM

Highland Park, 1979

She gets up early and sits at the kitchen table without coffee — coffee would come later — and faces not the graying windows but the rest of the house, where everyone lies asleep. No stranger here, but even so this isn't her house. She sits at the table wearing her frayed orange morning sweater. *I've lived here eleven years?* You leave a place long before you leave it. You float through the door a thousand times before you finally open it. She remembers the first time she saw this house, the long lawn stretching to the street, the iron benches outside the front door. The garage had these little red-and-white-striped curtains over the two small windows that had reminded her of the tablecloths at a roadside place her father used to take her for fried clams on Cape Cod, just on the ocean side of the Sagamore Bridge.

She thinks of Philip testing the drawers. "See this smooth slide? You can always judge the quality of a house by the bearings in the drawers. Do you like it?"

Yes, yes, how could anybody not like it? It's a wonderful house, Phil.

You think all you have to do is take root. Fill up the drawers with clothes, the cabinets with pots. She listens to the low growl of the refrigerator as the day begins to rise over the lip of the window.

Night Orders
March 5, 1946

En route from Ponape Is. to Yokohama in company with 29 LSTs. Base course 317° T. Speed 10 knots.

1. *Read standing night orders.*
2. *Be prepared for emergency breakdown signals.*
3. *Check watertight integrity throughout the night. Report every hour and <u>log it</u>.*
4. *Water the prisoners.*
5. *Wake me if in doubt or for any other unusual occurrences.*
6. *Do not stop for man overboard. No exceptions.*

S. Popper
Capt.

CARY AVENUE BEACH

You'll not find another place, you'll not find another sea.

—Baudelaire

Midwinter and the lake heaves ice slowly up the beach. Popper stands with his gloveless hands jammed in his armpits and watches the lake and listens to it groan. The remains of the jagged breakers rising out of the water like broken teeth. The cement sandbags at the bottom of the bluff, plumped and ripped, not stopping the erosion that will never be stopped. The lake is always east. East is always the lake. Anywhere else he's ever been he never knows where he is. Snow begins to fall slowly, like paint chips. Chunks of ice ride the bloated waves.

The lake is always smaller in January. It doesn't stretch itself out blue as far as you can see. It's contained, circumscribed, deadlier. If you fall in, you're a goner. It happens every year to one or two smelt fishermen, pulled down by the welcome weight of his clothes.

ACKNOWLEDGMENTS

The author wishes to express his gratitude to the Guggenheim and Lannan Foundations for generous fellowship support, as well as to the editors of the following publications, where some sections of this book appeared in a different form: *The Believer, Bomb, Canteen, Conjunctions, Granta,* Jewishfiction.net, *McSweeney's, New American Writing, Ploughshares, A Public Space,* and *StoryQuarterly.*

Thank you also to Katie Crouch, Phoebe, Ellen Levine, Pat Strachan, Rhoda and Dan Pierce, Ronald and Mitzi Orner, Edward Loiseau, David Krause, Alex Gordon, Rob Preskill, Chris Abani, Katsuhiro Iwashita, Nick Regiacorte, Melissa Kirsch, the Civitella Ranieri Center, and Anna Leube and Piero Salabe of Hanser Verlag. And to Eric Orner for the drawings.

In memory of Lorraine Spinner Orner, who danced (1915–2011).

BACK BAY · READERS' PICK

Reading Group Guide

LOVE
AND
SHAME
AND
LOVE

A NOVEL

BY

Peter Orner

A conversation with the author of
LOVE AND SHAME AND LOVE

Peter Orner talks with
Ted Hodgkinson of *Granta*

Reading this book got me thinking about the capricious way that memory often works: not necessarily in neat chronological order but associatively, moving outward in a starburst from one image to the next. I began to see the novel as a compendium of images that were bursting from the Popper family's memory banks. There's actually a scene in the book when Leo Popper eats a cookie as a parody of Proust's madeleine — clearly another writer fixated on being truthful about how memory works, or doesn't. Is there a truthfulness about the function of memory in this lateral structural movement of the book, and did you find it a challenge to trace the lines of memory across generations of a single family?

I've been thinking a lot about this lately. I wonder if the word *memory* itself doesn't somehow send the wrong message. There's something about it that suggests truth when it is so often not even close. Scientists and criminal lawyers have been proving this for decades now. Our memories lie like a rug, as my grandmother used to say, and then laugh her head off. Or did she? See, I'm doing it again. My grandmother, who we called Sally Grandma and not Grandma Sally, used to say, 'Don't lie like a rug.' But when she said it, she was saying, Don't be a lazy meshuggener. So she wasn't talking about memory and lying at all, but only about the fact that I was a slug. I still am a slug. Where was I? Our memories lie. And I've come to also believe that our own autobiographies are merely compilations of the greatest hits of our own bullshit. How often do we actually tell the truth about ourselves? I think in this novel I was trying to trace the strange way memory operates and how it's so tied up in fiction that they're almost indistinguishable. They are indistinguishable. The first fiction man ever created was when — for the very first time — a single hairy caveman began to recount something that happened yesterday. I wanted to build a book around a person who can't stop doing this, who remembers and lies and remembers and lies.

Though the novel certainly has a wholeness, it is constructed of lots of small moving parts: fragments of letters, brief vignettes, oblique and not exactly "plot-driven" chapters through which a large cast of characters move. Taken individually, the sections of the book operate in a way similar to your short stories — capturing a moment or an image and distilling it down to a potent essence. Did writing this novel allow you the possibility of seeing further into your characters' lives? Do you think of plot as something you have to resist in order to write fully realized people?

I'm not sure I resist plot as much as feel that the conventional definition of plot is a little cramped. For me, the strange moments that make up our lives are plot. I forget, but there must be some classic definition of what the word *plot* actually means. Hang on. I'm going to go look it up in an actual dictionary. *"A small area of planted ground."* No. *"An intrigue, conspiracy, cabal."* I like that, but no. Wait, *"The main story of a literary work."* That's it, but it's as dull as hell. It isn't that I don't think something should happen in stories, and I hope things happen in mine, but what fascinates me the most about living on earth are the people I will never know. All the people I walk down the street and see, I will never, ever know what they are thinking, what's gone on in their lives. So for me, character, the creation of a character on a flat page, is the most exciting thing. It's less the "what happened" and more the memories they lug around, the loves, the regrets.

And as you say, I guess I try to zero in on the quieter moments of their lives in order to give characters life. This morning at the coffee shop down the street, I watched a guy reading a little book. He was really into the book and he was holding it really close to his face. I wondered if this was because he was nearsighted or because he was loving the little book so much he wanted to get as close as possible to the words. It may well have been the first reason, something wrong with his eyes, but I like the second one better. And so I imagined (probably wrongly) that I had a small window into this guy's life. I'll bet he's still there, reading that little book.

Some of these characters reappear, albeit in a different incarnation, from your first book of stories. The character of Seymour Popper also appears in your short story "The Raft," but he seems very different in the novel: he's much less demonstrative in some ways. Did returning to the character prompt you to see him in a new light?

I'm sure you're right that he's different now. To be honest, I didn't go back and reread the stories about Seymour before writing about him again for the new book. I think I didn't want to be influenced by my previous imaginings of him. I do know that I missed him and I wanted to bring him back to life. The difference might be that "The Raft" is almost entirely from the perspective of a little kid, whereas in *Love and Shame and Love* I try to take in the totality of Seymour's life. And people change, of course. And our vision of the people we have loved changes. And I love Seymour. I love the fictional guy and the guy he's based on, too, and they never stay especially consistent in my head. I remember once

I was walking to my grandparents' house, my actual grandparents' house, and on the way this cat started following me. I must have been about ten. So the cat follows me to their house. They aren't home, but the back door is always open. I go inside and lock the cat in the bathroom with a little plate of dirt, you know, kind of like my own idea of kitty litter. Then I go and raid the refrigerator. My grandparents come home. By this time I've forgotten about the cat. My grandfather goes to the bathroom. He starts screaming. I mean, totally freaking out. This is a guy who captained a ship in World War II and a cat in the bathroom totally unhinges him. So our real people, as well as our fictional people, are always acting in ways they aren't supposed to, according to what we understand about their characters. My grandfather weighed something like 265, and he was no match for that cat.

Animals and sometimes insects in the book are often creatures whose plight seems to embody the whole of the human comedy and tragedy that encircles them. The fate of a fly seems poignant and absurd in a way that recalls the Popper family's struggle as the fly wanders across a desk lamp and wonders where all the other flies have gone. "And I alone," it thinks, "I alone lived to... lived to what?" The Popper family dog is a central character, and at one point is tellingly described as being more affected by silence than by hunger. Do you think that animals, particularly family pets, can be portals into the stormy core of a family, and does part of their power in the novel come from the way they seem to be often overlooked by the Poppers?

I love this idea of our pets as portals into the core of a family. Imagine if we could interview our pets and ask them about us. I think I had in mind, when I was writing about the pet dog in the book, Sir Edmund Hillary. The dog knows the Poppers too well, and he isn't especially fond of them. But what choice did he have?

He's their dog. Dogs can't choose their families any more than we can. I'm sitting here in my garage in San Francisco with my dog. Bud is very bored watching me type. Her name is actually Daisy, which embarrasses me when I am at the dog park, so I call her Bud, which she is happy to answer to if I have treats. Otherwise, she generally ignores me. But she knows everything about me, all the things I lie about. So I guess I'm glad she can't talk.

The Chicago you describe here has a particular, almost mythic quality, as if you're hooking up with an image of the city that belongs to a deeply American, Chicagoan tradition that includes writers like Saul Bellow and Stuart Dybek. When you're writing about the Windy City, how often are you conscious of wrestling your image of it away from those writers who have come before, or are you wanting rather to engage with that literary conversation about it?

I think maybe all the places we tell ourselves we love are actually myths. Chicago is impossible for any one book or piece of prose or poem or whatever to capture. So is London. So is Cleveland. So is the state of Delaware and the country of India. And Madagascar. And yet I think this is why writers keep trying. And we keep trying in spite of — or maybe because of — the fact that we are conscious of the great writers who have come before. In my case, Bellow, Algren, Dybek. I'd also like to mention the work of Aleksandar Hemon, a relative newcomer to Chicago, but a writer who captures its essence, or some of its essences, as well as anybody. I think I write with all these people in my mind, to, yes, as you say, have a conversation with them. But then, as you know, conversations sometimes run off the rails, and we move in our own directions. As far as place goes, I think we get a myth in our heads about a place and we try to convey this myth to a reader. So yes, for me Chicago is the mythical place I grew up in. Call it Chicagoland, which is one of my favorite stupid advertising slogans. But Chicago is also a very real place where, among other things that happen, young kids are killed at the most alarming rate imaginable. I try to address how hopeless this feels in one scene in the book: Kat reads about a young girl being raped and then can't figure out what to do about it. She feels so useless, all she can do is go sit on the stoop. She's paralyzed. She wants to act, to do something, but she doesn't know what to do. She's twenty-five years old and new to the city. What can she do? Raise her voice? March in the streets? Write a letter to Richie Daley? I relate to Kat's hopelessness in that scene. You write a story about a myth, your myth, the myth you love, and then you open the *Sun-Times* and you fall apart. Does this make any sense? Writers, like most everyone else, see what's wrong but aren't sure how to fix things. So we shine a little light. But I reserve my most profound respect for those people who actually make change, and there are people in Chicago who devote their lives, every day, to making it a safer place for all its citizens.

The book is very frank and funny about the difficulties of adolescence, particularly the difficulty of talking to girls. Do you recall that period of time fondly or with a grimace?

Fondly, at least concerning those few times things worked out in this particular area. With a cringe concerning the majority of it.

The book itself is chock-full of books, from Alexander's reading lists at college to the Rozencrantzes' pointedly impressive library. Is this in some ways the story of how books can shape lives and how they have shaped yours?

Absolutely. Popper is, from the very first scene, obsessed with his own personal library. Or the idea of his library. Another thing we lug around. Our books. Now I hear people boasting about how many books they have on their Kindle and isn't it great, no more books to carry! And my thought is, and I know I am rapidly becoming a dinosaur, books are made for carrying. Nancy Sinatra didn't walk in any virtual boots. Books are weight, the weight of our lives. Shove three or five or eight in your bag when you take a trip. They are supposed to ache your heart — and your back.

Adapted from an interview that originally appeared on December 13, 2011, on granta.com. Reproduced by permission.

Questions and topics
for discussion

1. The way memory wanders is one of the central themes in *Love and Shame and Love*. Popper is obsessed with the passage of time and the impossibility of going back — the closing off of options as time passes us by. How would you describe your relationship with memory and time?

2. Another important theme is love (or the lack of it) over the course of four generations in one family. Were notions of love (or the lack of it) on your mind while you were reading?

3. *Love and Shame and Love* features many wonderful minor characters. Do you have favorites? The Rosencrantz children? Coach Piefke? Manny Laveneaux? Hollis Osgood? Do you mind that some characters exist for just a few pages and then are gone forever, or do you think they worked to support the greater narrative?

4. Politics figures prominently in the novel — the autumn of Dukakis, the Democratic Convention, the mayoral races in Chicago. What's the relationship between politics and other concerns — love, for instance, or commitment — in the book?

5. In the *Washington Post*, Ron Charles wrote, "Orner is unusually gifted at creating freighted moments...that generate far more impact than their size would suggest." In what ways did the mosaic of short sections help or hinder your engagement while reading *Love and Shame and Love*?

6. "Only our disgraces are permanent?" (p. 259) is a powerful question, posed in the context of the Poppers' broken home. Do you think that shame outlasts love? Do you think that in the Popper family disgraces were the only thing that lasted?

7. Some elements of Alexander Popper's life reflect the author's — childhood in Chicago, University of Michigan, law school. Yet the author himself rejects the notion of autobiography as being any path to actual truth, saying that the more autobiographical the elements, the less truthful the fiction. If you were to write a novel based loosely on your own life, how might you structure it? What do you think are the benefits or disadvantages of using familiar material?

8. In a letter Alexander writes, "But we do tend to judge our fathers. For what exactly, we don't always even know" (p. 411). Do you think we judge our fathers more harshly than we do our mothers? Do you think Alexander did? If so, why?

9. Peter Orner is able to say a lot about his characters (Miriam, Kat, Seymour, and others) by listing the books they own. Do you think that your books say something meaningful about you? Can the books that people choose to read say something deeper about them that they might be unable to communicate explicitly?